Full Figured 9:

Carl Weber Presents

Full Figured 9:

Carl Weber Presents

Carl Weber with Paradise Gomez

and

Ms. Michel Moore

www.urbanbooks.net

Urban Books, LLC
97 N 18th Street
Wyandanch, NY 11798

ISBN 13: 978-1-62286-748-6
ISBN 10: 1-62286-748-3

First Mass Market Printing September 2016
First Trade Paperback Printing August 2015
Printed in the United States of America

10 9 8 7 6 5 4 3 2 1

Distributed by Kensington Publishing Corp.
Submit Orders to:
Customer Service
400 Hahn Road
Westminster, MD 21157-4627
Phone: 1-800-733-3000
Fax: 1-800-659-2436

Dear Reader,

As many of you know, the start of 2015 has been really tough for me, with the passing of my 101-year-old grandmother and also my father-in-law, a man I deeply respected. That's why I have to thank author Paradise Gomez for stepping in during a difficult time to finish my *Full Figured 9* story, "Daddy's Girl."

I'd also like to thank my co-author, Ms. Michel Moore, for bringing it with her story, "This Can't Be Life." If you haven't read her stuff yet, you are in for a treat. For more of her drama-packed writing, check out her solo novels, *Coldhearted and Crazy, Ruthless and Rotten*, and *No Home Training*.

Once again, thanks for all your support, and I'll see you October 1, 2015 when *The Man in 3B* hits movie theaters.

All the best,

Carl Weber

DADDY'S LITTLE GIRL

Carl Weber with Paradise Gomez

CHAPTER ONE

JAMELA

I felt like a princess as I sat in front of the first man I had ever loved—the only man I had ever loved and the only man who had ever loved me. Any who came after him would have a hard act to follow. Victor Long, owner of Long's Soul Food chain, was charming, sophisticated, and just like his last name, so were his pockets. Hands down, in my eyes he was the most successful, hard-working man in the entire state of California. Who gave a damn about real estate tycoons and A-list celebrities? None of them could hold a candle to the wealth and riches of Victor Long. Not monetarily, of course, because God knows some of the properties in L.A. that were going for millions weren't worth the drywall they were made with, and I could name at least five overpaid actors. But Victor was rich in other things. Things that mattered. Love, gentleness, selflessness, kindness: those were some of the things kept in the bank of Victor Long's heart and head.

I looked down at his hands reached across to the center of the table, cupping mine into his strong, thick ones. I felt so special and so secure, like I was his only girl. I looked into his soft eyes, knowing that I wasn't his only girl. That was something I'd have to live with though. He loved who he loved. Who was I to hold that against him?

He could do no wrong as far as I was concerned. He loved hard, so I endured and loved him anyway. Most would say that I was biased in my opinion about Victor. As I should be. After all, isn't a little girl's daddy supposed to be the first man she ever loves and the first man to show her just exactly what love is? My daddy—*the* Victor Long. I couldn't ever imagine having to live without him.

"I just wish your mother were here to see all your accomplishments," my father said with a sigh as we sat on the patio at Gladstone's Restaurant, overlooking the Pacific Ocean. Other than my father's restaurants, with its menu created from my deceased mother's recipes, Gladstone's was my favorite spot to eat.

"I know, Daddy." I squeezed his hand and noticed his eyes beginning to water. He pulled away and turned his head before a tear could fall. I'd never seen my father cry before, not even at the funeral of my mother: his first wife and the love of his life. He was too busy being strong for me. I knew he was in so much pain losing the woman who had been his high school sweetheart and the woman who stood side by side with him when he opened the first restaurant. Ironically, Daddy's credit hadn't been so great at the time, so it was my mother who had to take out the business loan.

Although my mother had been dead since I'd turned five, thirteen years ago, my father still missed her. Although my memories were becoming vague as the years passed, I missed her too.

My father used his hand to briskly dab away any tears threatening to fall. "She's looking down on you, though." He looked up in the clear blue sky.

"I know what you mean," I murmured, glancing upward, envisioning the angel-white silhouette of my mother hovering over us, her body dipping in and out of the puffy clouds. It broke my heart when my dad would talk about Mom. This was supposed to be a happy, celebratory moment, so I decided to change the subject. "I thank you for taking the time to have our father-daughter day. It reminds me of . . ." I allowed my words to remain tucked away in my voice box. I was about to bring her up, the other woman who was now my father's second wife. I hated to say it, but how I wished his current wife could trade places with my mother and be six feet under.

Before Glendora came into my father's life, I didn't have to take the scraps of time he had left after catering to her every beck and call. There was a time when father-daughter days weren't so few and far between, but my stepmother's last name might as well have been Timex, because she clocked my father's every second.

Just thinking about wife number two made me lose my appetite. I pulled my hand from my father's and pushed my plate away. This dinner was not going the way I had imagined it would. It was hard trying to stay upbeat. This morning when I woke up I'd told myself that I was absolutely not going to feel sad today. This was supposed to be a celebration dinner for my receiving a score of 2200 on the SAT. I'd also received acceptance letters from several top universities. I actually did have a lot to be happy about. Now if only someone could give my emotions the memo.

I looked at my father, who was looking at me. Whenever I was down, he felt like a failure. He'd told me so on more than one occasion.

"What's the matter, pumpkin?" my father would ask when I was younger whenever I appeared to have the blues. "Tell Daddy so he can make it better. That's what a daddy's job is: to make his little girl happy. If he can't, then he's not doing that great of a job at being a daddy. Now tell me what's wrong so I can fix it and make you happy again, because I won't be happy unless you are."

A tiny smile stole a moment on my lips as I thought about how my father would stop the world from revolving to make sure I was okay. That alone was enough to lift my spirits. "I'm happy to be here with you, Daddy," I said.

The corners of his mouth lifted into a smile. Inside I questioned, though, just how genuine it was. Unfortunately, in the last few years I'd seen forced smiles, usually to appease her. She wasn't here and he had no reason to fake it, so I would simply take his expression at face value and cherish the night.

I was so glad it was just us two on this beautiful April evening. When I was little we used to have father-daughter day once a month. It had been years since we could be that consistent.

We'd plan them, but something else always just happened to come up, or we had unwelcome guests—unwelcome from my end anyway.

I was so excited when Dad told me that it would just be him and me, alone, without the company of the Wicked Witch of the West. I almost broke out into a happy dance.

Daddy had married Glendora when I was ten. Ironically, he met her at the hospital where my mom spent her last days. Glendora worked as a CNA there, and my mom was often assigned as one of her patients. She was very nice when I first met her. I remember her giving me a card, a bouquet of daisies, and a box of chocolates the day after my mom died to try to cheer me up. She even showed up to the funeral and brought a tuna casserole to our house a week later. From that point on, she was a permanent fixture in our lives.

What I liked most about Glendora was that she made Daddy smile. That was a good thing considering he never really smiled much after my mother passed. Glendora making Daddy happy made me happy as well. Like I said, she was nice back then, so I had no qualms about having a stepmother when he ended up marrying her. Glendora seemed nothing like some of the horror stories I'd heard from friends at school who had a stepparent.

She and Daddy eventually got married, and she and her two kids—Brielle, who was two years younger than me, and Brendon, who was my age—moved in with us into our home. Even when the two adults sat the three of us kids down to talk about the whole marriage and blended family thing, I had no worries. Our four-bedroom home was plenty big. We'd just have to turn the guestroom into a room for one of Glendora's kids, and turn the bedroom we used as a library into a real bedroom. I was excited to say the least. As a matter of fact, I felt like the luckiest girl in the world. I had a mom again, and I gained a new brother and sister. I had lost my mother, but God gave me three new people to be a part of my life. I pictured family outings, sibling pranks, and late-night girl chats with my little sister.

Unfortunately the picture-perfect portrait I had fantasized about turned out to be anything but that. The moment Glendora, her children, and the U-Haul truck showed up in our driveway, things went downhill. Soon after she moved in, she quit her job to become a stay-at-home mom. I overheard her telling Daddy that this would allow her more time to do "mommy things" with us kids. Sounded good to me. What she should have said was that she would do those things only with her kids. She began treating me like I was an unwanted stepchild.

It all started when she forced me out of my princess-inspired room and moved Brielle into it. Brendon moved into the guest room and, well, remember that makeshift library? Well, that became my bedroom, which also just happened to be the smallest bedroom in the house. In all actuality, it didn't even feel like part of the house. It was located off the kitchen right before the garage door. I remember my dad once telling me that it was designed for a live-in maid or something.

Being kicked out of my bedroom wasn't the worst of it. Glendora offered to help me pack up my room and relocate, but only so that she could go through all my things and "throw them out." To her, throwing them out meant hanging them up in Brielle's closet.

"Hey, that's my BeBe sweat suit," I said to Glendora when I saw her taking it out of my drawer and putting it in the giveaway box.

"Girl, this is a size small, and you know you are a large all day long," Glendora said, ignoring my plea and tossing it into the box anyway. "I told you to lay off all that cake. You getting fat. Keep it up and no boy in his right mind is going to want you."

I looked down at my size-eight frame. What was she talking about? I wasn't getting fat. I grabbed at the side of my stomach. There were a few extra inches of skin, but still, I was no size large. Medium at best. And that extra skin was nothing a few side-to-side sit-ups couldn't get rid of. I just had to tone up a little bit. None of this mattered to her though. Not even the fact that Brielle was the chunky one. If anything, she should have been passing her outgrown clothes down to me!

Glendora's mind was made up though. She had every excuse in the world why this designer top needed to be thrown out or that pair of designer pants needed to go. Heifer even went through some of my jewelry, passing that on to her daughter as well. Now, a damn earring can fit in anybody's ear. That's when I realized that she had a hidden agenda. Underneath it all Glendora had to have truly liked me, I decided. Why else would she have wanted her daughter to be me?

I was starting to see a completely different side of my stepmother—a not so nice one. My father, however, was so caught up in Glendora's phoniness that he didn't even notice her evil transformation. She started doing little nasty things to me here and there behind his back.

Every time I even thought about telling my father about Glendora's antics, his jovial spirit would make me reconsider.

"Dad, I need to talk to you," I would say. "It's about Glendora."

"Isn't she just amazing?" he would say before I could drop the dime on her ass. "It feels so good to have her in my life . . . in our lives." He'd stare off as if he was in la-la land. "I never thought I would find love again after your mother, but Glendora was really there for me in my time of need. I don't think I would have made it through such a difficult time without her."

He looked to me for confirmation. I simply nodded.

"She was there for you too," my dad reminded me. "And now look at us." He pulled me in for a hug. "We're all one big, happy family who can be there for each other, right?"

What could I do? Take my foot and kick him so hard that he'd come tumbling off of cloud nine? "Right, Daddy," was what a good daughter would say. So that's what I said as I went to exit the room, head down.

"Jamela, what was it you wanted to talk to me about?" my father asked, stopping me in my tracks.

I lifted my head to face him, trying to decide one last time if I should tell him about that wife of his. Looking into my daddy's eyes, I just couldn't. "I . . . I forgot. It must have been nothing." I gave him a smile and then exited the room. Hopefully one day he'd see her on his own for the woman she truly was.

Once my dad noticed Brielle running around in my clothes, he did make mention of it. Glendora gave him the same song and dance that she gave me. The clothing issue wasn't the only thing he noticed. After dinner I was always the one clearing the table and cleaning up the kitchen while Brielle ran off to FaceTime her friends.

I remember hearing Glendora and my father arguing about it one night. She always had some excuse that he pulled out his wallet and bought.

"Jamela is the oldest. She'll be off to college here soon and will need to know how to take care of herself. Not to mention one day she'll have a husband she'll need to tend to. I know I'm not Jamela's mother, but I feel it's my job as her stepmother to teach her how to be a woman."

Bullshit! I could smell it through the door. My dad, on the other hand, thought her shit didn't stink. She made up anything to justify how she was treating me. Her explanation for putting me in the small room was that Brielle had dust allergies and needed a large and airy room. As for giving her my clothes, again, she told him it was clothes that I had outgrown. My father always believed her, to the point where he stopped questioning her at all.

Feeling as if my father was no longer concerned about the little things she did to me, and realizing that I wasn't going to rat her out, this gave Glendora free rein to treat me even worse than she already was. She'd talk to me like a dog on the street, at least when my father wasn't around. When he was around, she didn't talk to me at all. It was as if I wasn't even a part of their happy little family.

No one even noticed me. Dad was busy keeping the restaurants in order, Glendora was busy shopping and spending afternoons at the spa, and Brielle was busy being a spoiled brat. The only one who ever did notice me was Brendon. Ironically, it was when I was around him that I pretended to be invisible.

I stopped hoping that things would get better, and I learned to keep to myself and stay out of Glendora's way. Once she realized neither I nor my dad was going to speak up about her ways, she became even more bold and obvious. She had no problem letting it be known that her own blood children were her priority and I was just someone in the way of her seeing to it that her children had everything their hearts desired. Everything their hearts desired came with a price tag. Since my dad was the only one bringing in income, that meant he financed it all: everything from Brendon's old-school Corvette he'd found on eBay to Brielle's little two-door sport convertible. Me, I drove my mom's old car. She was never big on material things. She didn't even upgrade her cell phone unless the old one broke. So when I say her car was old, it was old. It ran just fine though. It got me to where I needed to be, which was pretty much just back and forth to school.

I loved driving the car. It felt good to have inherited a piece of my mom. When I first sat behind the steering wheel, I closed my eyes and inhaled. I swear I could smell my mother's scent: a mixture of eucalyptus lotion and fried chicken. Sometimes when I was driving I'd pretend she was in the passenger's seat. I'm sure folks who pulled up next to me at red lights thought I was crazy, because sometimes I'd even carry on a conversation with her. I couldn't talk to my stepmother about anything, so I compromised.

Even though my dad didn't speak on our divided household, I knew it was hard on him—trying to be fair to his ready-made family and making sure that I wasn't feeling like I didn't belong. What was supposed to be a happy family became more like a living arrangement. Whenever we went out to dinner together, we were just one big, dysfunctional family. Brendon and Brielle would spend most of the time on their phones. Every now and then Brendon would look up at me and wink. Perhaps that was his way of reminding me of my miserable existence. Lord knows I was invisible to everyone else.

I ate my dinner in silence while Glendora and Daddy made small talk. Here there were five people sitting at the table, hardly acknowledging one another, yet when it used to be just Daddy and me, the table would be full of laughter and conversation. It was a prime example of less being more. I quickly went from desiring a big family to wishing to be rid of Glendora and her kids. I made it my mission to try to arrange for me and Daddy to spend time together alone. Just the two of us.

At first I'd make plans to go to the restaurant he was working at that day and eat with him while he was on break. That never went well. Every five minutes one of his employees had an issue they needed him to tend to.

"I'm sorry, Jam-Jam," he'd say, using the nickname he'd given me. "Maybe another time." He'd get up from the table, leaving his not even half-eaten meal on the table. I'd find myself eating both my meal and his, just to at least be under the same roof with him for as long as I could.

Eventually I came around to the concept of if you can't beat 'em, join 'em. In between school and homework, I started working with Daddy at the restaurant. Even though my time with him was business, it was a pleasure, and it sure beat being at home, where Glendora always found something for me to cook or clean. I figured I might as well do it where I could get paid for it.

Needless to say, working at my dad's restaurant had other benefits, too, besides me just being able to spend time with him. A sista could get her grub on. Getting my work permit was like getting a food stamp card. Working at the restaurants, I had access to all the food I wanted. That's when I began to pick up weight. Food started to become both a comforter and a protector for me. It was a struggle, though, finding comfort in my size-eight clothes anymore. They were getting tighter by the day. If there was ever a time when Glendora had a reason to give Brielle all the clothes I was outgrowing, it was then.

A local paper ended up doing a write-up on Daddy's restaurant. That landed him a cooking segment on a morning show. The next thing we knew, one of his to-go desserts ended up as one of Oprah's favorite things. Business was booming so much that Daddy decided to open up another restaurant. This meant he was now much busier. He was always working and running back and forth between the two locations. He wasn't as accessible as he was when we were both working out of the same restaurant, which used to be the only one—the first restaurant he and my mom had started together.

That didn't deter me from trying to spend quality time with my dad. I would arrange for us to go to the museum or for a walk and picnic in the park or something. Whenever Glendora caught wind of it, though, she'd be sure to dig deep in her tool chest and pull out a monkey wrench to throw in our plans.

"Honey, remember, you have a meeting," Glendora would remind him. "You have a doctor's appointment." Then there was, "You promised me you'd take me out." Anything she could do or say, she did.

As the clock wound down to my appointed daddy-daughter time with my father, I'd sit back and wait for the infamous knock on the door.

The door would crack open, and he'd stick his head in.

"Honey, I'm sorry, but—"

"It's okay, Dad. Maybe another time," I'd say without him even having to finish his sentence.

I eventually gave up on planning anything. Glendora went out of her way to see to it that my dad didn't spend time with me—or even just talk to me. At one point I thought she had blocked my number from his cell phone because I could never seem to get through. I would text him and he would never get my text messages.

"I'll have Glendora call the cell phone company and look into it," he would tell me.

My father was a busy man. I knew he didn't have time to do it himself. There was just no use. Glendora was running things, and there was no way around her. But somehow, today, as I sat with my favorite guy at my second favorite restaurant (my father's restaurants were my number one, of course!) he'd somehow managed to make it through Glendora's maze of distractions to have dinner with his daughter.

As if he could read my thoughts, Daddy said, "I'm glad we've got this alone time too." He crunched his giant crab leg with the small pliers that accompanied his meal.

I had no idea where Glendora was today or how she'd allowed Daddy to slip through the cracks and land at this dinner table with me. Something or someone must have been keeping her quite occupied. I knew for certain that it wasn't either of her two spoiled children. Brielle, who was now almost seventeen, and Brendon who, like myself, would be nineteen on his next birthday, were doing their annual Easter weekend visit with their father in Long Island, New York.

I couldn't have cared less where they were. They could have been in Europe having tea with the royals for all I cared. I was just grateful to get this time with my dad.

"Things have been busy at the restaurants," Dad said. "Which I don't have to tell you." He chewed his food and then looked at me and said, "By the way, you are doing an excellent job, sweetie. I know you are just working there because it's the family business and it allows you a little bit of extra spending money, but, honey, you are doing a real fine job. Word gets back to me, you know. You take initiative, just like a true leader." Daddy pointed his fork at me. "You know, I could even see you possibly taking over the restaurants one day when I'm dead and gone or too old to fry chicken." He laughed.

"Daddy, don't say that," I scolded. I couldn't even think about anything happening to my father. If it did, trust and believe Glendora would go to the end of the world to make sure I didn't run those restaurants. Even though she knew absolutely nothing about the business, with the exception that it brought in enough money for her to own several pairs of red bottoms, she'd never allow me to be in charge.

"Anyway," Daddy continued, "it's nice to be able to spend some time with you, daughter. It's been a while."

"Same here, Dad, and yes, it has been a minute since you've been able to get away from . . ." I swallowed my last words and just left it at, "Been able to get away." I took a bite of my salmon. I closed my eyes and inhaled. I was taking in every moment, not just of the taste of the delicious food, but every second spent with my father. No telling the next time he'd manage to go missing without Glendora getting a whiff of it. I mean, you'd think I was his mistress or something the way she tried to keep my father away from me.

"Oh, yeah," my father said. "I can't believe I almost forgot," he said, wiping his hands on his napkin.

"Forgot what, Dad?" I asked as he started to feel around in his pockets. "What happened?" I was thinking the worst: that he'd forgotten about something he had to do for his wife, and now he was in search of his keys so he could go do it.

"I have a little gift for you."

I got excited. "Oh, what is it?" I might as well have been jumping up and down like a six-year-old. I loved it when my dad made me feel like his favorite girl. I guess I would always be a daddy's girl at heart no matter how old I got.

"Hold on. I'm going to give it to you." Dad held up his finger and chuckled at my excitement, shaking his head.

I intertwined my fingers and waited impatiently, shaking my knee under the table.

My dad looked over at me while he continued his search. "You're starting to look more and more like your mother each day."

Just that morning I'd said the same thing to myself. While getting dressed, I looked up at the picture of my mother I had hanging in the corner of my dresser mirror. I looked into her eyes and then at my reflection. My mother was a beautiful woman—a beautiful, hardworking woman. Even though for the most part she was always wearing an apron with her hair pulled back and a hairnet on her head, when she got cleaned up, she was drop-dead gorgeous. Like in the picture. It was one of those Glamour Shots photos. She looked like a movie star. I kept looking back from her picture to my reflection, pinpointing our similar features. The more I stared at myself, the more of my mother I saw in me, but no way could I possibly be that beautiful.

"You know your mother named you Jamela because it means beautiful," my dad said, bringing my attention from my bedroom mirror back to the dinner table.

"Huh?" I said, shaking out the thoughts from earlier so I could focus on my dad.

"I said your name means beautiful, and you are, baby."

I could never understand for the life of me how my dad always managed to address questions that rested in my internal thoughts.

"If a man can't appreciate your natural beauty, then don't deal with him."

I blushed at the compliment. It was the norm for a girl's father to think she was beautiful, but in the back of my mind I always wondered if the rest of the world felt that way. I had a warm, dark espresso complexion like my late mother, Jade. My father was a mocha brown, which meant I was considered dark-skinned by society's standards. Everybody knows that in this world, dark things are connected to negativity. Black cats crossing a path is bad luck. Blackmail.

Black ball. The verdict is still out on Black Friday considering people get crushed to death trying to get great deals on electronics. Nonetheless, my dad always made me feel like royalty.

On the other hand, Glendora and her children were all light-skinned. I've heard lighter-skinned blacks say they experienced the whole "not black enough" thing. I try to empathize, but for some reason, redbone just doesn't sound as hurtful as tar baby. In addition to that, my stepmother always made sure to remind me that my darker complexion wasn't the more "desirable" one. Here we were, living in 2015, and colorism still existed within the black community . . . within the black family!

"Before I give you your gift," Dad continued, "I want you to know how proud I am of you. You're a good daughter, Jamela. You could've gotten off your program, you know, with the loss of your mother, fitting in to a new family, but you stayed on track and now you're at the top of your high school class with the opportunity to go to almost any college you want. I know it hasn't been easy." He paused.

"That's all I've ever wanted to do, Dad, was to make you happy."

"And you've done a hell of a job doing just that," he replied with a smile.

"I must say, though, that I'm glad *they* didn't come because I know *she* wouldn't be happy—not really. Not with Brielle looking like she'll have to go to junior college." In spite of Glendora's constant efforts to make her daughter outshine me, Brielle could never compete with my academic success.

"Clear your mind of Glendora and the kids. Let's not talk about them right now," Daddy said sternly. He then quickly changed the subject to a good note—the reason why we were out celebrating in the first place. "You know with that SAT score you can write your own ticket now and go to any Ivy League college you want."

I smiled, but my mind was on what the gift was inside the box he was now holding in his hand. Was it a key to a new car?

"You could probably even apply to—"

"Da-aaa-d! The gift," I said anxiously, my impatience totally getting the best of me.

"Here's what I'd like to give you," he finally said, handing me the box. "This was your mother's."

I knew that whatever was in that box, it was priceless, because it had once belonged to my mother. With anticipation, I opened the box, and to my surprise, I found an antique-looking golden locket with a sepia picture of my mother encased in it. She was throwing her head back in her usual proud West Indian way, and she looked healthy and strong. A flood of memories rushed at me. These were happy days. In this picture, my mother was about twenty-five. She looked so radiant and strong. By the time she was thirty-two, which was the age she died from leukemia, she'd been just a shell of her old self. The photo in the locket was just the way I wanted to remember my mother.

"I love it! Oh, thank you, Daddy!" I got up and walked over to my father. I threw my arms around him. "This is beautiful." I looked down at the necklace I was twisting between my thumb and index finger. "I really do love it!" Tears welled up in my eyes, but these were tears of joy. Now I could always wear my mother near my heart.

My father put the necklace on me and I sat back across the table from him.

"Well," he said, "I understand you've already gotten acceptance letters from several different schools. Have you made any decisions?"

I knew my father would be happy with whatever school I chose. I could've gone south, west, or east, but after much consideration, I had decided to stay in California. I couldn't wait to get out of the house, but at the same time, I

wanted to stay close to my father. With my dad
getting older, I didn't feel comfortable leaving
him with her. I'd never seen her do anything bad
to my father, but with a woman like Glendora,
she could never be trusted. She was a manipula-
tive, sneaky liar. She was a leopard and a leopard
never changes its spots, just its location. If I
wasn't around, I could imagine her redirecting
all the hate she had for me toward my father.

I nodded. "I think I want to go to Stanford."

Dad smiled. I could tell he was pleased.

I knew my stepmother would be furious when
she found out I wasn't going away to college out
of state. I was sure she wanted me as far away
from her and Daddy as possible.

Speaking of my evil stepmother, at that
moment my father's cell phone began to ring
on the table between us. I looked at the screen
before he had a chance to pick it up, and I could
see Glendora's face on the screen. Ugh!

I rolled my eyes as I watched my father answer
the phone. Her mouth was so loud I could hear
her as if I was the one holding the phone to my
ear.

"Where the hell are you, Victor?" she snapped.

He cleared his throat. "I'm, uh, I'm with
Jamela," he answered in a constricted voice. He
probably would have had an easier time telling

his wife he was out with his mistress. I couldn't believe the way he was informing her of his whereabouts as if he was up to no good. "You know I told you we were going out to celebrate."

"Yeah, yeah. Well, it's almost six o'clock."

"The fundraiser doesn't start 'til eight," my father reasoned. "And it's not like we have to show up at eight o'clock on the nose."

"Yes, but the cleaner's closes at seven, and you still have to pick up your tux before they close."

"I thought you would have grabbed it while you were out."

"I can't do everything. I had to go to the salon to get my hair done, get a mani and pedi. Bella is here now doing my makeup. You don't want your wife to be on your arm looking like a ragamuffin, do you? But if you do, then fine. I'll send Bella away and I'll go pick up your tux. I can just do my own makeup. Who cares if I show up looking like Boy George?"

Talk about nails down a chalkboard. Her voice sent chills down my spine. In that instant, the entire atmosphere shifted. The sun disappeared into the ocean, and that was the end of our last happy moments together.

CHAPTER TWO

GLENDORA

First of all, let me say this: I couldn't stand my raggedy-ass stepdaughter. But not to worry, I was almost certain that the feeling was mutual. Cow wouldn't shoot milk on me from her titties if I were on fire. If I were a dog, I wouldn't piss on her if she were a fire hydrant.

When I first met my husband, I honestly had no idea that he and his dying wife had a child together. By the time I found out about her, he and I had already had a little spark flickering between us. There was no need to let it fizzle out. I had plans, and some brat of a daddy's girl was not going to make me stray from them.

I tried my best not to let the little troll get under my skin. It was difficult to maintain, though, considering my plan, I mean my marriage, would have been just fine if it weren't for her. He called her a daddy's girl, and it made me cringe. I, on the other hand, called her a home wrecker. The only disagreements Victor and I had were when it came to her. When it came to my kids, everything was hunky-dory, but with Jamela . . . Whoever said being part of a blended family was easy told a lie. We certainly weren't the Brady Bunch.

There was a light at the end of the tunnel, though. Soon she'd be graduating from high school and then taking her tired ass off to college in the fall. I couldn't wait. I had no idea how far across the map she was going, and I didn't care just as long as it was out of my house.

"Baby, you sure you can't stay out longer?" Jasper, my sexy caramel sidepiece called from the bed. He'd interrupted my train of thought as I dried myself off after having stepped out of the shower. I wrapped myself in the oversized Egyptian bath towel and then walked into the room where he was lying in the king-sized bed with his penis lying between his legs. Yes, that's just how packed his junk was. Shit was lying, like a girl lays out her prom dress before sliding into it. And damn did I want to slide onto that . . . again.

I glanced down at the clock on the hotel night-stand. It was 6:15 p.m. I was due at the UCLA charitable event at eight. I'd already called and hounded Victor about it before I got into the shower. I played it as if I'd been all day riding around town getting ready for the event when, in all actuality, I'd been all day riding Jasper's dick.

"No, I've got an important event to attend tonight." I looked down at Jasper's sculpted body. "I'll see you next week, though. Same time."

He frowned. Clearly that was unacceptable to him. He wanted more of me and he wanted it now.

"Don't get greedy." I kissed my fingers and touched his lips. This turned up the corners of his lips into a smile, but it also made his manhood stand at attention.

Jasper flexed his pecs. Damn it! He knew what that did to me. He looked so youthful lying there. Every time I climbed onto him it was like diving into the fountain of youth. Afterward, like now, him lying there without a care in the world with nothing to do in life but fuck, sleep, and eat made me remember how I was approaching the big five-oh. Although I worked out, had a physical trainer, and kept my grays touched up, I was still no longer in my twenties, like Jasper, or even in my thirties for that matter.

Don't get me wrong. I knew I looked damn good for my age, but Father Time was pulling on me. They say black don't crack, and so far, I hadn't had any work done—other than my boobs—but I don't know. Being with this young man was making me consider Hollywood's dirty little secret: plastic surgery.

I looked over at Jasper in all of his manhood. I then looked at the clock. Then at Jasper's dick calling my name. He was just so beautiful. *It* was just so beautiful, standing there in all of its glory. I loved sex, and granted, I could get sex from Victor easily after turning in from our function tonight. Despite my romping around with Jasper, Victor wasn't a bad lay. It's just that he was old school, still into shit like doing a sixty-nine. Jasper, on the other hand, was a new jack with tricks that would make the performers in Cirque du Soleil look like a beginners ballet class.

"Fuck it," I said, tossing the towel. A dick in the mouth was worth two in the bush. I climbed on the bed and immediately began slobbing down Jasper. I got it shiny and slippery before I slid onto it. Time was of the essence, so we didn't have time for any sensual foreplay acts. I bounced on it like I was in a potato sack race. He clutched my lifted D cups like he was a jockey whose horse had gone rabid and he was holding on for dear life.

"Damn, baby. Oh, shit," he moaned as his face twisted up.

Beautiful man. That's what I loved even more about my Jasper. When it came to getting it in, he didn't care about getting ugly. His deformed face let me know that he was on the verge of exploding inside of me. Knowing I had about twenty seconds max to get mine in, I leaned slightly forward so that my clit would rub against his penis with every bounce. This intensified the wonderful feeling I was already indulging in.

Five, four, three, two . . .

"Oh, damn! Oh, shit! Fuck!" We each called out our own expletives as we reached our climax and I fell onto his chest.

"Damn you," I scolded him after looking at the clock. "I gotta get out of here. For real this time." I got out of the bed and began wiping myself down with the towel.

Jasper grabbed the remote, and with a look of victory on his face, he turned on the television and began flipping through channels.

Bastard, I thought about his confidence, or maybe it was arrogance. Either way, he knew he'd have me one more time before I walked out of there . . . just like all the other times. I bit my bottom lip as I rubbed the towel between my legs. Looking at Jasper, I wondered how

long it would be before he wanted to leave me
for someone younger. After all, besides the sex,
I honestly didn't know what was in it for him.
He could fuck any- and everybody, and I was
sure he did, with the exception of our Thursday
standing appointment. Sure I footed the bill for
the deluxe hotel suite we had our little rendez-
vous in, but that was only once a week. Perhaps
the same way Jasper made me feel younger and
alive while we were having sex, I made him feel
like a man: older, mature. With all the mommy
issues young men had nowadays, no telling. All
I did know, though, was that Jasper was simply
gorgeous and could lay it down in the bedroom.
The sex was amazing, and I looked forward
to our weekly sessions. Never mind why we
were using each other, as long as we were both
happy. And I damn sure knew I was one of the
happiest women in the world.

I guess some would say that I was a cougar.
Now that word made a sista feel old. Every
week as I did the walk of shame down the hotel
hallway, I kept telling myself I was going to leave
this boy toy alone, but besides mind-blowing
sex, he made me feel wanted and needed. My
age actually had its advantage. With age comes
experience. Sure, Jasper knew some new tricks,
but I was experienced enough to know what to

do with it, so perhaps in retrospect, that's what Jasper admired about me and why he chose to connect with me out of all the other women that night.

See, I met Jasper six months ago at a charity fashion show event in Beverly Hills. He was one of the male models. I swear to God when he hit the end of that runway and winked before making his trek behind the curtain backstage, he was winking dead at me. His boldness alone made me get sticky between the legs. After all, Victor had been sitting right there with his arm around me.

I was afraid he'd felt me jerk at the tingle Jasper had sent running through my body. I feared we were about to reenact that scene from Robert Townson's movie *The Five Heartbeats,* when Leon and the lead singer were competing with one another by singing to a woman in the audience who was sitting there with her husband's arm around her. By the time they finished serenading her, she was sunk down in her seat and her man slowly removed his arm from around her, got up, and left her there to find her own ride home.

Ha! That was almost me, except Victor hadn't noticed, even though ironically he did end up leaving me to fend for myself that night. It was okay. I had Jasper there to take care of me.

Victor had to open up the restaurants early that next morning due to inspections. He'd hinted around for about a half hour that he was ready to go before I suggested he take the car on home and I'd use the driving service to cop a ride. No sooner than I was blowing Victor a kiss good-bye as he exited the building did I find myself back in the dressing room with Jasper getting my pussy ate out. Now see, that's how these young boys get down. They come out the gate letting a chick know that it's all about her, all about pleasing her and making her feel good. Of course, it can all be compared to the crack dealer who gives the crackhead his first hit for free. He knows that crackhead will be back over and over again on the chase for that very first high. And boy oh boy, was I high.

He did the craziest things with his tongue. Had me leaned up against the wall with my leg hiked over his shoulder like we were on *Dancing with the Stars*. Even though I wasn't at my peak, juices were just a-flowing. I was sloppy wet, and not just with his saliva.

Once he made me cum, though, I felt so indebted. I pushed Jasper onto the couch in the dressing room and I crawled onto him like a thief in the night. My Donna Karan pencil skirt was still hiked in the air, and I stepped out of the panties that had previously been resting at my ankles. I bent over and took him into my mouth: all the thickness and all the length. I needed him to know that I could hang with the best of them.

The warmth of my mouth sliding up and down his vessel made him harden in my mouth. With my ass tooted in the air, I began squeezing my breasts together, my nipples massaging his balls.

"Mmmm. Baby, that feels so good," he moaned.

I was working my tongue as if it was a brush and his manhood was my canvas. As I cupped my hand around him and concentrated on the head of his penis, he took in deep breaths like he was hyperventilating.

With all the dramatics, I wanted to be part of the act. I needed to feel him inside of me. I always get what I want, so without further delay, I turned away from him and dropped it on him backward.

"Grab my ass," I ordered him. "Good boy," I said after he followed my directions.

Not only did I like the touch of his hands cupping my ass, but I needed him to balance me as I rode him backward. I felt myself losing my breath with every stroke. When his fingers slid around my thigh and he began to play with my clit, I completely lost it.

"I'm about to cum. Baby, don't stop! I'm about to cum." I barely whispered it as I felt my body tense up. "You watching?" I asked over my shoulder.

"Fuck, yeah," he moaned. "Your cunt is so pretty," he said.

"It's a pussy, dear," I told him. "White girls have cunts. Black women have pussies." So he showed his age. I could get around that. I didn't mind being the teacher sometimes.

"Well, I'm about to fuck the shit out of this pussy," he said with each hard pump.

Young fella took offense at being corrected, so he was taking it out on my kitty. I loved it. The sound of my wetness and my ass smacking against his stomach shot fireworks through each of us. I could feel him releasing inside of me as I sat straight up on his vessel, allowing my juices to flow down him. He held me tight against him, his hands across my stomach, until he was empty and I was full. After that, there was nothing but the sound of our hearts beating and each of us trying to catch our breath.

I fell to the side of the couch and waited for the numbness in my legs to go away. Young buck had ol' girl putting in work. I had something to prove though: that an old G like me could hang with a boy who was still wet behind the ears.

"You can go in there to clean up." He pointed to a room that I assumed was the bathroom.

Oh, goodness. The dreaded ho bath. I had no choice though. Sometimes Victor could be spontaneous, taking me right when I entered the bedroom door. I couldn't take that chance, so off to the bathroom I went.

After cleaning up, I came back into the dressing room area where Jasper was doing what young guys did: checking his Facebook status and liking pictures on Instagram.

"What was your name again?" I asked as I picked up my panties and slipped them on.

"Jasper," he reminded me, looking a little hurt that his name had slipped my mind.

I really didn't need to be reminded. Hell, he'd engraved his name on my pussy with his tongue. I just wanted him to think that he was both replaceable and disposal. That's how a real boss chick keeps the fellas in line. Even an old girl originally from New Orleans knows that.

"Well, Jasper, it was truly a pleasure meeting you." I pulled my skirt down while looking around the room to make sure I'd gathered all my things. Then I clicked my heels right on over to the door.

"Hey, wait a minute," Jasper called out. "Aren't you even going to tell me your name?

What if I want some more of that?" he asked, licking his lips.

With my hand on the doorknob, I turned back to face him. "If you want more of this, then you'll figure out how to get it." I winked then made my exit. I wasn't the least bit worried about Jasper figuring out how to reach me. I'd left my cell number written in lipstick on the bathroom mirror.

Since then, Jasper and I had had more trysts than I could count, but if I did say so myself, this last one here at the LAX Airport Hilton had been one of the best.

While I waited outside the hotel for the valet to bring my Mercedes, I pulled out my phone and called my husband again. I knew he probably hadn't immediately gotten up from having dinner with that daughter of his after I'd called him the first time to remind him of tonight's fundraiser at UCLA. I was on the scholarship board, and I planned to make sure Brielle got into the school next year when she completed her senior year, so missing this affair was not an option, for me at least. Victor, on the other hand, wouldn't surprise me if he somehow managed to miss it just so he could be with Jamela.

He loved being with her. I did everything I could to keep him from spending too much time with her, though. I couldn't risk her getting into his ear. The financial security of me and my children depended on it. Usually I could manage to come up with a reason why he couldn't have dinner with her but instead had to cater to me, but this time there was a conflict of interest. His dinner with her would allow me time with Jasper, so I sacrificed. Still didn't keep me from calling to throw a monkey wrench into their evening.

When Victor had first told me that he was having a celebratory dinner with that brat-ass Jamela, I almost blew a gasket. He'd only told me the morning of. Again, though, I wasn't about to change my plans with Jasper, so I let him go. I knew that while they were dipping crab or lobster into hot butter, Jasper would be dipping himself into me, but I still hated the fact that he was with her. God only knows what venom she would try to spit about me. As far as I was concerned, he might as well have been out with another woman.

Although the two always spoke of how they never spent much time together, I knew it was a lie. The girl worked at one of his restaurants for Christ's sake. Made me wonder if they were trying to throw me off or something, keep me from being suspicious.

For years I felt as if Jamela had Victor under some kind of spell. I feared that whatever she might say to him, he would take a biscuit and sop it up. I was almost certain the man would drink my bathwater if I bottled it up and kept it in the fridge, but the two of them seemed to have a bond that not even the power of my pussy could break. I just wished I'd known that from day one.

I met Victor at the hospital where, at the time, I was taking care of his sick wife. I wasn't particularly attracted to or interested in him when we first met. I'd come in and tend to his wife, exchanging only cordial pleasantries with him, but then everything changed when I learned that he was Victor Long, owner of the most popular and infamous soul food restaurant in town. Then there was the fact that he was about to be a widower. From that point on, I looked at him as if he'd been heaven sent. God knew the life I should have been living, and it wasn't one taking care of sick people for the rest of my life.

I'd escaped a miserable, abusive relationship back in New Orleans. As luck would have it, Brielle and Brendon's father came to town on business. I was working at one of the hotels back then. I'd seen many a businessman from across the map come and go, but it had never crossed my mind to hook up with any of them. Cheating on my high school sweetheart, who wasn't so sweet, could have been the death of me, but there was something about the children's father that made me feel safe and secure.

When I'd go to his room to do turndown service, he treated me like a person, not a maid who wasn't good enough to shine his shoes. He talked to me. Asked me about my life and aspirations. He was the first person I told about wanting to go to college and get into the medical field. He encouraged me to quit dreaming and just do it. Of course it was impossible on the salary of a hotel housekeeper.

He always left me nice tips on the nightstand for cleaning his room, some equaling more than the cost of a one-night stay at the hotel. At first I tried to give it back, thinking he'd mistakenly pulled out a higher amount of bills than he meant to. He insisted I keep it, stating that I should consider it an investment in my college tuition. Right then and there I felt as though he believed in me. I was even more convinced when, after his two-week stay, he asked me to pick up and move back to New York with him, promising to marry and take care of me. Without a thing to lose, I slipped away from my old man and caught a red-eye to New York.

They say that if you can make it in New York you can make it anywhere. That might have been true, but two kids later and baby mamas popping up all over the map from everywhere the children's father had vacationed on business, I was done. A baby mama equaled child support. Bitches were cutting into me and my children's riches. The fairy tale life I dreamed of was never going to come to pass with that man.

I figured he was singing the same song and dancing the same two-step with every other housekeeper he could manipulate. I was pretty sure I was the first, but after making it so easy for him, clearly I wasn't the last. I put up with three baby mamas popping out of the wood-work, but when baby mama number four died during childbirth and the little bastard had to come live with us, that was the straw that broke the camel's back.

I took his ass to court and got what I could be-fore it was all gone, but no way was I going back to New Orleans where everyone would call me a stupid failure. So, I went to the next best place where I thought my fairy tale could come true: California. With my settlement from the divorce as well as grants and loans, I worked hard as hell to put myself through college. All had not been in vain with my relationship with my children's father. Upon graduating, I landed the job that would also land me in the lap of Victor, AKA the lap of luxury.

I wasn't thrilled about his "baggage," as I called Jamela, but if I wanted to change my life for the better, I had to take the good with the bad. At first the little tyke didn't seem like she'd be that bad, but once her mother passed, it was obvious that Victor felt the only piece of her left was with Jamela. Victor had been in love with his wife, so I didn't waste my time trying to compete with that. What drove me crazy was that it seemed like Jamela used her mother's death as a way to wrap her father around her finger.

Yeah, I felt sorry for the poor girl. She'd lost her mother, but Victor felt he could make up for it in material things. He bought her something new almost every day. Hell, he was going to be bankrupt before I could even get him to put a ring on it. That shit had to stop. That's when I fed him some line about how using material things to try to fill the void of her mother might someday turn Jamela against him. She might accuse him of trying to make her forget about her mother with the distraction of gifts. Being the soft, kindhearted fool in love he was, Victor fell back.

Then there was that stupid daddy-daughter day tradition they had. It wasn't so easy to put a crashing halt to that at first, but I managed. I called myself being Victor's unofficial assistant. I kept his calendar, started staying on top of his bills and things like that for him. He'd trusted me with the care and life of his former wife, so he had no problem trusting me with things involving his own life. Whenever he wanted me to schedule his time with Jamela, I'd tell him he was already booked.

With losing his wife and Jamela losing her mother, I knew they needed each other more than ever, but I'd already started showing Jamela my true colors. I just couldn't hide my disdain toward the little brat. I figured that it was only a matter of time before she'd start flapping off at the gums during one of their infamous daddy-daughter dates. I had to keep them apart, at least until he was into me way too deep.

I didn't know what their talks were like, but I just felt like every time he came home from having spent time with her, he was in a different state of mind. He was back to being focused on her and her achievements, talking about how proud he was of her. Everything would be Jamela, Jamela, Jamela. One time, it took me a week to clean up the residue of her from his mind. It was work.

The fact that he'd spent most of today with her had me slightly on edge. God knows what nonsense she'd put in his head this time. I was willing to bet she tried to talk him into buying her a new car. As far as I was concerned, that 1999 Ford she had was good enough. Besides, I already had my counter all worked out. I'd just tell him that she'd be in college soon and typically freshmen couldn't have cars when staying on campus, so it would be a big, fat waste. Besides, this summer I wanted Victor and me to vacation in Maui. Surely another car note would dip into my spending money. Buying one outright would probably put the trip on hold altogether.

Although Victor made money hand over fist, he wasn't a frivolous spender, so I was pretty sure my argument would convince him. At least that's what I hoped, until I got home and he told me his plan.

"What the hell you think you are going to buy her a new car for? We're just coming out of the recession. You just started the corporate delivery business a few months ago," I fussed at Victor. "What if that flops? You put so much money into it. We could take a really bad hit. We need to be smart. We need to be wise." I tried to calm down a tad. I walked over to Victor seductively and rubbed my hand down his cheek. He'd heard me roar. Now he needed to hear me meow. "I say we wait to see how the new business does. Let's give it a year. By then Jamela will be a sophomore in college. She'll be able to drive on campus. It just makes more sense," I reasoned, knowing that next year I'd come up with yet another excuse why we shouldn't purchase Jamela a new car. "We can't risk financing another car at this time. You're a savvy businessman, so I'm sure you'll agree." I began beating him down with the batting of my eyelashes.

Victor was already worn out from his long day. First work, then dinner with Jamela, a pit stop at the drycleaner's, and then a night at the scholarship event. We hadn't been home but ten minutes. Victor hadn't even gotten out of his tux yet. He stood in front of the mirror, removing his tie. I stood behind him, still rubbing my hand down his cheek, staring at our reflection in the mirror.

The event had gone very well. I was marking my territory for when it was Brielle's time to be considered for a scholarship. I had truly felt as though the night had been a success, until Victor dropped this bombshell on me on the way home.

He wanted to get Jamela a new car for her high school graduation. He swore it was his idea, that Jamela hadn't said a word about a new car, but I doubted that. That heifer had been working on him just as I had expected.

Victor kept his voice low and even. "I really did want to surprise her with a car. It's not every day you get a 2200 on the SAT. She doesn't ask for much."

On top of everything else, he wanted to throw how smart she was in my face. Really? "I don't care what she got on the SAT. We can't afford it. Period," I snapped.

"Please lower your voice," Victor whispered. "I don't want her to hear us."

She couldn't hear us. I'd made sure of that when I moved her ass into the maid's quarters.

"Why must you be so difficult?" Victor continued, now at his normal speaking level. "When she first started high school, I told her if she did well I'd buy her a car for graduation. I'm going to keep my word. She has kept her grades up in spite of all the things that she's had to deal with."

"Like what?" I said, a little paranoid. *That little bitch had better not be running her mouth about me.*

"She lost her mother at a young age. She had to share me with you and your children. She's worked for everything she has. I don't just hand her allowance. She works for it at the restaurant. She's earned it. It's just a car note. She makes enough money in tips alone to pay for her own car insurance and tags."

I was not used to Victor going back and forth with me. Usually I said what I had to say and that was it. "Look, I'm not going to stand here and listen to you make excuses for why she's too good for the car she's already driving. It works just fine. I just think this is you slipping back into the days of trying to buy her happiness. Money cannot buy happiness, Victor." Ha! Wasn't I one to talk? "And what's this about her having to share you with me and my children? You pay her more mind than you do my children!"

I knew as I said it that I was lying. The one thing I could say was that Victor was good to my children. Throughout the marriage, I could not think of a single time he ever treated my kids badly. He always treated them as if they were his own. Strangers on the street wouldn't known Brielle and Brendon weren't his blood children.

"That's a lie and you know it." Victor wasn't concerned about keeping voices down now as he raised his. "Your children get child support from their dad, and I still provide for them and get them things. All Jamela gets is a roof over her head and food. Any clothes she does get, hell, I see Brielle in them the next week."

Damn, he noticed that, huh?

"Jamela pays for the little things she wants and any activities she wants to do with her own money. Brendon and Brielle get to spend the money from their dad on whatever they want. And from what I hear, Brielle is spending her money on street pharmaceuticals, if you know what I mean." I could tell by the look on Victor's face that he wished he could take those words back. It was as if he'd been keeping a secret and had let it slip out.

My blood immediately began to boil. I knew he was getting worked up about his little princess, but how dare he try to throw Brielle under the bus in the process? "Don't you dare tell that lie on my child!" I yelled at him.

He came over to me and took me gently by my shoulders. "Honey," he said as he softened his tone. "I'm sorry. I honestly didn't mean to blurt it out like that. But I'm back and forth at restaurants across town. The kids come in, and kids talk."

"So you believe rumors, is that what you're telling me?"

"It's not that."

"Then by all means, please get to telling me just exactly what it is." I put my hand on my hips and stared him down. Using my daughter to change the subject was not sitting well with me at all.

"You can't tell me you haven't noticed how quickly Brielle goes through her money."

"Yeah, but she has things to show for it."

"Like what?"

I opened my mouth, but nothing came out. He'd asked me too quickly. Anything I could think of was something he or I had purchased for her.

"Exactly," he said. "Unless she left remnants of crystal meth somewhere in her room, we'll never see where her money is going."

"How dare you!" I hauled off and slapped Victor with all my might.

Victor grabbed my wrists while I tried to continue swinging on him.

"I know you're upset, Glendora. The truth hurts."

"Truth?" I yelled at the top of my lungs. "You said they were rumors. You're standing here accusing my daughter of being a drug addict based off rumors of what? Some stupid high school kids who are probably just jealous of her?"

"Based on rumors that I'm starting to believe, and that, if you were any kind of mother, you would start to look into."

If I were a dragon, I would have spit fire and burned the muthafuckin' house down. "You son of a—"

Suddenly our bedroom door flew open, just as I'd broken one wrist free from his grip and had my hand extended up in the air, ready to hammer down on Victor.

"Leave my father alone, you old witch!"

I looked up and saw Jamela coming through our bedroom door. The next thing I knew, she'd lunged at me and was now gripping my wrist. Now Victor had one, and Jamela had the other. I was in total disbelief. I looked at her hands on my flesh. *No, she didn't put the paws on me. Fuck that!* We were both about to be on some reality TV show shit.

"You little bitch, if you don't get up out of grown folks' business, I'll knock you out," I said to her.

Hearing me call Jamela a bitch must have stung Victor. Sure, I'd called her that name more times than I could count, but he'd never heard me do it. I'd gotten caught up in the drama, and in turn got caught slipping.

Victor's shocked reaction to my referring to his little princess as a female dog had him releasing my arm and stumbling backward. I immediately used my free hand to pry Jamela's fingers from around my wrist while I snatched away from her.

"What? You tried to hit me?" I said to her. "Did you see that, Victor?" I said without taking my eyes off of Jamela. "Your perfect daughter just jumped on me." I tightened my lips, still glaring at her. "I wish she would try to lay a hand on me. Try that shit again and see what happens. Your father already lost a wife. Would you really want him to have to bury his daughter as well?"

"I was defending my father," Jamela snapped. "So if keeping you from jumping him means jumping on you, then let's do this."

I watched as Jamela's eyes watered with anger. Her fists were clenched and her chest heaved up and down. Little bitch had heart. Who knew?

"I'm not a child anymore, Glendora," she spat. "I've only put up with you and not told my father what a mentally abusive bitch you've been to me because you were the only thing that seemed to make him happy. But now you wanna put your hands on him? That's where I draw the line. So let's do this. You and me." Jamela didn't even give me a chance to respond before she came charging at me.

I managed to catch both her wrists. I planned on releasing them so we could get it in, but there was something I needed to say to her first. "I've been wanting to whip your ass for years," I said, looking her dead in her eyes. "But out of respect for my husband, I didn't—that and the fact that I didn't want to go to jail for child abuse. But you just said it yourself: you're not a child anymore. So let's get it." I released her hands and then immediately grabbed her head of thick hair.

"Let go of me," she said, reaching around and grabbing a handful of my virgin silky hair extensions.

She pulled so hard that they came out in her fingers. *Damn this little bitch. I knew I should have gotten a weave instead of these hair extension clips.* The fact that I was going to have to spend unnecessary money getting it done all over again made the fire that had already lit up under me that much hotter. I was now smoldering.

We scrapped and tussled. This was more than a knockdown, drag-out fight. We were both determined that only death would end this battle. Not even Victor could tear us apart—not that he was trying. I was surprised he wasn't trying to get in between us. He was just standing there watching. At least I thought that's what he was doing. I couldn't tell. I had to keep my eyes on Jamela.

"Let go of my hair!" Jamela shouted. "Fight me like a real woman. Oh yeah, that's right. You're not a real woman. You're a gold-digging h—"

While she was poppin' off at the mouth, I managed to let go of her hair and quickly pop her on the jaw. This caused her to lose her balance, and we both stumbled backward.

Jamela wiped her mouth and looked down at her hand. The sight of blood turned her into someone I had never seen before, someone full of rage. Made me wonder if I could take her on.

"Didn't your mother ever teach you how to fight, little girl?" I smirked at her. I knew it was a dirty move on my part, but I had to hit her where it hurt.

"I'm going to kill you," she growled. She charged back at me. I stuck my hand out, scratching her face.

We continued round two of tussling, swinging, kicking, and scratching. When it comes to physical fighting, I'm not sure age and experience overpowers youth, but I sure as hell was going to give this chick a run for her money. I didn't give a damn if she was about to be out of the house on her own. Right now she was living under my roof. The nerve of a child, eating my food, lying up in my house, raising her hand at me. Even if I did get the worst end of this fight, oh, she was going to know better than to try this shit again.

I learned quickly that this bitch was stronger than I ever would have guessed. It got to the point where I couldn't keep up with her and had to go old school on her. I dipped my head, closed my eyes, and just began to windmill.

I felt like I had been windmilling for an hour, like I should have taken off like a helicopter, but she was still coming for me.

Eventually, I heard a loud thump and a crashing sound. At first I thought I had managed to knock her out or something. That couldn't have been possible, though, because I could still feel my fists landing on her.

"Daddy!"

Jamela yelled for Victor, her attention now on him instead of me. This would be my chance to take her down. I could sneak her the same way Floyd Mayweather had done that Latino boxer. Protect yourself at all times. Well, that was a rule Jamela wasn't following right now. There was something about the look of horror on her face, though, that made me decide to follow her eyes instead of sneak-attack her.

I turned my head to see Victor sliding down the dresser. His eyes were blank, and he was slumped over.

It was at that moment that Jamela and I were no longer concerned about being the last man standing. We each raced over to him.

"Victor, honey. Are you okay?"

"No, he's not okay," Jamela said. "Look at him," she yelled. She was yelling out of fear, so I let it go. "Call 911," Jamela said to me as tears began to spill from her eyes. She started patting Victor's cheeks. "Daddy, please be okay. Stay with me, Daddy, please. Not you too, Daddy."

Believe it or not, standing there watching that poor girl plead for her father's life really did break my heart. Yes, we had our differences, but I couldn't help but feel sorry for her in that moment. She'd already lost one parent, which had benefitted me greatly. In all honesty, I didn't want her to deal with the death of two. Not this soon anyway—for her sake and for mine.

With Victor being older than me, I figured he'd be the first to go, but we hadn't even gotten to the point where he was worth more dead than alive. He still had a few good miles left on him—and money to make for me to burn.

"Please, Glendora. Call for help."

Jamela's cry tore me out of my daze. Victor's lips were starting to turn blue. "Okay, yes, okay." I panicked, running over to the nightstand and grabbing the house phone. When the operator answered, I gave her our address and said, "Please hurry. It's my husband. He's lying on the floor. His lips are blue." I looked over at Jamela, crying over her father.

"Daddy, Daddy, wake up. Don't do this to me."

At that point, the operator walked me through the steps that would enable me to determine whether Victor was breathing. In my current mental state, all my years of nurse's training did me no good. I couldn't think straight. "No!" I yelled. "Dear God, he's not breathing."

Jamela began giving Victor CPR. I watched as she tried her best to breathe life into him, then placed her hands on in his chest, pumping up and down.

All of this felt surreal. I listened numbly as the operator told me that an ambulance was on the way. My only concern now was, would the help be on time?

CHAPTER THREE

BRIELLE

(Long Island, New York)

"Mom, what's wrong?" I asked when she called me at my father's house. She usually sounded so happy and upbeat, especially when she was calling to tell me about a purchase she'd made. Today, she sounded like she was crying.

"Bri," my mom said. She swallowed so hard I felt like I was traveling down her windpipe. "It's . . . Victor."

Okay, now she was scaring me. She needed to say whatever it was she was trying to say. I was all the way in New York with no connects. The last thing I needed was to get all hyped and anxious and not have anything to bring me down. "Mom, what about Victor? Is he okay?"

I could hear a swishing sound as if my mom was shaking her head.

"Ma, please tell me." My voice began to tremble.

"Victor had a stroke, sweetie."

My stomach plunged as if I'd been kicked. I pulled my iPhone away from my ear and looked down at it like a snake handler. I couldn't believe the words that had had the nerve to slither into my ear. Not that I wanted to, but I needed to hear them again. I needed to make sure of things. "What did you say?"

"Victor had a stroke," my mom repeated in a shaky voice. In spite of what Jamela wrote in her diary about my mother being a gold digger, I knew Mom loved Victor. There were so many times I'd wanted to call Jamela out on the things she said about my mom in that stupid diary she kept hidden in her sock drawer, but I couldn't let her know I'd been reading it. Hearing how broken up my mom was right now just proved to me how wrong my stupid stepsister was about her.

"When? What happened? Where is he, Mom?" My anxiety rose with every question I asked. "Is he in the hospital? Is he . . ." I couldn't even bring myself to say the word. It would have been harder for me to accept Victor's death than that of my own father. After all, it was Victor who saved us from living the life of a low-income family, with Brendon and me having to walk through the doors of public schools every day. Yeah, our pops paid child support, but that's where the support stopped. No extras, with the exception of the health care the courts forced him to provide for us and the roundtrip flight tickets he provided every spring break.

I didn't really trip about it all that much. Hell, I knew my dad had kids all over the map he had to pay child support for. I couldn't imagine he had any left over to give, especially with trying to maintain the New York lifestyle he shared with his current wife and their child.

Brendon, on the other hand, despised our father for not doing more. I don't think he meant doing more when it came to money. I think Brendon would have taken more father-son time with our dad than anything. He was a growing boy becoming a man. Victor was a great example of a hardworking man who took care of his family, but I guess for a boy, there is nothing like having your biological father take you under his wing and teach you how to be a man.

"It happened last night," my mother said. "He's in the hospital and, baby, it's not looking too good." She started crying loudly.

I put down my turquoise fingernail polish. My toes were only half done, but my hand was shaking so bad that I wouldn't have been able to finish.

"Last night?" I yelled. "Why didn't you tell me?" I shrieked. "Why are you just now calling me?" Here I'd been sitting out on the patio by the pool—even though it was still down for the season—in my North Face fleece outfit like everything was just fine, all while my stepfather was on his deathbed.

My mom paused, swallowing her tears. "It was touch and go for a moment. So much was going on that I didn't have time to call you." She went on to explain the events of the night before. "They did emergency surgery He's in intensive care now. I just got home a few minutes ago."

"Mom, are you okay?" I asked, hearing the strain in her voice.

"I'm exhausted," she said. "I haven't slept a wink since the ambulance took him away. I'm going to try to take a nap while he's in recovery."

I heard the fear in her tone, something I almost never witnessed from my mother. My mom was a beast. A lioness. I'd watched her work hard to provide for us pre-Victor. She was always so sure, confident, and fearless. To hear her sounding almost . . . weak . . . Oh, I knew without a doubt that I needed to get my ass home so that I could be there for her.

"Oh my God. I'm coming home to be with you right away," I said, gathering up all my things and stuffing them into my nail polish storage case. Suddenly, a part of me was overcome with excitement. In the words of Biggie Smalls, I was going back to Cali!

Now don't get me wrong. I really was worried about Victor's well-being. My stepfather had been a good dude to my brother and me over the past eight years. He was a stand-up guy, and I couldn't wait to get there to see him. My mom had already said things were touch and go, and I wouldn't be able to live with myself if Victor passed and I wasn't there to say my good-byes. Then there was my mom, who needed me there to help her be strong. But truth be told, I had been dying to get back home for other reasons.

It was so boring out here on Long Island. I never could figure out what the big deal about the whole "weekend in the Hamptons" was about, or why people spent money to travel here. There was never anything to do if you asked me. The people seemed so uppity, acting like life was good all the time. As a matter of fact, they stayed so high off of life itself, I couldn't find one single person who needed that extra boost in life, if you know what I mean.

This was made clear the first time I tried to go out and see if I could find someone selling ice, AKA crystal meth. Talk about a lost cause. I wasted hours befriending kids my age and dirty old men, and I still came up dry. I could live without the stuff definitely. I just used it because I wanted to, not because I needed it, but it had been frustrating as hell knowing that if I did want a hit, I was shit out of luck. But it looked as though my luck had just changed. Now, all I wanted to do was get back to Cali so I could buy what I needed and get white-girl wasted.

Before heading into the house, I stopped at the door and prepared to put on the best performance of my life. I really was feeling bad about Victor, but I had to lay it on thick if I was going to convince my father to let me cut my time with him short to go see about my stepfather.

I worked up some tears before I rushed into the house in hysterics, crying about how Victor was about to die and I needed to get home.

"Your dad's at work," my stepmother said, putting her arms around me in an attempt to calm me down. "But you go ahead and start packing, honey. I'll talk to your father and tell him what's going on."

When she planted a kiss on my forehead, I couldn't keep the smile from spreading across my lips. White chicks were so easy to manipulate sometimes. Now, a sista from the streets who's always on top of her game never would have fallen for that shit, at least not that quickly. That was the difference between my moms and Sky, my dad's current wife. Dad had gone black with my mom, but despite popular opinion, he never went back. Hell, my dad was what some would consider to be a pretty boy. He could pull women of all races and nationalities . . . and he had.

After wiping the smile off of my face for getting one over on Sky and then all the tears I'd deliberately worked up just to work her, I went to my room and immediately started to pack my suitcase. It was my goal to leave before my dad got back home from work. The last thing I wanted him to do was try to talk me into staying. This girl was not packing her bags to go on a guilt trip. I was not trying to let him make me feel bad by reminding me how I lived with Victor all year long and he only had this little bit of time with me, blah blah blah. Later for all that. I was on a mission. Besides, I was not ready to deal with the fake, phony lies from my dear old daddy. Yeah, I might have been staying under the same roof as him during spring break, but I could barely stand to stay in the same room with him.

Truth be told, I couldn't stand my father ever since he got married to Sky. She was cool, but keeping it one hundred, her being a white chick probably had less to do with her being a pushover than her age did.

Sky was only in her early twenties, but she looked like she was still in high school. Then there was the boob job my dad got her for her birthday, and the ass job for Christmas. One year I came down for spring break and both her chest and ass were as flat as the diving board out at the pool. The year after that, I came back and could set my soda bottle in her cleavage. And that butt! I could set my whole nail polish kit on her ass and do my nails without anything falling off. She'd already had a nice body, one that could make an older man such as my pops spend all kinds of money on her ass—literally.

Anyhow, my father, who had turned forty-nine on his last few birthdays, tried to act young in his new marriage. Sky even got that fool taking tennis lessons. He had the nerve to text me a selfie of him and Sky playing doubles with another couple. My dad sending selfies. Ha! How embarrassing.

My dad told everyone the two of them had met through work, but I knew better. With a name like Sky, I was willing to bet that he'd met her at some rinky-dink strip club while away on business. With Sky being from Texas, no one could really poke holes in his story, but game recognizes game, so my mother knew the story was probably bullshit. After all, he made up the same kind of story about how he met my mom, when she was really just the housekeeper in a hotel he stayed at.

I would never tell my dad what I really thought about him and wifey though. I acted like an innocent little Miss Goody Two-shoes around him, because I didn't want to give him any reason to cut off his monthly child support. But after the first couple days of being here in New York with him, I got so sick of pretending to be this perfect little California girl. I believe my dad even thought I was still a virgin. What a crock of shit! But I had to give myself a pat on the back. The City of Angels had taught me how to be what people wanted me to be. After all, wasn't everybody in Hollywood an actor?

I was just a girl trying to fit in—and fitting in was pretty easy for me. I was able to do what Blacks call "pass." Depending on how I wore my hair, in its natural kinky loop curls or flat-ironed bone straight, or how much I'd tanned or hadn't, I could pass for either black or white. Bitch was like a chameleon for sure. I was a little thick on top of it all, so it made me appear older than I was. One day I'd drop a few pounds, but for now, the weight came in handy. It had helped me really look like I was twenty-one on that fake ID I'd managed to get.

Speaking of the ID, that thing had gotten me into so many places it wasn't even funny. They have clubs in Hollywood that all types of stars and young people hang out at, and I was always right there in the scene. Thank goodness my mom wasn't into TMZ, Instagram, Twitter, or any of that stuff. Lord knows how many incriminating photos she might have spotted me in.

I couldn't help myself from overindulging and getting caught up sometimes. Heck, what teenager wouldn't want to be in the clubs every night if they were spotting people like Justin Bieber, Selena Gomez, and Taylor Swift? I swear on everything I even saw Willow Smith trying to stay incognito in the VIP section one time. I'd learned to fit in and roll with the best of them, and I was fiendin' to get back to the scene.

Sky called the airline for me and helped me change my return flight. She explained to them how ill my stepfather was and how I had to get back home, and of course, I turned on the waterworks in the background. Brendon decided to stay for the rest of spring vacation, but sent his well wishes that Victor would recover. Not only did big brother want to maximize his time with our father, but I think he had a little sidepiece he was knocking off back in the Big Apple. So, I was headed home alone.

Within ten minutes of calling the airline, Sky was racing me to the airport for a flight that was scheduled to leave New York in three hours. With the city traffic, my nerves were on edge, hoping we'd make it in time. There was a God, because even after I got all checked in, I still had an entire hour before boarding. I texted the entire time, putting the word out to my peeps that Queen B was on her way back to home sweet home. That meant it was going to be turn-up time for sure.

My phone rang and my dad's name popped up on my screen, interrupting me in the middle of one of my texts.

"Yeah, Dad," I answered, sounding annoyed at first, but then realizing that wasn't the role I was supposed to be playing. "Sorry to sound so bothered. It's just that Mom's been calling me every five minutes to see if I was on my way home yet. She's so torn up. Now I'm not only worried about Victor, but I'm worried about her as well." Even though my dad couldn't see my face, I wore a grim and exasperated expression to match my tone. Damn, I was good!

"I'm going to miss you, baby girl. Have a safe flight," were the last words my dad said to me before he hung up the phone. I knew my dad wouldn't really miss me. That was just the proper thing for a father to say to his daughter. I mean, I guess he liked having me around for a few weeks to visit, but we didn't have a tight bond or anything. Trust me, I'd seen a real daddy-daughter relationship with Victor and Jamela. Therefore, I knew a fake one when it was smacking me in the face.

After boarding the plane, I sent out one last tweet before the captain told everyone to turn off their electronic devices: Home sweet home #CaliHereICome #IrunLA

That's right. The boss bitch was on her way back!

When my Delta plane landed at LAX, I pulled out my phone to call my connect from the airport. We made arrangements to meet up so I could get my weed and my ice. Before you get the wrong idea, yes, I was going to the hospital first. After all, I didn't know if my stepfather would be alert, and I didn't want to risk visiting him with a buzz. I just wanted to get all my ducks in a row so that as soon as I left Victor I could enjoy my high with my girls.

Lately I thought Victor was getting suspicious of my recreational drug use. My mother, on the other hand, didn't have a clue. She was not one to bite her tongue, so if she thought for a minute that her "perfect" daughter used drugs, she would have flipped. No, I worked hard to perfect my image so that she still thought I was a California angel. To make sure my charade stayed intact, I rented a car from Enterprise. After all, what would I look like having my mother drop me off when I went to cop a fix later?

With my fake ID and the emergency credit card Victor had given me on my sixteenth birthday, I was in a rented sedan and headed to the hospital within forty-five minutes. I was definitely glad to be back on home turf, but the moment I stepped into the hospital, my entire demeanor shifted. Seeing all the sick people waiting around to be checked by a doctor, or taking walks through the corridors in their hospital gowns, reminded of exactly why I was here: Victor. Worry suddenly came over me.

I hadn't heard from my mother since before I got on the plane in New York. Was no news good news . . . or bad? Suddenly I felt guilty for not checking in with Mom as soon as I got my bags after the flight. I'd been so caught up in making sure I had what I needed to get my mind right that something bad could have happened to Victor in the interim and I wouldn't even know it. I immediately picked up my pace and raced over to the elevator.

Looking at the hospital map above the elevator buttons, I saw that the ICU was on the second floor, so I pushed the button to go up, jumping in as soon as the doors opened. As they began to close, I could see an older lady hobbling to the elevator with her walker.

"Please hold that—"

I'd already put my finger on the CLOSE DOOR button before she could finish her request. *Sorry, old lady.* She was moving way too slow, and my anxiety was about to get the best of me. I needed to see about Victor.

Even though I only had to go one floor up, it felt like the longest elevator ride ever. What if something had happened and I'd already missed out on the chance to say good-bye to Victor?

When the elevator arrived on the second floor, I couldn't wait for those slow-ass doors. I squeezed through them before they had a chance to fully open, and I went straight to the nurse's station.

"Victor Long. My father," I said, out of breath. "I'm here to see my father, Victor Long."

The nurse looked at me, then turned to click a few buttons on her computer, then looked up at me again. "You said you're his daughter?" she asked in a way that had me suddenly irritated as hell. "But his daughter is already in there with him."

"I'm his stepdaughter. My mother, his wife, is Glendora Long," I explained, although what I really wanted to do was tell her to mind her own damn business. I had as much right to be there as that pain in the ass Jamela.

The nurse retrieved a file and then flipped through it. "Brail?" she said with a raised eyebrow.

"Yes, but it's pronounced *Bree-elle*," I corrected her with plenty of attitude.

"Sure." She dropped the file on the desk, giving me attitude right back. "Your father is in room 212," she told me, pointing down the hall without bothering to look at me. I was so happy to hear that he was still alive that I didn't even bother to call her out on her rudeness.

Everything was going by me in a blur as I made my way to room 212. The numbers were taking their sweet time getting higher—something I wished I could be doing at that moment. Finally I stood in front of a plaque that read 212, with Victor Long's name underneath it.

Like all the other rooms in the ICU, this one had no door, but there was a curtain around the bed to give a patient some privacy. I stood in the hallway and took a moment to catch my breath. You would have thought I'd just run in a marathon. Definitely made me rethink keeping this weight on. Maybe it was time to get rid of the baby fat.

As I stood outside the curtain I could hear Jamela's voice.

"Daddy, please don't die. I won't have any reason to live if you're not here." I peeked around the curtain and saw her on her knees at her father's bedside, holding his hand. "I don't have anybody on this earth who cares about me but you, Daddy. You can't leave me. You just can't."

She looked so pitiful, and her words almost made me feel a little bit of regret. I hated to admit it, but I hadn't been the best stepsister to Jamela. When she said those words about not having anybody on earth who cared about her, I kind of understood why she felt that way.

When we first moved into Victor and Jamela's home, I was so happy. Having a big sister was awesome, and she was so generous to me. I'd be so excited whenever my mom brought in another box, saying, "Jamela just cleaned out her stuff and said you can have all these things."

It wasn't no junk either. Jamela had some nice stuff. Some of it I knew for sure she hadn't outgrown, but I figured she was just totally into being a big sister and wanted to make me happy. I got so caught up in stuff, a trait I definitely inherited from my mother, that I never took the time to tell her how much I appreciated her welcoming me with open arms and treating me like I was her very own blood sister. I know if the tables were turned, I wouldn't have given her half the stuff she gave me, if anything at all. In spite of the distance that had grown between us over the years, I knew Jamela had a good heart, which was why hearing her feel so alone made me feel that much worse.

I stood there for a few more moments listening to her cry and pray over Victor.

"God, I really need you to heal my father," she prayed. "I need him as much as he needs me. I'm his princess. I'm his daddy's girl."

Immediately, a frown covered my face and envy covered my heart. Just that quickly I was reminded of why I never did voice to Jamela how much I appreciated her when we first moved in. See, it hadn't taken long for Jamela to show her true colors and make it clear that while she might share clothes, she wasn't interested in sharing her daddy. She always wanted to be alone with him and have what she called daddy-daughter time. It started to make me feel left out, and before long my appreciation turned to resentment. No matter how much Victor tried not to show any favoritism and to turn us into one big, happy family, Jamela would demand louder that he spend time alone with her.

It didn't help my attitude to know how my mother felt about Jamela. Once, in passing, I overheard her talking to one of her friends on the phone about it. "I swear that fucking brat wants to spend so much time alone with him so she can try to get rid of me and my kids," she said.

I remember laughing under my breath because I'd heard my mother curse, but deep down, it scared me. What if Victor really did decide to get rid of us? My own father called me once in a while, but we barely had a relationship, so I couldn't stand the thought of losing Victor, the only real father figure I'd ever known. So, underneath it all, who could blame me for being jealous?

After witnessing what a true father and daughter relationship was supposed to look like, I did try to create that with my own father. For two whole months I called him every single day. After that, I purposely stopped just to see if he would miss me and call to check on me. It never happened. That's when I had to accept the fact that my father was nothing more than a spring break father and probably always would be. Victor had been more of a father to me in these last few years than my father had been my entire life.

I thought of my last conversation with Victor before I left for Long Island. "Brielle, you know I love you like you are my own child, and I only want the best for you, but I've been hearing bad things about you and the crowd you hang with. And I don't like the hours you're keeping." The night before, he'd closed up the restaurant and come home at 3 a.m. He felt the hood of my car, which was still warm, so he knew that I had been driving it not too long before—way past my midnight curfew.

I had hung my head, hoping he'd take that for an apology and drop the subject. No such luck. He continued, "Your grades are starting to suffer from it as well." He lifted my chin and looked me straight in my eyes and asked, "Is there anything you want to tell me? Is there anything you are into that you might not want your mother to find out? Because you know you can tell me anything and I'll help you."

Thing was, I believed every word Victor said. I didn't feel as though he was trying to get me to confess to something so that he could trap me and go rat me out to my mother. Victor truly did seem concerned about me. It was the look that every girl hopes to see when she looks into her father's eyes. I'd waited years for that look, but I couldn't even take it all in for what it was worth, because I knew damn well that, as a father, he had every right to be concerned about me. I was hanging with a suspect crowd, my grades were shitty, and I was getting a craving for those ice chips.

No way was I going to have that look in Victor's eyes be replaced with disgust and disappointment, so I did what I do best: I lied to that man right in his face. I told him everything was fine and that after spring break I'd hit the books harder than ever.

He didn't press the conversation after that. He just kissed me on the forehead, patted me on the shoulder with a smile, and told me how much he'd miss me and my brother while we were gone. But I could tell he didn't believe me. I could tell he knew something was up.

I cringed, just thinking that this might have been our last conversation. I told a man who never wanted anything but the best for me a lie right to his face. How could I live with that? If God would just give me one more chance to . . .

Who was I kidding? If I had to do it all over again, I'd still lie. I mean, I couldn't admit to Victor that I dibbled and dabbled in drugs here and there. He'd look at me as a hardcore druggie and probably start hiding things in the house. No way would I be able to convince him that it wasn't that serious, even though never once had I stolen anything to get high or even borrowed money. I'd usually just treat myself to a little something whenever Mom turned over my portion of child support to me.

Don't get me wrong; I wasn't any kind of addict. I bought just enough to last me. You'd never find me lying out in a sweat, scratching at my neck, fiendin' for the stuff. Although another week in New York might have been a different thing. But still, believe me when I say I wasn't hooked or anything. Like I said before, it was just a recreational high. I could quit any time I wanted. It's just that life was so much more fun when I was high.

As I stood there listening to Jamela cry over her ailing father, though, no drug in the world would have made that sight fun.

I listened a little longer to Jamela.

"Daddy, don't leave me. I'll do whatever I have to do to take care of you, just so long as you live. I won't go away to college. I'll be here for you like you were always here for me. I love you, Daddy. Can you hear me?"

I couldn't take it anymore. The girl was crying and snotting all over the place. Hell, if she kept it up, I was probably going to end up having to ask the doctors if they could prescribe something to calm her down. Hmm, had I copped my ice first, I might have been able to solve that problem. For now, though, I guessed I would have to see if a few comforting words would do the trick.

"Jamela," I said as I entered the room. "I'm so sorry, sis." I decided to call her sis like I did back in the day when I was younger and smaller than her. Somehow, in all my thickness, I'd managed to surpass Jamela in size. Guess it was time for me to start giving her all her old clothes back.

"How is Victor?" I reached over and put my hand on her shoulder. Since she was still on her knees, I couldn't give her the fake hug that I would have sacrificed doing. What can I say? I was not the hugging type, although I was sincere as far as her father went. I really did care about him.

Jamela looked up and noticed for the first time that I was in her presence. "Oh, hey, Brielle," she said. "You're back early." She was surprised to see me. I didn't interact with Jamela that much, and she and my mother didn't communicate, so there would have been no way for Jamela to know I was coming back home early.

She began to wipe away her tears with her hands. I spotted a small box of tissue, grabbed a couple out of the box, and handed them to her.

"Thank you," she said, extending her arm limply. She looked so weak and helpless, just the way my mother had sounded on the phone. In this state, Jamela looked nothing like the confident person I'd always seen her to be.

In my opinion, sometimes her confidence was laced with a little cockiness. She always walked around the house unaffected by anything, her head held high and nose in the air like she was better than all of us. She never gave me a direct attitude, but I just couldn't stand how she acted like her shit didn't stink. I imagined her being at school telling all her friends how I had to wear her hand-me-downs. Now that I think about it, she probably only gave me her old things as an excuse to get her daddy to go out and buy her an entire new wardrobe. I could just hear her now: *"Daddy, I had to give Brielle all my clothes. I have nothing to wear to school. Do you expect me to go to school and get straight A's if I don't look good?"*

Well, I would have said it like that, anyway. Jamela was so proud of herself. She even acted like her dark skin was better than my light skin, when we all know it should be the other way around. Just look at the music videos. The light-skinned girl is always the pretty lead. But I thought her father probably had something to do with that. I was sure he'd instilled in her to be proud of her complexion, to be proud of herself period, because he was always telling her how proud he was of her. I bet he never lectured her about the kinds of people she was hanging out with, the way he did with me.

Watching her crying and begging for her father's life was sad though. For the first time since I could remember, I really felt for Jamela. Truth be told, she had never really done anything bad to me, nor had she ever been mean to me.

If I was really being honest with myself, I could admit that I had allowed my mother to shape my relationship with Jamela. I loved my mother. In my eyes, she was right about everything. I watched how she was with Jamela. I listened to the things she would say about her, and I guess I allowed those things to influence my feelings about Jamela. I started seeing her differently—through my mother's eyes.

"I came back early when I heard," I said to Jamela. She turned her attention back to her father, and so did I. Seeing Victor lying there, tubes coming from his nose, IVs from his arm and machines beeping, I grew weak in the knees. "I'm sorry that this happened, Jamela. I know how much you love your dad."

She turned around and looked at me. I felt like she was examining my face for sincerity. "You love him too." Her eyes were questioning.

"Yes." I nodded and smiled.

"I appreciate you being here."

Neither of us said anything for a minute as we both watched Victor lying motionless in the bed. After a few seconds, she pushed herself up off the floor. She stretched her stiff body.

"I'll sit with him and give you a break, if you'd like." I looked around. There was a chair on each side of his bed. The one closer to me was a regular plastic chair. The one closer to the window was a little nicer, almost like a mini La-Z-Boy.

"No, I don't want to leave him." She walked over to the less comfy-looking chair, so I headed over to the recliner. "I want to spend as much time with him as I can."

She sat down and said, "Your mom is funny about how long I stay in here with him. She went home to shower and change, so I want to spend as much time with him as I can before she gets back and starts regulating." She let out a small chuckle.

I chuckled too, but I knew shade when I heard it, and that chick had just thrown some shade. I wasn't mad though. My mother was very controlling and protective of those she loved, so I knew what Jamela meant.

Jamela took her father's hand and just sat there staring at him. This was like a depressing scene from one of the soap operas my mom used to watch. I wanted to sit here and keep Jamela company, but this was too much. I shot back up from my chair, rubbing my palms down my jeans.

"Okay. I'm going downstairs to grab a coffee then. Do you want one?"

"I'd appreciate that. I haven't slept a wink since yesterday. I could use a boost."

You and me both, I thought, rolling my eyes up in my head. I headed over to the curtain to exit. "Sure you don't want to come with me? Just to walk and get your blood flowing?"

She shook her head. "I want to be here when he wakes up. *If* he wakes up."

I nodded my understanding as I exited the room, making sure I'd wiped every last one of my escaped tears away before I got on the elevator.

I returned to the room about a half hour later, surprised to see that my mom wasn't back yet. I knew she said that she was going to try to take a nap, but she must have been so exhausted that she was still asleep.

I gave Jamela her coffee and then sat back in my chair with mine. I pulled out my cell phone to call my mother.

"Those aren't allowed."

I looked over at Jamela, who was pointing to a sign on the wall. It was a laminated picture of a cell phone with a circle around it and a huge slash through it.

"Oh," I said, then opted to send my mother a text instead. I told her that I was at the hospital and asked when she was heading back up. She replied a couple minutes later, letting me know that she wouldn't be back any time soon.

"My mom's not coming back until the morning," I informed Jamela. If I wasn't mistaken, I think she perked up a little bit at the news.

"That's fine," she said. "I'll just stay with him all night."

I suppose I could have offered to stay with her, but no way was I spending the night at that hospital. It wasn't like Victor knew we were there anyway. What was she going to do, just sit there and stare at him all night? Sorry, Charlie. It wasn't happening.

The nurse came in to check on Victor. By then I'd finished my coffee and figured I'd been there long enough. I stood up to leave.

"I think I'm going to get ready to head out," I said, stretching. "I'm still jet-lagged and everything from that long flight."

"I understand," Jamela said. "Thanks again for coming."

"No problem." I threw my cup into the trash. "You sure you don't want to go home, change clothes, and get cleaned up or something?" This was my last offer, and I was hoping and praying she'd decline—which she did. On that note, I told her good-bye and left the hospital.

As soon as I walked out of those sliding automatic hospital doors, I hopped on the phone with my BFF, Lyric, who was also a fellow cheerleader. We were polar opposites but complemented each other in so many ways. I was the thick cheerleader; she was as skinny as a rail. I was the popular black girl, and she was the popular white girl.

Although she was a straight-up white girl, she was real cool. We met each other in second grade after my mom married Victor. She also lived in Bel Air, with both her parents and younger twin brothers. Her parents had beaucoup money. They were both in the movie industry. They stayed on sets or on location. Most people thought the housekeeper/nanny was her mother, because she was more visible in Lyric's life than her own parents. Lyric had no complaints though. She said they rarely saw her, so when they did, they could never differentiate whether she was high. Made it easy for her to keep her little meth habit under wraps.

"Girl, what are you doing in town so soon?" she screamed into the phone so loud that I pulled the phone away from my ear to make sure I hadn't accidentally put it on speaker.

"Didn't you get the text I sent you?"

"I didn't get a text from . . ." She said the words slowly. I could tell she was searching through her phone while she was talking. "Oh, here it is." I heard her mumbling as she read. "I don't know how I missed this."

"Yes, my stepdad had a stroke, so I came home early." I reiterated what was in the text I'd sent her as I approached the rental car.

"I'm sorry to hear that. Is he okay?"

"He seems to be holding his own. I'm at the hospital now. Well, I'm just leaving the hospital."

"Will you be able to make it to the club tonight?"

"Hell, yes, and after being up in this depressing bitch, there is nothing more I need right now than a drink—well, maybe there is something I need more than just a drink." Lyric knew exactly what I was talking about as we both shared a laugh. "Girl, I can't wait to get my drink on. I just have to drop off this rental, go home and pick up my car, and then it's on. We gon' party tonight, bitch!" I got in the car and started it up.

"That's what's up," Lyric said, using ghetto slang in her white voice.

"All right then. Let me handle my business and we'll hook up later. Deuces." I ended the call and pulled out of my parking spot. I couldn't wait to get my stuff. I didn't want to think about my mother, Jamela, my father, or even Victor laid up in the hospital. All I wanted to do was go have fun. I'd caught my second wind, and now I was about to flap my wings and fly high!

CHAPTER FOUR

JAMELA

Three Years Later

The day after Daddy had his stroke, Brielle flew back from New York. She sat with me in Daddy's room for a little while, but then she left. Glendora, his own wife, didn't even show up again that night. It was just me alone with my father near death. That was the scariest time in my life, and there I sat, dealing with it alone. Even now, three years later, I still felt alone. Yes, Daddy was back home now, but the stroke had done so much damage that he couldn't care for himself. And even though Glendora, Brielle, and Brendon were under the same roof, it felt like it was always just me and my pops, because no one else seemed to be around to help take care of him. Glendora was off spending as much money as she could; Brielle was busy getting high and thinking she was hiding it from everyone, although Glendora was the only one still in denial about the extent of Brielle's problem; and Brendon . . . I didn't care what he was doing as long as he was staying away from me.

Call me an "old soul," but I didn't mind spending any free time that I had next to my father, reading the paper to him or reporting to him how well the restaurants were doing. He'd been a good father to me, and I did everything I could to make sure he was comfortable. Although he had two full-time nurses, I spent as much time with him as I could. He and I were family. Even as ill as he was, he was still a comfort to me. The same way it had been hard for me to tear myself away from his hospital bed, it was just as hard to get me away from his side now.

When I wasn't with Daddy, I was working at the restaurants to continue his legacy. Three years ago I was just a high school senior with an after-school job helping out in the restaurant. Now I was a grown woman who had taken Daddy's place in actually running the restaurants. Glendora had tried for a while to manage the books, but between her expensive tastes and her lack of self-control, she was running the place into the ground. Half of our profits went to pay off her American Express bill every month. I finally convinced her to let me take over, and to my surprise, she relented pretty quickly. She actually admitted that she was glad to let me do it because, as she said, "I am too cute to be spending so many hours on my damn feet every day." On top of taking over at the restaurant, I was going to school part time, squeezing in night classes whenever I could.

With all that I had going on in life, you would think I didn't even have time to sleep and eat. Well, you would be partially right. I didn't have much time to sleep, but eating wasn't a problem, considering I spent hours each day surrounded by food. So I was no longer that girl sitting by my daddy's hospital bed in more ways than one. I was twice the girl—literally.

I'd put on so much weight that it was ridiculous. As always, my stepmother did not bite her tongue in reminding me. Just last week she'd said, "Girl, you better do something about that weight if you ever want to get a man the way I got your daddy. You already a dark shade of black," she said, referencing my complexion. "You don't want to be fat and black. You can't do anything about your skin unless you got Michael Jackson money, but you can do something about that weight."

As much as I hated to say it, she was right; not about my skin tone, but about my weight. There was no reason why I was allowing myself to get out of control like this. My father needed me, and if God saw fit, he'd be needing me for years to come. I needed to get healthy so that I could always be there to take care of him. I didn't want to get so big and unhealthy that I was lying right up next to him, needing someone to take care of me.

With that being said and with my gym bag strapped over my shoulder, I pulled up to LA Fitness in West Los Angeles. I climbed out of my car. My mother's old car had finally clunked out, but I didn't get a new one. I just drove Daddy's, since his medical condition prevented him from driving. I was sure Glendora would have rather I walked, but somebody needed to keep the restaurants up and running, and I couldn't do that using public transportation. Besides, that was the income that still allowed her to shop like there was no tomorrow, so she handed over the keys to his Cadillac.

As I approached the facility, I got a glimpse of my muffin top in the mirrored windows of the building. Even with a black stretch girdle under my sweat clothes for my workout, it was obvious that I wasn't just thick; I was fat.

It never failed that whenever I ran into old classmates at the restaurant or something, they'd have this look on their face as if to say, "Girl, what happened to you?"

If any of them had been bold enough to ask out loud, my answer would have been simple: "Life happened."

At five feet four inches, I now weighed almost 220 pounds. When I was in the department store trying on clothes a few months ago and had to go from buying size sixteens to my first size eighteen, I knew then that I had to make a change. I didn't mind being curvy, but I knew I was becoming unhealthy. My doctor had even informed me that I was borderline diabetic, but I still hadn't made time to change my habits. I'd been trying to work the gym into my schedule for the past six months, but it just never made it to the top of my priorities.

I'd decided that having a personal trainer might motivate me to work out more regularly, so here I was, going into LA Fitness for my first session.

I stepped up to the front desk, feeling a little nervous. "I have an appointment with Isaac Butler," I said to the man behind the counter, who was buff as hell. Looking at my figure, you could tell that I practically lived in a restaurant, and looking at him, I guessed that he pretty much lived in the gym. Lord have mercy, I wouldn't mind having someone like him working me out!

That's when it hit me. What if he was Isaac? He would probably think I was some kind of pig. Now a woman, she'd be able to empathize.

Almost every woman has dealt with the weight fluctuation issue at some point in her life, but a man like this with his bionic metabolism could never understand. Why hadn't I hired a female trainer?

"Isaac is—" the man behind the counter started, but then a voice behind me finished.

"Right here."

I turned around to face the beautiful man whose cut muscles were visible even through his spandex workout gear.

"Hey, don't I know you?" he said, extending his hand to me. "I'm Isaac."

I looked him in the face as I shook the hand of this strangely familiar man.

"You don't have a better line than that, man?" joked the gentleman behind the counter before the phone rang and he took the call.

Isaac chuckled. "Oh, snap, that probably did sound like a line." He smiled, and I promise you little sparkles and ding sounds shot from his mouth like on a cartoon. I'd never seen such a perfect smile in all my days. Actually I had, and that's when it dawned on me where he might have known me from.

"The restaurant," I said, snapping my finger.

"Long's," he replied.

"Yep," I confirmed. I looked down and realized that I was still shaking this man's hand. I quickly pulled it away. I didn't want him to think I was trying to flirt or be touching all on him or anything.

"See, it wasn't a line," he said. "I knew I knew you from somewhere. I never forget a face."

"I'm not good at remembering faces, but I never forget a good tipper." I winked, trying not to focus too much on that beautiful smile of his.

Like me, he looked to be in his twenties. If I recalled correctly, he usually wore glasses, but today he didn't have any on. That smile of his stole the shine from all of his other features anyway.

"You're Jamela, right?" he said.

"Right."

"I know that not only because I have an appointment with a Jamela scheduled for now, but I remember it from seeing your nametag at the restaurant." He stared at me for a moment. I looked downward, feeling slightly awkward. "Oh, I'm sorry, I was just realizing that this was the first time I'd seen you with your hair down. It's beautiful. Glad to know that you're not one of those women who's afraid to sweat her hair out." He smiled, then as quickly as the smile had appeared on his face, it disappeared. "Oh, umm,

I didn't mean it like that. I just meant . . ." He scrambled around for words.

I put my hand up. "It's okay. I knew what you meant." I ran my hand down my hair. I was shocked that he'd paid close enough attention to me to know the way I normally wore my hair. I usually kept it pulled back in a bushy ponytail. The only reason it wasn't pulled back today was because I couldn't find a scrunchie within my messy room. I didn't particularly like to walk around with a ponytail all the time. It's just that I didn't have time to fix myself up in the morning before I headed out to start my extremely busy day.

"So, what brings you here today?" he asked, changing the subject before things got any more awkward.

"Well, I need to get healthy. My dad had a stroke a few years ago, and I know I need to start taking care of myself so I can be there to take care of him," I explained.

"I'm sorry to hear about your dad," he said. "But sometimes it takes things like that to give us a wake-up call."

I nodded, forcing myself not to get emotional. Even three years later, I still got teary-eyed whenever I thought about my dad.

Isaac must have sensed my emotions needed a pick-me-up, because he sounded extra cheerful when he clapped his hands together and anounced, "Well, shall we get started?" I appreciated that he was trying to keep things upbeat for me. I was already nervous enough about working out in front of his fine self.

"I'm as ready as I'll ever be," I said.

"Good. Then let's get to work. Follow me."

I can't believe that all the times this guy came into the restaurant, and I never once noticed that ass before, I thought as I watched him walk in front of me. All of a sudden, I felt self-conscious about the fact that I hadn't bothered to put on any makeup. I didn't wear that much to begin with—usually just eyeliner, mascara, and a little lip gloss—but I would have felt more confident around this fine man if I had some on now.

He stopped in front of an area full of paddded flooring and turned around to look at me. If he'd caught me staring at his ass, he didn't comment. As good-looking as he was, he was probably used to it from all of his female clients.

"Let's start here with some stretches," he said.

"Cool." I looked around for a place to put my gym bag.

"Here I'll take it for now," he offered, extending his hand. "When I give you your five-minute water break, I'll show you where the locker room is."

I nodded and smiled even though inside I was thinking, *A five-minute break? I signed up for a full hour. A sister is only going to get one break?*

Not wanting to complain and whine when I hadn't even done a leg lift yet, I just sat on the mat waiting for further instructions.

It just so happened that since I was sitting and he was standing, his package was right there in my face. Now, that might have been the biggest muscle of them all. Brother was packin' for real, so much so that I had a quick mental fantasy of me unwrapping it. I felt a tingling between my legs and the little jerk of my thighs tightening in an effort to keep the juices from flowing. How in the hell was I going to be able to lose weight if I lost my mind daydreaming about the Black Captain America? And why did I have to take note of everything about this fine specimen of a man right now?

I wondered why I had never noticed him in such detail before. I supposed he had been nothing more than a backdrop in my busy day. My life moved so fast that most of it was a complete blur, but I could definitely see clearly now—and it went without saying that Isaac was very easy on the eyes.

"Before we get started, let me just say that I'm glad to be working with you. It's truly an honor."

"Same here," I replied.

He squatted down. "Yeah, you say that now, but trust me, in an hour you'll hate my guts." He winked and then stood up before he proceeded to instruct me on stretching out. This stretch thing went on for about ten minutes, and by the time I was done, I honestly felt as though I didn't need fifty more. That shit felt like a workout in itself. A chick was sweating like she'd already done an hour on the treadmill.

"Here you go." He handed me a towel.

I took it and wiped the sweat off my forehead.

"Why don't you go ahead and take a break before we really get started?" He stood to the side of the mat. "I'll show you to the women's locker room. Grab a drink and I'll be outside of the locker room waiting on you. Sound like a plan?"

I could only nod. I needed to save every last freaking breath.

He extended his hand and assisted me up from the mat by pulling me up. I thought for certain with all this body-body it would have taken him two hands and someone to spot him, but he pulled me up with one hand like I was a rag doll. Very impressive. I was impressed with myself as well for not taking a moment to visualize him lifting me up in the air with that one hand while I rode him.

I brushed my bottom off as I strolled behind him to the locker room. I noticed how most of the other women in the gym were a size two or four. What the hell were they doing here? If they lost another ounce they'd be invisible! And I didn't want to hear any of the BS about maintaining. Once I attended the gym long enough where I had lost some weight, I was going to suggest a new gym rule: thick girls only . . . and fine-ass men!

As I entered the locker room, one of those skinny girls stopped to talk to Isaac. He'd probably forget all about me even being in the locker room and run off to chat it up with her, I thought. This was why I never came out and did anything. This was why I stayed in my own element, oblivious to all that was going on around me. L.A. and Hollywood were where the beautiful people lived . . . the thin, beautiful people.

I looked at myself from the side as I stood in front of the long mirror in the locker room. Ugh. I felt like the damn duck who'd seen his reflection for the very first time and discovered that he was nowhere near a beautiful swan. New rule number two: no fucking mirrors!

Now feeling like the big ol' cow Glendora made it sound like I was, I tried to suck in my stomach. That didn't make much difference. There wasn't that much sucking in the world. I thought about how my stepmother was turning into an old hag by the day, even though she was fighting it tooth and nail. But there was still one thing she had over me: her figure. How did I let my sorry-butt stepmother end up looking better than me? At least she didn't look better than me in the face though. Ugh, did I just justify what skinny people think is a compliment to big girls? "You have a cute face though."

But in Glendora's case, I did look better than her. In her effort to fight Father Time, she looked like she'd gone under the knife. Her facial skin looked tighter and kind of strange if you asked me. Talk about cosmetic surgery gone wrong. She definitely thought more highly of herself than she ought to, so I don't even know what made her want to get plastic surgery. It surely wasn't to look good for her husband.

Ever since my father's stroke, she barely spent time with him, because she was too busy spending his money. Being that she was a CNA when they met, one would think she'd be taking great care of him, but when he came home, she wouldn't even help him feed himself.

Glendora's tired ass didn't care if my dad lay in his own shitty diaper all day. One time not long after his stroke, I had come home from school and found him in a soiled bed. From that day on, I took over. I'll never forget the stench that assaulted my nose when I walked through his bedroom door. I knew right away that Glendora was waiting for me to come home to change him. God only knows how long he'd been lying in his own mess. I just knew that it would never happen again. Not under my watch.

Over the years, I had basically just let Glendora be Glendora, not calling her on her mess. Still, seeing the way she treated my father, or wasn't treating him, pissed me off to no end. One day I confronted her about the lack of care he was receiving. It was supposed to be a hint for her to act like a wife and take care of her husband; instead, it resulted in her agreeing to allow me to hire two nurses. Well, at least something good had come from the conversation.

I tried to get some help from the government to pay for his home healthcare, but because of his businesses, he didn't qualify for anything. When I told Glendora how much we would have to pay for the help, she did two things. First she flipped out about the cost, and then she tried to distance herself from any responsibility. Selfish as she was, her biggest concern was that if something happened to Daddy or to the restaurants, the healthcare workers would come after her for their money. "I don't want them bitches coming after me for payments for them wiping your father's ass," she had told me.

So, to my surprise, she came up with the idea of giving me limited power of attorney over some of Daddy's affairs. She got a lawyer to draw up paperwork that basically gave me the right to make decisions concerning his healthcare, including the hiring and payment of health workers. She said it was only temporary, until everything was in order, but I knew there was no chance in hell she was going to ever choose to take over the responsibility once she'd thrown it on me. As long as she continued to have money to live her fabulous lifestyle, she couldn't care less what was happening to Daddy.

So, Glendora continued prancing around like everything was kosher. She continued attending all types of fancy charity events. What's that saying about charity starts at home? Ha! She missed that memo. She had the entire community thinking that she was the caring wife when underneath it all she was pure evil.

Another skinny chick brushed past me as I stared at my reflection in the mirror, pulling me away from the thoughts of my wicked stepmother. I remembered fine-ass Isaac was waiting for my outside the locker room, so I grabbed a drink from the fountain, stashed my bag in a locker, and went back out to meet him.

"Did you get all squared away?" he asked.

"I sure did," I told him.

"Good. Now we can really get it in."

Isaac worked me into a sweat on everything from the elliptical to weights. I wound up bicycling almost ten minutes near the end of the hour workout. I know that might not sound like a lot, but the bike didn't have no damn seat for me to sit on. Last but not least, we finished the same way we had started. I was on the mat doing a cool down.

"You did good today," Isaac said as he sat in front of me, pulling my arms to help me stretch. He was looking me dead in my eyes.

It took everything in me not to blush when I said the words, "Thank you." Him holding my hands and pulling me toward him as he stretched me out made me feel a certain kind of way. I know he was just doing his job, but tell my feelings that.

As much as I was enjoying the way he looked into my eyes, I was sure without a doubt that this was one-sided. He'd probably already made plans to meet up with the Little Miss Size

Two that he was talking to when I went into the locker room. I bet when he looked at her he thought of sex; when he looked at me, he probably thought of fried chicken, collard greens, and candied yams.

"We're all done," Isaac said, getting up and then helping me into a standing position as well. "I hope I didn't scare you off."

"Not at all," I told him. "I committed to the gym special of three months, three times a week for thirty dollars a week, and that's what I'm going to do."

"That's what I like to hear," he said proudly. "Dedication."

On that note we said our good-byes and I headed back to the women's locker room. I showered, the entire time thinking about the way Isaac touched me—holding my hands when we were stretching, resting his hands on my waist to help me twist, or touching areas of my body to show where I should be "feeling the burn." Before I knew it, I was touching myself, imagining that it was Isaac's hand between my legs and not my own. I trembled as the juices flowed down my leg and into the shower drain. This was the first time I'd ever cum where and when I wanted to—where I wasn't ashamed that it felt good to do it. I felt so good after this physical release that I refused to let my mind go to that shameful place it usually traveled to whenever I thought of sex. I quickly got dressed and headed out of the gym, wanting to hold on to the good feelings for as long as I could.

Sitting in my car outside of the gym, I felt fresh and renewed. As I started the ignition, I heard a faint beep. It was the notification that I'd just received a text. I unzipped my gym bag and pulled out my phone to read the message: I usually don't mix business with pleasure, but since I eat at your restaurant anyway, I was just wondering if you would join me.

Initially I was a little confused. I didn't recognize the number. That's when I got a second text message: BTW, this is Isaac.

I thought I was going to die. Had this man just really asked me out, or was someone playing a cruel joke on me? For a minute I wondered how he'd gotten my number, but duh! I had to give all that information when I signed up for the trainer, in case he needed to get in touch with me. Well, thank the Lord he'd decided to reach out and touch me.

I was excited for about all of one minute as I considered whether to text him back. As I sat in my car and watched all the fit, pretty girls com-

ing out of the gym after their workouts, I started
doubting myself. What if Isaac was just trying
to be nice to a new client? Or what if he was
only looking for free meals at the restaurant? I'd
heard somewhere, or maybe read it on the inter-
net, that male personal trainers are only one
step removed from gigolos. They sleep with half
of their clients, so even if he was really hitting on
me, maybe it was just to add another notch to his
dumbells. I wasn't that type of girl. And even if I
was, I had nothing left to give. It had been hard
enough squeezing him in for business; pleasure
was out of the question.

With that final thought, I began my reply to
his text: Thank you but I don't think

The rapping on the window not only halted
my fingers from declining Isaac's invitation, but
it had scared the shit out of me. With my heart
pounding, I looked up to see Isaac's face at my
window.

"Sorry," I could hear him say through the
glass, raising his hands up in defense.

I leveled my breathing, then rolled down the
window.

"I'm so sorry," he apologized again. "It's just
that the more I thought about it, the more I
regretted sending you that text."

The look on my face went from fear to hurt.

"Oh, no, I didn't mean it that way," he said in an apologetic tone. "It's just that, well, who the hell asks somebody out for the first time via text? That was lame, corny, and something a high school boy would do." He stood up tall for effect. "And I'm a man."

And there his junk was, once again in my face, confirming that he was all man indeed.

"So I wanted to catch you and ask you out in person," he said. "You were my last client for the evening. I was going to go grab a bite to eat, ironically at your restaurant. So I figured, why not go together? Just dinner. I'm not trying to push up on you or anything. I just . . ." He paused for a second. "I don't want to start things off based on lies, so yes, I am trying to push up on you. So will you go to dinner with me or not?"

He was so determined and matter of fact, and even though I had been prepared to decline the invitation, just looking at him standing there in front of me gave me a change of heart. "You know what?" I said. "I think I will join you for dinner, Isaac. Do you just wanna meet at—"

He cut me off, shaking his head. "No, no, we're going to do this right. I want to take you to dinner, so why don't you hop in my car and I'll drive? I'll bring you back to your car afterward."

I just stared at Isaac for a moment, so many questions squirming through my head, allowing doubt to creep in again. Why me? Did he really see something in me, or had he just put two and two together when he saw my last name on the gym registration? He probably figured I was some kind of heir. Maybe he was looking at me as nothing more than a come up. He saw me as a meal ticket that could end his days of being a personal trainer, having to deal with fat, sweaty girls like me on a daily basis.

"What? What's wrong?" he asked me after I'd stared off so long.

"Nothing, I just . . ." It was me who, this time, didn't want to start things off with lies, so I kept it real and asked him what was on my mind. "Why do you want to go out with me?" I pointed back toward the gym. "There are dozens of girls in there right now who you could be with, and they all look like they fit in with the Hollywood scene. Why are you choosing me?"

He didn't even hesitate to answer. "Baby girl, I ain't looking for the chick who fits in. I'm looking for the one who stands out, and as far as I'm concerned, that's you."

Something in the way he looked at me when he said it made me trust that he was telling the truth. I felt a spark of electricity from his gaze, and suddenly all insecurity disappeared. I couldn't jump out of my car into his fast enough.

"Wow, nice ride," I said as I looked around his fully loaded SUV. There were TVs, and the dashboard lit up and had tons of gadgets. I felt like I was in a spaceship and he was about to take me out of this world. "If this is the type of vehicle being a personal trainer can afford you, I'm in the wrong business," I said, totally impressed, and that was a big deal considering I wasn't into material things.

"No, personal training is something I do in my spare time," he said.

"Huh?" I asked, not quite knowing how to take that. As a stranger to the gym, I had a hard time understanding how someone would choose to spend his free time there.

"I'm a true advocate for health and fitness. I enjoy helping others achieve their goals in that area," he explained.

"That's awesome," I said. "So I guess I'll be a good challenge for you, considering how far I have to go to get healthy."

"It's never too late to start," he said, sounding every bit the fitness coach.

"Well, I haven't always been this big," I said, "but I've been busy taking care of my father for the last few years, and I stopped taking care of myself. I realized I better do something, though, when my doctor told me—" I stopped myself, realizing this was not exactly the kind of conversation to make an impression on a first date. It was more like a way to insure that I didn't get a second date. What guy wants a woman with a growing list of health problems?

"Told you what?" he asked.

"Oh, never mind. You don't want to hear about medical stuff."

He smiled at me. "I guess now would be the time to tell you that I'm a doctor."

I tried not to go bug-eyed with surprise, but it didn't matter, because I stupidly blurted out, "You don't look like a doctor."

He laughed. "Well, what's a doctor supposed to look like?"

I twisted my lips. "I guess that was judgmental of me, huh?"

"No, you're fine," he said.

"I have plans to go to medical school, but it's going slower than I'd hoped. With the restaurant, I can only go to school part time."

"You should—"

He was interrupted by the ringing of my phone. I looked down at the caller ID, which read: RESTRICTED.

"Sorry. I have to answer it," I said. "I never know when it's somebody calling about the restaurant or my dad."

"I get it." He nodded. "You've got a lot on your plate."

I hit the TALK button. "Hello."

"Jamela!" It was Brielle, and she sounded frantic.

Brielle and I hardly ever talked anymore. I had thought for a minute that my father being ill would bring us closer, and we did share a few sentimental moments, but soon enough she went on with her own life, being the party girl she was. We had next to nothing in common.

"Yes, Brielle, what's up?" I asked, feeling annoyed that she was interrupting my date.

"I need you to come get me . . . now!" she said.

I could hear the fear in her voice. Brielle had always been the happy-go-lucky one. It took a lot to get her shook up, so this must have been bad. "What's wrong? Where are you?" I asked, genuinely concerned.

"I need you to come get me out of here," she answered. "I'm in jail!"

CHAPTER FIVE

BRIELLE

The last thing I remembered clearly was that I was planning to get all the way turned up at this college party in Brentwood that some senior was throwing because his parents were out of town. The party was jumping; the place was packed wall to wall with people. We were doing fireball whiskey shots and Jell-O shots, and I was so plastered it was ridiculous. All I knew was that I kept waking up in different rooms. Liquor and ice didn't mix for me, if you know what I mean.

I blacked out after I did a chugalug, and when I came to, I was covered in blood. I looked and felt around on my body for any cuts, wounds, my period . . . hell, something. There was nothing, though. I wasn't hurt at all, so the blood hadn't come from me.

I just remember Lyric coming into the room saying something about how some chick had gotten so drunk that she fell down, cut herself on a bottle, and bled on me. Shit had gotten out of control to the point that the neighbors ended up calling police. By the time Lyric was able to get me halfway cleaned up and out the front door, the police were already swarming the place.

When they asked me my name and birth date, my stupid ass gave them my real info. I couldn't hide the fact that I was as high as a kite. The fact that they made me take a breathalyzer test didn't help matters much either. They threw the cuffs on me while reading me my rights and took me in for underage drinking, which was how I now found myself in L.A. County jail. Well, leaving it anyway.

I'd been there since the wee hours of the morning. Even the arrest didn't kill my buzz. I was totally fucked up, so much so that they couldn't even put me in with the other cellies. They had to put me in the tank to let me sleep it off. I was in no shape to defend myself if something went down, so I was glad that at least they looked out for me in that sense.

I was even happier that they let me call Jamela instead of my mom. I told them that Mom was dead and my dad lived in New York and that my big sister had custody of me. Since I was over eighteen, I was legally an adult, so I really didn't have to lie about my mother being dead. I just didn't want the chance of her getting involved in this mess in any way, shape, or form.

Not that I felt much better about having to tell Jamela. I never called her, so I wasn't even sure if she would answer the phone. And if she did answer, I couldn't blame her if she hung up in my ear. I had no other choice though.

I couldn't call Brendon to come get me, because knowing his ass, he had a few warrants and wouldn't come anywhere near the jail to pick me up. All of my friends had been high at the party just like me. Hell, for all I knew some of them were behind bars too. This left me with no one to call but Jamela. Luckily, she agreed to come get me once I was released.

They let me out on my own signature or something like that. They said I would have a court date in a couple of weeks. I had never been in trouble with the law before, so I really had no idea what to expect.

As soon as they processed me out of jail, I headed outside to look for Jamela. I didn't see her car anywhere though. *What the fuck?* She'd told me she would come pick me up. Where the hell was she? I reached into the bag of my personal effects they'd given me and found my cell phone so I could call Jamela and ask her where she was.

"Fuck!" I said, realizing it was dead. It was now getting dark outside. I did not want to try to get home in the dark. I turned around and faced the jail. That really was the last place I wanted to go back into. What would I look like going back in there, asking for another free phone call? But I had no other option.

Just as I put my foot on the first step to the building, I heard Jamela calling my name.

"Brielle, right here."

I turned around and saw a huge black SUV. The passenger window was rolled down, and I recognized Jamela in the passenger seat. Who was driving?

I made my way over to the truck. "Jamela, is that you?" I said, talking to her but looking at the driver.

"Yes. We were heading out to dinner when you called, but when I told my friend it was an emergency, he agreed to come get you." She looked to the back door. "Get in."

I heard the clicking of the locks. I opened the door and climbed in.

Jamela turned her body around and asked, "What happened?" That's when I noticed her clothes. She looked like she'd just left the gym or something, in her sweats and a baggy T-shirt, but I knew the gym was the last place her hungry ass would be at. Besides, she had said she was going out to dinner.

I just couldn't believe she would go out looking so busted, although I didn't really care enough to ask. Plus, who was I to judge? I knew that I must have looked like shit. A bitch couldn't wait to get home so I could shower, get into some comfy pajamas, and sleep off this hangover.

"I'll tell you all about things later," I told Jamela. "Right now I just want to get to the house."

She nodded her understanding and smiled before turning back to face forward. I had to admit to myself that even if Jamela's gear wasn't all that, she was kind of glowing. It was a sad day when Jamela looked better than me and she didn't even have on a drop of makeup.

I looked down at my own outfit, which was covered with dried blood, and shook my head. I was looking like a crackhead, not the debutante my mother had raised me to be. *I've got to get a grip on my life,* I thought. I knew I was bullshitting myself though. I'd managed to get into college on a scholarship thanks to my mom and some scholarship board she sat on, but I was jerking off my schoolwork. I got put on academic probation my second semester. My mom knew nothing about it. I had to get it together. If I lost that scholarship, she'd probably disown me.

I never thought I would say it, but I believed my recreational drug use was the cause of everything bad that was starting to happen in my life. I mean, don't get me wrong. Things weren't *that* bad. It's not like I was some junkie always wanting to get high. So I still fucked with that bitch Crystal. What was the big deal? I was serious when I said I could stop when I wanted to, and I had. Before the party, I hadn't done it in God knows how long. I only did it when I over-partied and things got out of hand. Like last night. What I really needed to do was cut back on going out.

As I rode in the back of the vehicle, I started thinking about what punishment I might receive. "I could get sentenced to jail," I said out loud.

Jamela turned around at my outburst. "You sure you don't want to talk about it?" she asked, looking sympathetic.

Ah, why not just tell her and get it over with? She deserved to know why I spoiled her dinner outing. "See what had happened was . . ." I stumbled over my words, trying to find the right thing to say. I paused for a moment, knowing how stupid I must sound. "I was at this party that the police raided—"

"Wait a minute." Jamela stopped me before I could finish sounding stupid. "Did you say *raid*, as in drug raid?" She shot me a stern look. "You're not using again are you?"

Jamela had found some of my stuff on the floor outside of my door one time. I must have dropped it there. At first I lied to her and told her that I was holding it for a friend, but she looked at me like I was stupid, so I fessed up. I told her that I did it occasionally and that I hadn't done it in a while, that what she found must have fallen out of the trash I'd taken out because I'd decided to stop. I'd managed to lie to her with a straight face then, but the truth was written all over my face now.

I couldn't look her in the eyes, so I looked downward in shame.

"But I thought you told me you were going to get clean and sober." She sounded disappointed, and I was surprised that I felt actual remorse about it.

"I know." I shook my head. "I guess I fell off the wagon."

"Fell off the wagon? You look like you've been hit by a train."

"I know, but—"

"But nothing, Brielle. If your mom found out after she spent all that money on that rehab place she sent you to in Malibu . . . and that was only because she thought you were smoking weed. God only knows if she knew the whole truth!"

Damn! Why did Jamela have to rub it in? I already felt like shit. What I couldn't figure out, though, was if that was because of the restless night I'd spent in jail or because I had gotten caught up in the drug thing again.

"Relapse is part of recovery," I said defiantly, taking my designer sunglasses out of my bag of belongings and placing them on my face. That was the only thing I had that I could hide behind.

All of a sudden a thunderbolt of pain criss-crossed my head. "You have any aspirin for this headache?" I asked Jamela.

She dug around in her purse and handed me a bottle of Tylenol.

"This will work," I said, accepting the pills.

"If you look down in the console on the floor, you'll see a little compartment. There should be a couple water bottles in there." Up until now, the driver of the truck had remained quiet. I'd been so busy carrying on with Jamela that I honestly hadn't paid him much attention at all.

"Here, let me turn this on for you." He reached up and turned on the lights in the car. That's when I realized that I was being chauffeured by one of the finest brothers who was walking the planet. I mean he was *foine*. Simply put, I wanted him. But I was looking real crazy right about now. It was better to be heard and not seen at this point.

I looked down and fumbled around until I found the compartment. "Thank you. You can turn the light off now."

As I took a sip, I stared at dude. That's who Jamela was on her way out to dinner with when I called. Had the tables turned, I would have let that bitch rot in jail while I presented myself to him on a platter as dessert. I had absolutely no clue how Jamela had managed to pull a guy that hot. To be honest, I thought she was in the closet. She had never brought a guy home before. I didn't even recall her ever saying she was going out on a date. Besides that, she carried herself like an old lady, so who would have thought she could get a man at all, better yet one who looked this good?

I suddenly hated the fact that I looked so crappy. Pushing my shades up on top of my head to make it look styled or something, I tried to wipe away the mascara that I was sure was smudged all down my face, but without a mirror to check myself out, I figured it was best to remain quiet for now. I would come at him when I was fixed up and looking like the diva and boss chick I was. Once he saw me at my best, he'd be saying to himself, "Jamela who?"

I knew I could pull him without a doubt. I had long gotten rid of my baby fat. With my long, good hair and fair skin, I knew I could easily steal him from Precious. *When I throw it at him, he won't be able to resist. He won't know what hit him once Hurricane Brielle touches down on him.* Timing was everything and now was not the time, but one way or the other, I always got what I wanted.

CHAPTER SIX

JAMELA

"I really appreciate you taking me to get Brielle," I said to Isaac as we pulled up next to my car, which was still parked at the gym. When Brielle had called me and needed me to come get her, I'd told Isaac that he could take me back to my car and I'd get her myself, but he insisted. He didn't want me going to the jail alone.

Brielle had fallen asleep and was sprawled out in the back seat.

"It's okay. I was happy to help," Isaac said.

I was glad Isaac was so understanding, but that didn't prevent me from being embarrassed. How did my first date with him end up being a drive to pick up my sister from jail?

"Although I do hope a rain check on dinner comes with this." He put the car in park and looked over at me with a big grin on his face.

"What are you grinning about?"

"Huh?" he asked as he glanced past me and tried to get serious.

I turned toward him, crossed my arms, and tilted my head slightly to the side. "Don't play with me! I know you heard the question!"

He started grinning again. I gave him a playful shove and he broke out in laughter.

"Okay! Let's not get physical now!" he joked. "I was just thinking about how cute you looked when you was playing momma bear with your sister. I could tell you are a genuine and caring person. I like that." He smiled.

"Well, let me try to wake this girl up so we can get into my car," I said, taking off my seat belt.

"It's late, so if you don't mind, I'd like to see you and your sister home."

I gave him the side-eye. "You trying to find out where I live on the sneak tip?" I asked.

He sucked his teeth. "Woman, no. I'm a gentleman. What would I look like sending you two off in the middle of the night?"

I looked at the clock on his dashboard. I couldn't believe it was almost midnight. "Wow, it is late." I looked back at Brielle. She was a feisty one when she was clean and sober, but right now, she would be no good helping me out in a carjacking.

"You've already done so much," I said, looking over at Isaac.

He cupped my chin in his hand and spoke sincerely. "And I want to do so much more."

Whew! It was about to get hot up in there. I turned back around in my seat. "Well, okay. If you insist."

"And I do." Isaac smiled before getting out of the car and helping me wake Brielle and escort her from his truck to the back seat of my car.

She simply sprawled out back there while I drove to the house, Isaac following close behind. I'd be lying to myself if I didn't admit that I loved the fact that Isaac was such a gentleman. It felt good to be cared for, instead of always being the caretaker.

Before I knew it, we were pulling up in front of the house. I got out of the car, and Isaac got out of his and started walking toward me.

"You need help getting her out?" he asked.

"She's waking up. Give her a minute. I think she'll be all right."

Brielle stretched and then opened the back door to get out of the car. She stood there for a moment, catching her bearings, then wiped her eyes and looked up at Isaac.

"Thanks for the ride," Brielle mumbled before stumbling toward the door.

I watched her, hoping and praying she didn't land flat on her face. Once I saw that she'd made it to the door and was fumbling with her key to unlock the door, I turned my attention back to Isaac.

"Yes, thank you so much, Isaac. I really appreciate it."

"You are most welcome. It was no problem at all," he said. "So when can I take you out for dinner?" He stared into my eyes, his just a-glistening like he was looking at the most beautiful sight ever.

I suddenly became very self-conscious about the way I looked. I hadn't even changed out of my gym clothes after our workout. I nervously ran my fingers through the sides of my hair.

"You look beautiful," he said as if he'd read my thoughts.

"No, I don't," I said as I looked into my hands. "I look a hot mess right now. I really need to get inside and take a shower."

"Jamela, you are a naturally beautiful woman. You really should give yourself a little more credit."

"Thank you," was all I could muster without turning into a blushing puddle. I wasn't very used to getting complimented like this, so it felt very strange for me.

"Now back to my question," he said. "Dinner?"

"My goodness, you are persistent!" I exclaimed. "This Friday night after my shift."

"Okay, great," he said happily. "Friday night it is. I will meet you at the restaurant. You let me know which location," he said with a big smile on his face.

"I'll do that," I assured him, then turned toward the house. My stomach began doing somersaults. I was both excited and scared all at the same time. I hadn't gone out with a guy in a long time, so I was nervous about it. Earlier it was just a spur of the moment thing, but now it was a real date-date, where he would expect me to be dressed to the nines. I became filled with anxiety, wondering if I even had anything decent in my closet to wear—or anything in the closet that fit me right, for that matter. Right then and there, I decided to go out and buy myself something nice. To hell with Glendora if she didn't like it.

I entered the house and closed the door behind me. I was so deep in thought that I hadn't even realized someone else was in the room with me.

"Where the hell have you been?"

My euphoric feeling quickly dissipated when I heard her voice. Next I heard her feet padding on the carpet as she stomped over to me. My stepmother was in my face before I could even reply.

I took a step back, not comfortable with her being in my face. The last time we were that close, we ended up fighting so badly that we gave my father a stroke—literally.

"The last time I checked," I said to Glendora, "I didn't have a curfew. But if you must know, I was picking up your junkie of a daughter from jail." Damn, I hated that I had thrown Brielle under the bus like that, but Glendora just made me so damn mad.

"Don't you dare call my daughter a junkie. She's been clean for a while now. And you know what? If she is on anything, whatever it is, maybe you should try it too. It might just help you lose a little damn weight."

Usually I didn't care what my stepmother said to me, but this whole weight thing was starting to sting a little bit. I didn't need her making comments about my weight. I felt bad enough about it as it was. I'd finally given her something to hold over my head when it came to comparing me and Brielle, who had lost all her baby weight years ago. She'd managed to keep a nice slim figure. I don't know if it was from the drugs she was doing or her body had just thinned out naturally; either way, if I put her in my pant leg, she'd still have room left.

"But this isn't about Brielle," Glendora said. "Your father is sick and you've been out galli-vanting all night."

"What? Sick?" I wasn't expecting her to say that. I didn't wait to hear anything else. I ran past her and into his room so his nurse could fill me in on what was going on. I didn't trust what Glendora had to say.

"Nancy. What's going on?" I asked the nurse, who was sitting in the corner. Nancy had been his nurse for almost two years now. She was a real sweetheart and always took great care of him.

She put down the book she'd been reading and walked over to my father's bed. "He complained that he was having trouble breathing earlier, and his oxygen saturation levels had dropped, so I put the oxygen mask on him. He's had the mask on for about an hour, and his levels are staying steady now."

I looked over at my father. His chest was rising up and down hard, as if he was struggling to breathe even with the oxygen tank on. "Have you called the doctor yet?"

"Of course she called the doctor. She's not a total idiot," Glendora interrupted as she entered the room.

"Yes, I did call the doctor, Jamela," Nancy replied. I was glad she hadn't acknowledged Glendora's outburst. "The doctor said we need to monitor him closely and if his condition worsens, we are to take him immediately to the hospital."

"Okay, Nancy. Thank you," I said, moving toward a chair to settle in for the night.

"You know you don't have to stay," Nancy said. "He's resting comfortably right now, and you look like you could use some rest."

"It's that obvious, huh?" I asked. After dealing with Brielle's nonsense and then coming home to drama with Glendora, I truly was feeling exhausted. On top of that, I was starting to feel the aftermath of my workout creeping into my muscles and bones. I knew I would be aching by morning.

Nancy nodded. "Yes, it's obvious. Go to sleep. I promise I'll come get you if anything changes."

I got up. "Thanks again for everything, Nancy. You've been a godsend," I told her as I brushed past Glendora, fighting the urge to add, "unlike my wicked stepmother here."

I headed to my room, eager to take a long, hot shower after which I would fall into a deep sleep, hopefully filled with dreams of Isaac.

CHAPTER SEVEN

GLENDORA

"I'm sorry, Mrs. Long," the black lady with the huge Diana Ross hair said, accompanied by a smug look of self-importance. "But the bank cannot extend your credit line anymore. Your home already has two mortgages, the second of which is behind on payments." She cleared her throat. "We've allowed you to use your husband's restaurants on your individual loans."

I cut her off right then and there before she could go any further. "They are my restaurants too. I'm his wife. By law we are one person."

She gave me this "are you finished yet?" look and then proceeded as if she was not moved one bit by what I'd just said. "Either way, your loan has been denied." She shuffled her pile of papers, avoiding eye contact.

I gasped in shock. No loan meant no money. How the hell was I supposed to pay bills with no money? I guessed I should have thought about that while I was spending Victor's money all these years. I should have known that eventually the well would run dry. I couldn't even tell you how many of hundreds of thousands of dollars were in Victor's three bank accounts combined.

After he had his stroke, I went through his home office and retrieved the information for his bank accounts, including the checkbooks. After all, I was the one who would have to write the checks to pay the bills, especially the credit cards that I always managed to keep at max.

I really had no idea how much I was spending until that day my credit card was declined when I was trying to purchase shoes. Humiliating. I raced home and immediately started going over all the account information. The money wasn't gone, but damn near. I was in trouble, and I had no idea what to do. But I guess that's what happens when the only thing being made with the accounts are withdrawals and not deposits. Now that's something I hadn't thought about before.

"That fucking Jamela," were the first words that came out of my mouth. She was running the restaurant, so she should have been making some type of deposits. I immediately went to her room to get to the bottom of things, but I knew I wouldn't get anywhere with her, so I went to see Victor's attorney.

That was a waste. All he told me was that the majority of the money Victor would deposit was his salary, which had been quite large, but it was mostly from sources other than the restaurants. He'd made money from appearing on shows and traveling as a consultant to hopeful new restaurant owners. There were so many other things Victor had been doing to bring in income that I had no idea about. Hell, I'd never cared where it came from; all I cared about was how much of it I could spend.

"Well, the restaurant itself must be making money," I told his attorney. "Victor owns the restaurant."

"True, but he does not have one hundred percent ownership. And he's being penalized for the time you took over the restaurant and ran it into—" He stopped himself once he saw me give him the side-eye. He knew better than to bring up the brief time after Victor became disabled that I tried to run the business. Hell, was it my fault if I didn't have a good head for numbers? Plus, how was I supposed to make it to the bank to make deposits when I was spending so many hours running the damn place? That place could suck the life out of anyone.

I stood to my feet. I wasn't going to sit there and listen to this bastard tell me the reason I was broke was my own fault. "Look, I'm his wife and we have children who still need to be taken care of. There has to be some type of proceeds coming in."

"They are," he said.

Now that's what I was trying to hear. I perked up.

"But they all go toward the salaries of his nurses."

I wanted to spit fire. Again, that fucking Jamela. It was her idea to hire them.

"Mrs. Long, have you ever thought about getting back into the work force?" the attorney asked. "If I recall correctly, weren't you yourself a nurse? Why not take care of him yourself and you get paid to do it, versus some strangers?"

This prick actually had a point. I mean, it wouldn't really be work, and I'd make sure I saved all the shitty diapers for Jamela. My stomach was too weak for that. After all, I guessed as his wife I should have tended to him a little more, so maybe this whole financial situation was just wake-up call. "You're right. I could do that."

"Good, then just talk to Jamela and have her replace the current nurses' information with your own, and the money will start coming to you."

"Jamela!" I shouted. "What does she have to do with any of this?"

He began shifting through papers. "She has this to do with it." He handed me a paper.

Damn it! I'd forgotten all about this stupid power of attorney affidavit thingy. I let the paper fall between my fingers and float back onto his desk. "Have a good day." I smiled. "And thanks for nothing." I walked out of his office door and stepped my ass right back into square one.

I know that Victor was a good man, but this caregiver shit was wearing me out. I'd convinced Jamela to give the nurses a two-week vacation. For those two weeks I was going to go above and beyond in taking care of Victor. I figured I could show her better than I could tell her. Once she saw how well I was tending to her father, she would have no problem replacing those nurses with me. As soon as I convinced her to do that, I'd slack up and let her eventually do everything. Hell, her and my own entitled brats. I never thought the day would come where I would say this, but I was really starting to get tired of my kids.

I had just sent Brendon to stay with his father to keep him out of trouble. He'd gone to jail twice already. Some gang-related shit. I don't know how he got involved with the Bloods . . . or maybe it was the Crips; I can't keep up with gang names and turfs. But all I know is he got involved with a gang in Compton and his car got shot up. How he got into trouble in Compton is beyond me considering we lived in Bel Air, but he somehow managed to piss off the wrong people and almost got himself killed. I believe it was drug related, too.

I didn't understand how both of my children wound up with drug problems. I gave them everything they ever wanted. What void in their lives did they possibly have to fill with drugs and gangs? It didn't make sense.

After learning that he had survived the shooting, I knew Brendon had to get out of here, and so I sent him to his father in New York. I put him on a Greyhound at one in the morning, and now here he was in trouble again. I needed $5,000 right away so I could pay the attorney handling the case for Brendon in Las Vegas. I still didn't know how he had managed to get himself in trouble when he was supposed to be on his way to his father's in New York.

I had been able to get him out on bail, but I had used the last stash of cash I had at the house.

Now, his court date was coming up next week, and if I didn't pay the attorney fees immediately, they wouldn't be able to get all the paperwork done in time, and Brendon would be shit outta luck.

If having to deal with Brendon wasn't bad enough, I had to worry about dealing with Brielle. Two years ago, I'd sent her to a rehab facility for thirty days after they found marijuana in her locker at school. Marijuana leads to bigger drugs, and so I needed to nip that in the bud.

For a while I thought the rehab had helped, but lately I'd been noticing a change in my daughter. She had been acting nervous and fidgety. Some of the things she said at times were so strange that the night Jamela claimed to have picked Brielle up from jail, well, I believed her, even if I would never admit it to Jamela. Poor Brielle. She was still convinced she didn't have a problem.

The only one doing well was Victor's little black princess. I hated to say it, but she was really doing well in managing college, working full time at the restaurant, and taking care of her dad in her spare time. Speaking of her working at the restaurant, I thought that perhaps it was time she started chipping in on the bills. After all, she was a grown woman now. She'd been living for free for years, so no telling how much money she had been stacking, money that would come in handy right about now. Hell, I might even charge her ass back rent.

I needed this money to pull through our latest crisis with Brendon being in trouble. What I really wanted to do with the money, though, was get some more work done on my face. With all the stress of having a sick husband and unruly kids, I could use a touchup. Botox alone wasn't cutting it anymore.

The more I thought about it, the more I realized that I deserved to do something nice for myself. Even if Jamela started contributing some of her income to the household, though, I knew her uppity self would want me to account for where it was going. I was not about to have to answer to her, so I had to come up with another plan to get my needs met.

I walked into the bank and went to the manager's desk, sitting down in the chair across from her without waiting to be greeted.

"Good morning. I need to deposit this check, and I need it to clear immediately," I said to her as I slid the check across the desk.

"Good morning, Mrs. . . ." She hesitated.

"Long. Mrs. Long," I reminded her. She knew damn well who I was. I didn't know why she was trying to act as if she couldn't remember.

"Yes. Mrs. Long. I will be glad to help you deposit your check. Just to let you know, in the future you can go to any of the bank tellers at the windows and they can help you with your deposit transactions as well."

"I know what the tellers are there for. I just wasn't sure if they are allowed to work with large checks such as mine," I replied.

The Diana Ross wannabe grabbed my check and started working on her screen without saying anything further to me. I noticed her cheap weave was starting to show wear and tear, and her edges were looking a hot mess. I could never let myself go like that. I always made sure I looked good wherever I went.

"Mrs. Long, I can deposit the check today, but because the check is written from a different bank, it will take three days to clear."

"No. That is unacceptable. It is a check with my name on it. That is my money, and I need it right away." I was desperate. I had taken a check from Victor's credit union account and written it out to me. I figured by the time it cleared, bounced, or did whatever it had to do, I would have come up with a way to cover it, even if I had to start selling stuff out of my home. Brendon needed my help—and my face needed some work. I would do whatever it took to meet our needs.

"I'm sorry. There is nothing we can do on how long the check will take to clear."

"You're sorry? No, I'm sorry. I'm sorry that my husband and I ever decided to bring our business into this good-for-nothing bank. Every time I walk in here you give me a problem."

"I apologize that you feel that way, Mrs. Long, but it is company policy that out-of-bank checks get a seventy- two-hour hold before being cleared. Would you still like me to make the deposit for you?"

"Forget it. I'll take it to the bank it was written on. This one was just closer and I'm running late to an appointment," I lied, snatching the check out of her hand.

"Well then, is there anything else I can help you with, Mrs. Long?" she asked, sitting there batting her eyes, winning round two with me.

"Yes, you can. You can fire your stylist. Your tracks are showing, boo." With that, I stormed out of the bank.

CHAPTER EIGHT

JAMELA

"Don't tell me you forgot to bring your umbrella."

I jumped at the sound of a male's baritone voice. I had just finished my Friday night shift at the restaurant, and I was at the bar area cashing out. I was so focused on my task at hand that I hadn't even noticed Isaac approaching me. Staring up at his fine-looking self, I pulled off my gingham apron and hairnet.

"Sorry. I didn't mean to scare you," he said then gave me a hug. "It's good to see you."

"You're going to have to start wearing a bell or something when you approach me," I said. "But it's good to see you too." I looked at the dapper outfit he was wearing. "You look good."

"Thank you," he replied, popping his collar. "And you look . . . like you forgot your umbrella."

"Umbrella?" I questioned. "But it's not even raining out."

"It looks like you forgot all about our rain check. Get it? Umbrella? We were supposed to be having dinner tonight."

I threw my hand across my mouth. "Oh, my gosh. I'm so sorry, Isaac. I truly did forget. This week has just been so crazy."

I wasn't lying about my week. Glendora had decided she wanted to send the nurses packing while she did what she should have been doing all along, which was taking care of my father. That threw me for a loop. I wasn't sure whether she was sincere or just wanted to save money, but she was his wife. I at least had to give her a chance. I figured that her being around more often might even lift his spirits.

I almost lost my mind, though, when I came home the night before to find that Glendora's car was nowhere in sight. That meant she wasn't home, which meant my father was alone. I raced into the house screaming out my father's name. I was huffing, puffing, in a sweat and out of breath by the time I entered his room. When I barged in, I saw Glendora sitting next to my dad on his bed, reading him the paper. Now, that took me by surprise. Was it possible she had really changed?

"I didn't see your car outside," I said to her as I tried to catch my breath.

"That's because it's in the shop," she said, not looking up from the paper.

"Oh, okay then." Everything looked fine, so I backed out of the room, feeling a little awkward about how I'd panicked for nothing. "I'll be back in a few."

Glendora nodded, again not looking up from the paper. Just as I was about to close the door she called out, "Jamela."

"Yes?"

"There's leftovers in the kitchen."

Had I heard her correctly? She'd actually cooked and hadn't stopped off at one of the restaurants for take-home dinner like she usually did? I had to see this for myself. I went down to the kitchen and sure enough, there was a homemade Louisiana spread, gumbo and all. It smelled so good I had to scarf up a bowl before hitting the shower.

All day I'd been wondering what alternate universe I'd stepped into, where Glendora was properly caring for my dad and being nice to me. It had me so confused and preoccupied that I'd totally forgotten about my date with Isaac.

"No worries. We can reschedule dinner for some other time," Isaac said. "You're a busy girl. I get that."

I felt so bad—but I looked so bad too. For once I would have liked to look halfway decent in front of this guy. Still, I felt like it would be rude to bail on a date with him again.

"Can we at least have a cup of coffee?" I asked.

"Sure. Sounds good to me. I mean, I was supposed to have a dinner date with this hot chick I met at the gym, but she stood me up."

I smiled. Thank God he had a sense of humor. "Her loss. My gain."

We both sat down at the bar and ordered a cup of coffee from Amanda, the barmaid.

"I want to thank you again for the other night," I said as Amanda placed our cups in front of us.

He held his hand up, letting me know there was no need to thank him. "So, how is your father?" he asked, taking a sip of coffee.

"He's not doing so well. He's been having breathing problems." I thought about how weak he'd been looking lately. He was so stubborn though. He kept refusing to go to the hospital.

"I want to stay home," Daddy would protest. "If it's my time, then it's my time. When I go, I want it to be in my own room and in my own bed."

"I'm sorry to hear that," Isaac said. "I'm sending good wishes and prayers to him."

"Thank you very much." For a moment, my mood lifted.

"What does your sister have to say about all this? She looked rather . . . messed up." Isaac shook his head as if he didn't want to say too much.

I laughed. "Well, for starters she's not my biological sister. She's my stepsister. And about that day, it's a long story. Let's just say she's got issues."

"Well, that explains a lot. From what I saw that day, it didn't seem like you two were that close. And she came off like . . ." He seemed hesitant to keep talking.

"It's okay. You can say what's on your mind. I won't be offended," I encouraged him.

"Okay. Well, she came off like a spoiled brat, whereas you seem like a very dedicated and disciplined individual. I've seen you study on your breaks when I've been here at the restaurant. That shows a lot about a person."

"I didn't know you were watching."

"Yes, I've taken notice. Don't get me wrong; I'm not watching you on a stalker status, but I've had my eye on you here and there," he said as he leaned in and smirked. I wasn't sure if he was flirting with me on purpose. If it hadn't been for my complexion, he would've realized I was blushing.

"I've noticed you too," I said, deciding to flirt a little. "Noticed you haven't been wearing your glasses."

"Oh, those. They're just reading glasses," he said. "I only need them to read the menu here, although as much as I eat here I should know the menu like the back of my hand." He shrugged. "I don't need glassses to see how kind to your customers you are. And you always keep a smile on your face, even the times when you look like you haven't had any sleep," he continued.

"Well, thank you," I said shyly. "Now, I'm going to be paranoid that I look sleepy while I'm at work."

"Stop it! You know that's not what I was implying at all!" He laughed. "Why do women have to be so complicated, twisting up words and stuff?" he joked.

"I'm just messing with you!" I assured him. "Seriously though, I know I should be getting more sleep. It probabbly doesn't help that I love coffee as much as I do," I said, taking a sip and savoring the rich flavor.

Even though the warm beverage slid down my throat, an icy chill rippled through me. My stomach plummeted. The good mood I was in was eclipsed by this dark feeling that came over me. I shook my head to try to get rid of the bad feeling.

"You okay?" he asked, noticing the way I shivered.

"Yeah, I'm fine," I said. "Probably just a little too much caffeine in my system."

As soon as the words left my mouth, my cell phone started to ring, and something inside my soul just knew it was not good news. I picked it up automatically, without even apologizing to Isaac for the interruption.

"Hello," I answered, and immediately my ears were assaulted by Glendora's screeching.

"Glendora, please calm down." I stood to my feet and started pacing. "Slow down and tell me what's the matter."

"It's your dad. He had a heart attack." She burst out crying.

I struggled to keep it together. "What do you mean? I just saw him this morning. He was . . ." I couldn't say he was fine, because he wasn't. He'd been the weakest I'd seen him in a long time. "What hospital is he at? I'm on my way."

Glendora only said, "I'm sorry, Jamela. I'm so sorry."

"What do you mean, sorry? Where is he so I can get to the hospital?"

"You don't understand. He didn't make it. The EMS people could not revive him. I'm sorry, Jamela, but your father is dead."

Suddenly the room began spinning and the phone slid out of my hand onto the bar. I felt like the wind had been knocked out of me and I couldn't breathe. The last thing I remembered was everything going black and the sound of Isaac's voice calling my name.

As fast-paced as my life had been for the past few years, now time moved in slow motion. It might have had something to do with the Xanax and Ambien that a doctor had prescribed for me after my father's death.

I couldn't believe Daddy was gone. Each day I walked into his room it broke my heart to see his bed empty. All that was there was the medical equipment. I would have given anything to hear the sound of the heart monitor beeping the way it did when it was attached to my father, but that sound was gone, just like my father. I would never be able to hear his voice again, or see his big, wide smile and the wrinkles he would get on his nose when he laughed hard.

Glendora had been handling all of the funeral arrangements because I'd been too out of it. This was the first time in a long time I'd been relieved of the duty of having to do everything. It was a double-edged sword though. I was appalled when I found out my stepmother was being so cheap with the funeral arrangements. She wanted the cheapest casket and was asking for the cheapest package at the funeral parlor. It was insulting to see what she was doing, especially after everything my father did for her and her no-good children. My father was a good man, and he deserved better. I refused to allow her to do him like that, so I went behind her back and began handling the funeral arrangements.

I somehow managed to set my emotions aside and move forward with finances and paperwork. I went through the motions as though I was looking down at someone else. Almost like I was having an out-of-body experience. I don't even remember what was said between me and my crazy stepmother when she confronted me about taking everything over. I just remember that she finally stepped out of my way when she realized how determined I was to give my father a proper burial.

I picked out his suit. I picked the flowers. I chose the songs. I can't remember all the food that the neighbors brought to the house, and I can't remember all the flowers or the cards from his employees, his church, or his friends. I can't even remember how packed the church was. I was just existing, doped up and high. It was hard to believe Brielle had a drug problem, that she actually liked feeling this way, but I also wouldn't want to be going through this unmedicated. For me, it was either this or facing the unbearable pain of losing my father. In time, I knew I'd be all right and be able to function on my own, but not yet.

During the funeral I didn't pay my phony stepmother or my drug-addict stepsister any attention as they put on a show, screaming and hollering. I vaguely remember that Brendon wasn't able to come to the funeral. He couldn't leave the state he was in, out on bond or something crazy. I couldn't have cared less. I'd been so happy the day I found out he was moving out, and the last thing I wanted was for him to come back—especially now. God forbid he would try to stay and become the so-called man of the house.

Throughout it all, I couldn't cry. I was so numb.

The only thing I remembered clearly through this dark fog was standing at the gravesite, listening to our minister, Bishop O'Conner, intoning in his deep voice, "Ashes to ashes. Dust to dust. We commit your beloved son, Victor Long, back to the earth."

Through a mist, I vaguely remember feeling an arm go around me. I glanced up to see Isaac's face. It was amazing how God had put him in my life at just the right moment. Otherwise, I wouldn't have had anyone to lean on during my time of bereavement.

Exhausted, I leaned my head on his shoulder as we walked back to the funeral cars. I didn't know what it was about this man that put me at such peace. He had no obligation to be there for me. We had only spoken to each other about three times, yet he was the only person at the burial who was there for me.

There were no words exchanged between us. We just walked in silence. When he arrived to the black Lincoln Town Car, he leaned in and wrapped his arms around me. I wasn't expecting him to do that, and it felt a little strange at first, but while he kept holding me close, I turned my head to the side and laid it on his chest. In the serene quietness of the cemetery, I could faintly hear his heartbeat. I closed my eyes and took a deep breath. He scent was intoxicating. I couldn't pinpoint what the cologne was, but the smell was familiar to me.

Just then, he grabbed my head and made me look up at him. Again, he didn't say anything. He looked into my eyes and leaned his face down toward me, placing a soft kiss on my forehead.

"It's all right, Jamela. Let it out." He finally spoke as he put my head back down on his chest.

That's when I completely lost it. I broke down and cried. I cried because I was not there for my dad when he took his last breath. I cried because I hadn't sent him back to the hospital. I should have never agreed with Glendora to give the nurses a break. Maybe he would've made it. I cried because I didn't get a chance to say good-bye.

"My dad was my rock," I said, sobbing.

"He's still your rock. I know your dad is watching over you," Isaac said as he continued to hold me, "and I am here too, Jamela. I'm not going anywhere."

In a world where I felt alone most of the time, his words were exactly what I needed to hear. The only man's arms I'd ever felt this safe in were my dad's. Looked like God hadn't wasted any time in replacing him. Unlike Brielle and Brendon, I wouldn't have a void in my life that I had to fill with drugs and gangs. I had Isaac.

CHAPTER NINE

BRIELLE

I'd never understand how the fat girls were always getting the best-looking guys these days. Whenever I was out shopping, I would see some big girls walking hand in hand with a fly-looking guy. Now, don't get me wrong, I had nothing against big girls. I just couldn't get why or how they could pull good-looking guys like that. Guys are supposed to like tall, skinny girls for the most part, not the frumpy, chubby-looking ones.

So why did it bother me so much to see Jamela being comforted by Isaac? Perhaps because I didn't give a damn about the dudes in the mall, but this Isaac—my Lord! I hadn't crushed this hard since I was in high school.

I remember back in eleventh grade, I had the biggest crush on this boy named James. I would see him in the cafeteria during lunch, and I always made sure to flirt with him and sit at his table. As much as I would try to get his attention, though, he didn't really pay me any mind. Instead he would laugh and crack jokes with my friend Jackie. It would piss me off when he ignored me and talked to Jackie almost the entire lunch period. Heifer wasn't even pretty. She was my ugly friend, which was why I always brought her with me whenever I would try to talk to James.

You see, my mom taught me from when I was a little girl to always make sure I was the prettiest and best-looking one in my circle of friends. You can have friends who are kind of pretty or easy on the eyes, but you never keep girlfriends who look better than you. And no matter what, you have to make sure to have that friend who, no matter how hard she tries to dress up or wear makeup, she's still either fat or ugly. That way when you go out and boys or people see the group, you will always be the best-looking one. It was a lot for me to take in when I was little because I just wanted to have all my friends and I didn't care if they were pretty or any of that, but the older I got, the more I understood what my mom meant.

For the most part the plan worked. Whenever I would go out with my friends, I was the one who garnered the most attention from guys. In high school I had the best looks, clothes, and body out of all my friends. The only time the plan didn't work was with that asshole James. I guess he liked them ugly, because by the time we graduated, I heard he and Jackie were dating and they even planned on going to the same university. People found it cute, but I found it sickening. If he was planning on going away to school to get a degree and start a career, why would she want to do the same? If I were her, I would've just stayed with my parents and waited for him to get his shit together so that I could be a nice little housewife and he could just take care of me.

Speaking of taking care of things, things around the house had been very strange ever since Victor died. It had been a few weeks since his passing, and my mom hadn't been herself. She would sleep all day and leave randomly at night. I had no idea when she would get home, because I was usually too busy getting my rocks off.

Since the night I got arrested, one of my homeboys had talked me into popping E pills. That shit would make us horny as rabbits. I still did my crystals every now and then, but the E pill was my new favorite. He would come over, and we would each take one, chill on the couch until it took effect, and before we knew it, we were in my room going at it.

With my mom being gone so much at night, we pretty much had the entire house to ourselves. Brendon had finally made it to my dad's house in New York. Mom told me the attorney made everything "go away" and Brendon was released the same day of the hearing. She didn't want to take the chance of him getting into any more trouble taking the Greyhound bus cross-country, so she booked him a one-way flight straight to LaGuardia Airport in New York where my dad could pick him up.

Now that Victor was gone, I didn't have to worry about running into any nurses in the house. I had to admit, that was taking me a little bit of time to adjust to. Victor had been bedridden ever since he had that stroke a few years ago, so I had gotten used to him being in the house. Whenever I wanted to talk to him about things, I would just go to his room, take a chair next to his bed, and we would talk.

I was sad when he died. He wasn't my biological father, but he was good to me. All my real dad did was send money every month and send a plane ticket for me to go visit. Victor was the one who went to almost all the games I cheered at, and he always made sure to make time to listen to me when I needed to talk.

The day of the burial, I felt like shit just thinking about seeing him get put into the ground, so I smoked some crystal and popped a pill before we left. That was a mistake. I had never done the two at the same time, and it made me more emotional than I had expected. I started screaming and crying along with my mother, and the two of us looked like a couple of crazy women. I didn't know if my mom was being real with the way she was carrying on, but I knew I was. It's like the drugs made me feel every emotion and magnified the feeling to the point I felt like I would explode if I didn't let it all out. I cried for Victor, and I think I was crying for myself in there too.

Surprisingly, Jamela didn't cry when she saw the casket getting lowered. Come to think of it, I don't think I saw her cry at all throughout the funeral or burial; that was until Isaac wrapped her in his strong, loving arms. Ugh. Even in my high state, I couldn't help thinking that a man that fine should have wrapped his arms around someone who looked like me and not Jamela.

Jamela was another one who had been in and out of the house the last few weeks. I never knew if she was coming or going. What I did know was that she had been spending time with Isaac.

In fact, I had been listening to Jamela and the mystery man grunting and laughing for the last twenty minutes, and it was driving me up the wall. This guy was hot with a capital H, and instead of being in the living room chilling with me, he was in the sunroom with my fat, dark-skinned sister. That's exactly why I was sitting on this couch frustrated as hell.

My stepsister never fixed herself up. She didn't wear any makeup, usually kept her hair pulled back in a tight ponytail, and the most she would ever dress up would be if she wore some granny blouse and pants outfit instead of her usual college hoodie, jeans, and sneakers look. The girl shopped in the women's section at Macy's, for God's sake. I knew because my friends and I had been making fun of her for that since the day we saw her shopping there a while back. So how was it possible that she was getting this guy's attention over me?

When he first arrived and I opened the front door, he barely smiled and looked my way when he said hello; but when he saw my stepsister, he was quick to give her a big smile from ear to ear. I was so annoyed hearing them giggle and laugh with each other that I felt like walking over toward them just to curse them out. I couldn't do that, though, if I was still going to try to get me a piece of that sexy chocolate man.

"What are you guys doing?" I asked casually as I stood in the entryway of the sunroom.

"Hi, Brielle," answered an out-of-breath Jamela. "I'm just getting my workout done. I don't think I ever officially introduced you to Isaac," she said as she pointed toward that fine specimen of a man. "Isaac, this is my sister Brielle. Brielle, this is Isaac," she said before she resumed doing her squats.

"Hi, Isaac," I said as I waved at him with a twirl of my fingers.

"Hello, Brielle," he said nonchalantly. "It's nice to officially meet you."

"Likewise," I said as I looked him up and down. This man had perfectly toned arms. He was wearing a cut-off shirt that emphasized his tight abs. His skin looked as smooth as a baby's booty, and he had little traces of sweat that looked more like baby oil glistening in the sun coming through the windows. Man, I was getting wet just standing there looking at him.

I must have been staring, because he cleared his throat and gave me a very strange look.

"Well, it was nice to formally meet you. I have to get back to working out with your sister," he said and turned back toward Jamela.

"Okay." I decided to go back to the living room, where I took out my phone and made a quick Twitter post: Never let anyone stop you from taking what's yours #Mrs.StealYourMan #Don'tGetMadWhenIGetHim

"What are you doing?" The sound of my mom's voice startled me. I put my phone back to its home screen.

"Hi, Mom. I didn't know you were home."

"I'm home. I've just been sleeping all morning. I didn't get home until late last night. I was very tired when I got in," she said as she sat on the couch next to me. Just then we both heard Jamela let out a shriek, followed by laughter.

"What the hell is she doing?" my mom asked with an attitude.

"She's working out with *Isaac*," I informed her, rolling my eyes and twisting my neck while scrunching my face up.

My mom laughed. "Why did you say it like that?"

"Like how?" I asked.

"I don't know. You sounded let down. Like you were sad about it."

"Oh, it's nothing I guess." I tried to shrug it off.

"It's not nothing if you sound this down about it. What's going on, Brielle?" Mom pushed the subject.

"I guess I'm a little down because I like Isaac, but Jamela keeps interfering," I said. My mother didn't need to know all the true details.

"Jamela?" my mom questioned, twisting her face up like she smelled something foul. "I'd be willing to bet all my handbags that she's no threat to you. What man in his right mind would want a big, sloppy burger over a New York strip?"

"That's what I thought, but apparently Isaac does. I've only met him twice, but both times he didn't even look my way. Well, whenever he tried to, she'd interrupt." I was lying, but a girl's gotta do what a girl's gotta do. I was going to get this man by any means necessary, even if it took my mother's help. She knew all about roping in the man of her dreams.

"That sneaky little bitch," my mom said with venom dripping in her voice. "Well, we will just have to do something about that, won't we then?" she said as a sinister smile crept across her face.

Now with my mom on board, I knew it would only be a matter of time before Isaac was mine.

CHAPTER TEN

GLENDORA

I was driving like a maniac toward the dry-cleaner's. I overslept this morning and now I was at risk of being late to the attorney's office. Except for the days I married my first husband and Victor, today was one of the most important days of my life. At two o'clock this afternoon, I was expected in Ivan Chester's office for the reading of my late husband's will. I was anxious and excited to hear what the inheritance would be. It had been a long time coming, and I was ready to move into a new phase in my life.

The three years after his stroke had been nothing but a downhill battle for us, and I'd be lying if I said I was devastated when he died. I was never in love with Victor. I met him at the hospital, saw the opportunity for me to marry into a better lifestyle, and I went for it. Over the years, I grew to have love for Victor. He was a good man to me and my children after all. I know he loved me unconditionally, and he always made sure we were taken care of and were getting the attention we needed. No matter how busy he was at the restaurants he never missed any of Brendon's games or Brielle's cheerleading events. He even managed to spend time with that good-for-nothing daughter of his, even though I tried so hard to keep them apart.

After he became completely disabled, though, I personally thought he would've been better off dying. Who wants to live a life lying in bed and moping around the house sick all the time? I could never do that. I was a busybody. When I stopped working at the hospital I kept myself busy. Between the kids, the gym, and my personal sex life, I barely had time to sit.

Thank God Victor never caught me cheating. Who knew how that would have unfolded if he ever had? You might find this strange, but when Victor and I got married, I signed a prenuptial agreement. The only reason I signed it was because it had a single clause: that if the marriage did not work, I could walk away with whatever the judge deemed fit, unless I'd been unfaithful. I never worried much about being caught, though. Even back when he was as healthy as a horse, Victor was too busy to try to figure out what I was up to. But then again, Victor was so oblivious to what really went on, and he was so weak when it came to standing up to me, that if I had ever been caught, I would've been able to get away with it with no consequences.

I reached the drycleaner's, picked up my Alexander McQueen pantsuit, and was racing down the highway to make it back home. I couldn't wait to put on the suit. I had just purchased it a few days ago. It cost me close to two grand, but it was worth every penny. I had been named the beneficiary on his million-dollar life insurance policy, but I knew that was only the beginning, so what was two grand?

The material of the suit felt smooth as butter against my skin, and I looked amazing in it. I took it to the drycleaner's to have the pants hemmed and the width of the jacket taken in so it could fit me a little tighter. I had a size five waist and, thanks to my implants, 36D breasts. I was very proud of my figure, and I liked to show it off everywhere I went.

When I reached home, I ran up the front staircase toward the front door. With the exception of running a little bit late, I felt great about today. I was sure Victor had left me very well taken care of.

When I walked through the front door and saw Jamela standing in the living room, my good mood and vibes went out the window.

"I was just sending you a text. Ivan moved the meeting to three o'clock this afternoon," she said while she looked down at her phone. "Something about him running late with another meeting," she continued.

"Wait. Why is he calling to tell you about my meeting with him?" I asked.

"It's not just your meeting, Glendora. I am supposed to be there too," she informed me.

This really threw me off. As far as I was concerned, Victor and I had always spoken about not including any of the kids in any of our wills until they were older. He agreed because he said he did not want to leave the kids with anything they were not old enough to handle. Soon after his stroke, we decided to update his will in the event that he was to pass before me, and we both agreed to leave me as the sole beneficiary of his entire estate. Of course, I told him I would disperse the money and accounts evenly among the children, but I knew I would make sure Jamela never received a dime. I paid my dues by having to raise her from when she was a little girl and having to put up with her prissy ass all these years. With me being the only person in his will, it guaranteed me that Jamela would never get anything from him. Learning that she was invited to the meeting really pissed me off.

"Listen well, you little bitch. Don't think for a second that you are going into this meeting because your father left you something. I was his wife for over ten years, and I know all of his affairs and documents," I said as I walked toward her and waved my pointer finger in her face. "Now, I don't know what your sneaky ass is up to or how you managed to get yourself involved in this meeting, but I do know this: When we get back from this meeting, you are to pack up your things and get the hell out of my house. I'm not a landlord, and you are not my tenant. Screw a thirty-day notice. You have two days to get all your stuff out of here. After that I am changing the locks and I will file a restraining order against you if I catch you on my property." Before she had a chance to say anything back, I went to my room to prepare myself for the reading of the will. The days of me needing a man to house, clothe, and feed me were over!

"Mr. Chester will see you now." The lady at the front desk pointed us in the direction of Ivan's office.

"Mrs. Long!" Ivan exclaimed as soon as I entered. He greeted me with a confident handshake. "You look fabulous today," he complimented me.

"Thank you, Ivan."

"And it's good seeing you again too, Ms. Long. It's been a while," he greeted Jamela.

God, I hated having to share my last name with her. But now that her father was gone, I wouldn't have to put up with her for much longer. Soon, Jamela would just be an insignificant thing of the past. Maybe I'd even go back to my maiden name. Really start life over from the beginning.

"Ladies, shall we have a seat at my desk?" Ivan suggested. After he got us bottled water and took out all the paperwork, we were finally ready to get the meeting started.

"Ladies, before we begin, I must inform you that this entire proceeding will be recorded for legal purposes. This is the device that I will be using to record." He pointed down to a small rectangular device that had two small lights on it, along with a stop and go button. It reminded me a little bit of a cassette player from back in the day. "When the light is green, that means the meeting has commenced. Please let me know when you are ready to begin."

"I am ready," I said as I straightened up in the chair.

"Ready," said a nervous-looking Jamela. It brought me joy to see her so uncomfortable.

Without saying anything further, Ivan nodded his head and pressed the go button on the device. The green light turned on, and Ivan leaned in toward the recorder.

"This is Ivan Chester from Chester and Chester Attorneys at Law. Today is Wednesday, October eleventh, and we are here for the reading of the will for Victor Long. Present at the reading of the last will and testament of Victor Long is the surviving lawful wife as registered by the State of California, Glendora Long. Also present is his surviving biological daughter, Jamela Long."

Ivan picked up the will and brought it to his face. He began reading directly from the document. "As written in the will: 'I, Victor Long, residing at 1201 Rancho Alisal Drive, Santa Ynez, California, declare this to be my will, and I revoke any and all prior wills and codicils I have previously made with the exception of privileges made in my will created with my widower Arlene Long concerning Jamela Long's inheritances.'"

I was beginning to lose my patience listening to all the legalities. I wished Ivan would just skip to what I came here for.

"Remaining privileges exempted from the will concern the transfer of ownership of Long's Soul Food chain of restaurants. When Jamela Long reaches the age of majority, I authorize the transfer of ownership for Jamela Long to become legal CEO of all Long's Soul Food restaurants and possible future chains."

"Wait a minute!" I interrupted. "What the hell do you mean *CEO?* I'm his wife, and I am fully entitled to *everything!*" I couldn't believe what I had just heard. Did he really just say Jamela would be the CEO of the restaurants? "Does that mean his ownership goes over to her as well?" I was confused, but more so livid! Here I was thinking he might have left her an insurance policy, some jewelry, furniture, or maybe his car, but here he'd turned over his entire empire, his legacy to her.

"Mrs. Long, you cannot interrupt during a last will testamentary reading," Ivan commented. "This is a recorded event for full disclosure purposes," Ivan continued. "Now, allow me to do my job without interruption." Ivan rewound the recording to a point before my outburst. I was fuming inside, but I knew I had to keep my composure. The nerve of my husband to have gone behind my back and created this foolishness.

"Ahem. Please take into account that this recording has been altered to strike out verbal mistakes. Continuation of the reading of the will . . ."

I couldn't understand a single word of what he said for the next five minutes. I was pissed beyond belief. The entire time I sat in my chair fighting the urge to slap the color off of everyone's face in the room. That was until I heard the mention of my name.

"Glendora Long has been given all and exclusive privileges of my bank accounts," Ivan read.

I didn't give a shit about that. I'd already drained them dry. "Keep it moving. I already know that," I said, getting impatient.

"Glendora! If you disrupt my reading one more time, I will have you removed from my office and you will have to get your results from Jamela when this is over! My schedule is packed, and you are wasting valuable time that I cannot afford and neither can you. Do I make myself clear?" A clearly agitated Ivan surprised me with his authority.

"I apologize about that, Mr. Chester. It won't happen again. Please continue." And I meant it. I couldn't wait to hear the details of any other assets Victor might have had. I just couldn't imagine he'd leave the restaurant business to Jamela and leave me with less than her.

All of a sudden, I realized that I shouldn't have expected anything else. I'd never really shown an interest in the business, so Victor probably figured I didn't want to be bothered with it. I never cared for those restaurants anyhow. I couldn't even remember the last time I set foot in one of them. The only time those restaurants mattered to me was when I was making the daily deposits into the account . . . or not.

"For the record, we have altered this recording for the second time," Ivan continued. I heard my name again, and so I perked up again. He was mentioning something about brokerage accounts. "The amount in each brokerage account will be undisclosed for the will, as the values vary for each of the personal accounts. All other accounts relating to the restaurants will become the responsibility of the new CEO, Jamela Long. Effective immediately, Jamela Long is sole beneficiary of the Long's Soul Food restaurant account as well. She is to pay the widower Glendora Long a fifty thousand dollar severance."

Fifty thousand lousy dollars? Really! At least that time I'd managed to keep the thought in my head and not speak it out loud, but this was some bullshit to the tenth power. I know I had given this man the best years of my life, and for what? For shit, that's what!

Ivan went into the next portion of the will. "Concerning the estate property in Santa Ynez, Glendora will become the deeded owner of 1201 Rancho Alisal Drive . . ."

That was all I needed to hear. I hoped Jamela still remembered my words from this morning. It was time to start looking at the glass half full. I did get a million-dollar life insurance policy, fifty grand, and a house that I could sell for almost a million and a half. And I didn't have to mop floors at a restaurant. Everybody in L.A. was so damn health conscious these days, it was only a matter of time before Long's Soul Food restaurants were long gone.

Nothing else Ivan had to say could make things any better than this, unless the next words he read were that Jamela inherited a noose and a tree to hang herself.

"This concludes all matters of allocation of the deceased, Mr. Victor Long. May he rest in peace, and may his family find comfort in what he has left for each."

He couldn't end this meeting any faster for me. *I need to hurry to the bank to find out how much money I have to play with, because Momma needs a new pair of Jimmy Choos for when she goes out to celebrate.*

CHAPTER ELEVEN

JAMELA

I bet Glendora's ass thought she'd hit the lottery back in Ivan's office. In a sense she had, but not the mega-million lottery I was sure she'd thought she bought the ticket for when she married my dad.

She raced out of Ivan's office so quick she caused a breeze. She was probably headed straight to the bank. Me, I had to sit there in his office for a moment and let everything register. I was officially the CEO of my father's restaurants. I would be the sole decision maker, under the guidance of Ivan, of course. Fortunately, Ivan had been guiding me for a while now, when he started to see the way Glendora was treating the restaurants like her own personal bank account.

Ivan had suggested that I should take the time to learn everything about my father's affairs. I had gotten right on that, never knowing when

Glendora would talk my father into revoking my power of attorney. I couldn't believe how she was going through everything my father had worked for like it was water. That's when Ivan had helped me to immediately begin shifting money around into various names, protecting them under his corporation. She was ruining Daddy's personal credit. That was a rope I was willing to let her hang herself with, but Long's restaurants was a legacy that I could not, would not, let her destroy.

My father was a decent man. He never would have wanted to leave this earth without making sure Glendora and her children were taken care of the same as me. That's why we decided that instead of having a $5 million life insurance policy, he would have five individual million-dollar policies for each of us. The fifth one would be divided among the restaurant employees who had helped make Long's what it was.

As far as Brielle's and Brendon's policies, they were none the wiser. I'd retrieved them out of Daddy's safe deposit box ages ago. I didn't trust the three of them not to conspire to have Daddy killed if they knew they could run off with $3 million. Beecause I didn't let Glendora and her kids get to me, she never saw me as a threat. Little did she know, I was a quiet storm.

***

"You still here?" Glendora said from the doorway of my bedroom.

"Don't worry, I'll be out of here shortly," I said as I closed the plastic bin that held some of my personal items, like my journal, pictures, and other keepsakes.

"Ha, not from the looks of things." Glendora looked around my room. Everything was still pretty much in place. The only things I'd packed were personal items. My clothes were still in the dresser drawer or hanging in my closet, as well as any shoes, purses, et cetera.

"Brielle," she yelled. "Come help your sister pack." She looked at me, then with a grin on her face, said, "Oh, yeah, with Victor being dead and all, I guess that means you and Brielle aren't really sisters anymore."

I shook my head. "You really don't know who you're fucking with, do you?"

My words wiped the smile right off of Glendora's face. She wasn't used to me holding my ground.

"You're right, my daddy is gone. It does mean that Brielle is no longer my sister, and thank God it means your perverted son is no longer my brother either. But you know what else?" I glared at her and began walking toward her.

"It also means that you're not my stepmother anymore either. Now you're just another bitch on the street. I've respected you for all these years because my father really loved you. Why? I'll never know. You might think you're the shit, but trust me when I say that you really don't want to find out what happens to a bitch on the street." I was now nose to nose with Glendora. "Up underneath all this fat you love to criticize me about is a broad who will beat your ass and leave your children spending the rest of their lives trying to figure out where the body is at." I pulled back away from her.

"Now, why don't you just go on out of here? Isn't it Wednesday? Don't you have a standing appointment on Wednesdays?" I smirked.

Ohhh, the look on her face. Priceless! I could see the wheels in her head churning now, trying to figure out how I knew about the little boy toy she'd been screwing—until recently, that is. "Tell Jasper congratulations on graduating summa cum laude. Guess he won't need me tutoring him anymore—which also means no more nookie for you. Isn't it funny how he paid for my tutoring by doing me the favor of sleeping with your old ass?" I let out the most annoying laugh I could muster up.

"Wha . . . what are you talking about?" Glendora began rubbing her chest as if she was about to have a heart attack of her own.

"During one of my meetings with Ivan about the whole power of attorney thing, he might have accidentally made mention that you and Daddy had a prenup . . . with a stipulation. Something about adultery," I continued to tease her. "I honestly never expected my father to die, but I didn't know how much longer I could take having your evil ass around. So just in case I needed to help him see the real you, Jasper was going to be my backup plan. I'd been collecting evidence of your affair for longer than you would believe. Lucky for you I never had the heart to reveal it to Daddy."

"You're lying," she said weakly.

I had to put the nail in the coffin. "Do you really think someone as fine as Jasper would want an old wrinkled-up prune like you?" I laughed. The more I laughed, the angrier she got.

"Fuck you!" she spat. "He clearly didn't want a fat, black bitch like you."

I put my finger on my chin then looked upward in thought. "Actually, you're right. Do you know how hard it is to get a gay man to have sex with a woman?"

Okay. I needed a spatula to be able to pry Glendora's fucked-up face up off the ground. Splat!

"You never wondered why he always opted for oral sex first, hoping that he could get you off to keep from having to screw you?" I shook my head in disgust.

"You trifling—" she started before Brielle walked up behind her, looking like hell. She'd probably been high ever since the night before. That girl was headed nowhere in life real fast.

"Did you call me, Mom?"

Glendora stood there glaring at me with the look of death. Her chest was heaving up and down. "Hurry up and help this bitch pack before it's me who gets locked up."

Brielle looked around the room. "Pack what? In what? There's no boxes or anything."

"That's because I'm leaving it all," I said, looking at Brielle. "To you. I know how you like my sloppy seconds."

Brielle turned red.

"Yeah, Isaac told me how you showed up at the gym trying to get with him," I said to her, unfazed. "He also told me how you went on and on about how he must be gay if he didn't want you, blah blah blah." I looked at Glendora. "I'm sure your mom can vouch for the fact that even a gay guy will play in the kitty litter if there's a buried treasure within." I guessed that was the straw that broke the camel's back, because the next thing I knew, Glendora came charging at me.

"Ma, no," Brielle said, grabbing a hold of her mother before Glendora could put her hands on me. I hadn't even backed away. She could come get some of this if she wanted.

"This pig isn't worth it," Brielle spat at me, holding her mother's arm and trying to calm her down.

"You're right," Glendora agreed. "She's just bitter, black—"

"And fat," Brielle said.

"And my Creole momma back in New Orleans always taught me that fat girls finish last."

Those two stood there sounding like some high school mean girls, or those girls from the movie *White Chicks* trying to tell "yo' momma" jokes. Lame. I grabbed my plastic bin and my purse and stepped toward the doorway.

At first Glendora and Brielle stood there like they were going to try me. I twisted my lips and dared them to go for it. They could tell by the look in my eyes that I would drop that bin and go to work on them. My size would definitely come in handy. The two parted like the Red Sea, one on each side of the doorway, allowing me to walk through.

"Fat bitch," I heard one of them mumble under her breath.

I stopped in my tracks and then turned to face them. "I need to just remind you both of one more thing before I go," I said. "Big girls might not finish first because we had to stop and get a chocolate milkshake in the middle of the race, but damn it, we finish!" And with that, I strutted my fat ass right on out of that house.

I sat in front of the fireplace of my home I'd just closed on earlier that afternoon. I stared at the flames as I looked back at my life over the years. I think I honestly was the black Cinderella. My father married the wicked stepmother then turned ill, eventually passing away, leaving me having to fend for myself.

But just like Cinderella, my Prince Charming came and saved the day. Isaac and I had become inseparable over the last six months since my father had passed. I had taken a leave from school, but I was still working harder than ever in the restaurants.

"I have more wood out back if you need to keep up the fire," Isaac said, entering the room.

I looked down at the last piece of paper I had in my hand that I was about to ball up and throw into the fire. "No, this ought to do it." I tossed the final page of Brendon's insurance policy into the fireplace and watched the flames devour it. Brielle's was the first I'd burned to a crisp. I knew Daddy wanted them to know how he never saw them as any different than me, which is why he'd left them a policy identical to mine, but I'm almost certain Daddy wouldn't have wanted to be responsible for Brielle's death. She would have spent all the money on drugs until she was found dead in an alley somewhere. And Brendon, the stepbrother who, after living in our home for just a couple months, woke me with his hand over my mouth as he rammed himself inside of me—well, if I had ever told Daddy the truth, I don't think he would have been too keen on taking care of Brendon either.

I never told anyone about what Brendon was doing to me. At first it had only happened that one night. My body didn't react to the rape the way I thought it should have. I actually came. I thought that meant that maybe a part of me liked it, therefore I never screamed rape. Once Brendon saw I wasn't going to say anything, he came back another night, and then another. But then things started getting more and more violent, until I would just shut down.

That's when I started to gain weight. I was subconsciously hiding the thin, weak girl up under all this skin, while at the same time hoping that eventually Brendon would get so disgusted with my weight that he would leave me alone. When that didn't work, I just stayed away from home as much as I could. I was busy on purpose. Then finally Brendon's time was more occupied with gangs. That's why I was so happy when he moved away for good.

So, I can't honestly say that I felt bad about burning up their policies. My only regret was that I hadn't burned up Glendora's, but I made it a point to use hers for the funeral. That bitch needed to pay for a proper burial for the man who'd taken her from the hood life to the good life.

She might as well have been left with nothing anyway. When she went to sell the house, she had a rude awakening. With two mortgages, the house was way in the red. Even after listing it for its full value, she still owed the bank a balance. It was her fault for taking out a second mortgage and letting it get delinquent. As Daddy's wife, she was also responsible for any outstanding debts he left behind, so all those charge cards and loans, yep, she had to pay all of them off, plus the vacation pay for the nurses. Ha! She couldn't afford to keep the house, and she couldn't afford to sell it either. Go figure. By the time everything was said and done, she'd ended up with exactly what she'd contributed: nothing!

I ended up buying the house through a short sale. The longer she kept it, the more of a deficit it became. Glendora had no idea it was me who was purchasing the home. I made sure that she didn't find out until after the fact. Ivan put her on speaker when she showed up at his office, cussing and fussing. Payback was a mutha indeed.

I exhaled as Isaac slid behind me and held me in his arms while we listened to the crackling of the fire. Just then my cell phone beeped, alerting me that I had a text message. I reached for it and read the words that appeared across the screen: You look nice and cuddly lying up in my house with the man who should have been my daughter's.

My heart immediately began racing. I shot up from Isaac's arms.

"Baby, what's wrong?"

I stood up to walk over to the window. Before I could even make it over there, I heard my phone letting me know that I had received another message: Don't get used to it. That's my life, bitch, and I'm going to live it even if it means I have to take yours.

I hurried to the huge picture window that gave a view of the front yard. I looked at the trees and bushes, but I saw no one. I did, though, see the taillights of a car driving away just as I received another text: You might have thought your fairy tale had come true, but so has your worst nightmare.

"What is it?" Isaac walked up behind me and wrapped his arms around me.

I looked into his eyes, wondering if I should fill him in just yet. I decided against it though. I wasn't about to scare him off with this drama. I knew it was Glendora having a hard time letting go. She'd just have to get over it, though, because no way in hell was I letting her steal another second of joy from my life. I had put up with too much from her over the years, and I would do whatever it took to protect myself and my new life now. All those years of doubting myself because of her mistreatment were over. Everything I'd been through had made me a stronger person, and I would never let someone like Glendora keep me down again.

"Nothing," I told Isaac, "I just thought I heard something." I smiled at him. "I'm going to go grab us a drink. I'll be right back, okay?"

He kissed me on the forehead. "Sure, honey. I'll be waiting by the fire."

I headed into the kitchen, truly amazed that six months had passed and Glendora hadn't found her another sugar daddy. Well, if it's true what they say that it's not over until the fat lady sings, then I suppose I should start taking singing lessons, because when all was said and done, I would make sure to have the last word in this story. . . .

THIS CAN'T BE LIFE

by

Ms. Michel Moore

CHAPTER ONE

I swear I despise Tori. My mind, body, and soul simply hate her. Matter of fact, hate is not a strong enough word to describe how I truly feel about my little sister. However, it's the only one that constantly haunts my daily existence. I promise every single bone in my body aches when even speaking Tori's name.

Ever since that child was born, I knew her dimple-having, green-eyed, bony ass was gonna be trouble. I should have socked my mother in the gut or attempted to shove her down two flights of stairs when they broke the supposed blessed news to me. I should've pretended I was sick and had to sleep in my parents' bed for a month straight to stop them from even creating Tori's spoiled, annoying self in the first place. If I could only turn back the hands of time, my life would be so much better.

First the manipulating trick took over my bedroom, forcing me to take the smaller one, *then she turned all my friends against me, and now she even got Mommy and Daddy to spend half their retirement nest egg on a lavish wedding she doesn't deserve. I had to work part time to help pay for college, but they had money to spare for that three-ring circus. What part of the game is that?*

Yeah, if you hadn't guessed, here comes that word hate *again. For once I wish I would win and that sneaky, man-stealing monster would lose.*

It doesn't matter that we are both grown women now. Who gives a shit? Not me! The time limits on being a bitter bitch never run out, and trust, I stay on the clock.

With her ear firmly pressed against her younger sister's bedroom door, Tami grew more irritated as the seconds dragged by. Seething with jealousy, she quietly ate several Double Stuf Oreo cookies, surely adding a pound or so to her already big-girl frame. *Oh my freaking God! Listen to these two going at it. They make me downright sick to my stomach. Well, at least she does.*

Dark crumbs fell down onto the lavender-colored maid of honor dress she'd felt obligated to wear. Fed up, Tami's true emotions were boiling to the surface. Heated, she wanted nothing more than to kick down the door. She yearned to slice her own blood's face and snatch the man she secretly loved out her conniving clutches.

Tami's true colors were definitely ready to be revealed. The older sibling was done keeping up appearances for appearance's sake.

I promise one day the tables gonna turn on Tori's fake ass. She knew I liked Vance. I told her I thought he was cute, and she still went after him, but that's okay, I'm gonna be good. It's a special place in hell waiting for li'l Miss Perfect Tori. Females like her always get theirs in the end! I should've stopped the wedding when the damn minster asked the million-dollar question. Shit!

"Bae, shhh, come on now. Please, you have to be quiet. I'm not playing around with you." Glancing at the closed bedroom door, which still had a poster of Usher, her teenage crush, taped to it, she squirmed, fighting to keep a straight face. "Come on now, boy, I'm serious. You're gonna mess around and let my parents or Tami hear us. Then what?"

"Then it's whatever. Let 'em watch if they want to. You belong to me now, girl, and you know I can't slow down once I get started loving my queen. I be in my zone!"

"Oh my God! Vance, you know you straight crazy, right?" Tori playfully teased, whispering in his ear.

"Well, let a brother just be crazy then!" With one thing on his mind, he was determined to have his way. After all, it was their wedding night, and what else were they supposed to do but bang like there was no tomorrow?

Ignoring Tori's pleas, Vance's strong hands groped in places his new wife never knew she had, causing her to shiver. "And besides, queen, I know you love this here I got for you. I can tell by the way you been looking at me all day. You wanted this meat. You liked seeing a guy flossing all high profile in a tuxedo."

In the midst of Tori giggling, Vance once more kissed her neck, running his fingers through her expensive one-day-only hairstyle.

Feeling as if she was fighting a losing battle, Tori ultimately gave in to his wishes. Allowing her man to have his way with her, she silently prayed her overly protective father was fast asleep and wouldn't come busting through the door acting like Rambo on a mission.

"Bae, I wish we wouldn't have missed our flight. We could have been on our honeymoon, on a beach lying underneath the stars and the moon instead of being so hush-hush in my old bedroom, like we kids sneaking to do it."

This was the night he'd been waiting for since originally meeting Tori and her older sister at a temp agency. Amazingly to some, six months after he and Tori started dating, Vance knew it was time to settle down and make it official. She was the one for him, and he wanted the world to know. Despite opposition from a few of his lifelong friends sworn to be bachelors, the once wild womanizer popped the question, and without a moment's hesitation, Tori accepted.

"Look at you, girl, all sexy in this twin bed," he teased, mocking their current situation. "With your main man Usher on the back of the door, watching us about to get it on!"

"Shut up, silly, and tell me you love me." Tori admired the diamond ring she'd been blessed with and smiled. Stroking his perfectly lined beard, her eyes lit up. Living in the celebration of being someone's wife, her world seemed perfect. Feeling as if Vance was her knight in shining armor, the new bride felt safe, as if nothing could ever bring harm or separation to their bond.

"Vance, tell me this is gonna last forever. Tell me you got me no matter what. Please tell me again. I love when you say it."

Vance smiled, showing the small gap between his teeth. "Come on, girl. I love you from the left side, right here." He closed his fist, pounding it twice against his chest. "Sweetheart, if it ain't gonna be me and you for a lifetime, then it ain't gonna be shit. Trust me; I've got your back the long way. Ain't another woman walking these streets who can take your place in my heart."

I can't believe he's in there saying all those mushy, meaningless things to that tramp he should be saying to me.

Tami grew enraged. In her heart of hearts, she believed if Tori had just fallen back for once, giving her the opportunity to at least try making a play for Vance, it could've been her wedding everyone in the family was celebrating earlier, not the other way around. Ripping the cheap satin-like dress from her body, she let it fall to the floor.

Tori got him fooled just like everyone else she comes in contact with. She's nothing but a conniving manipulator. She fumed as her thoughts took control. *This truly can't be life. It's not fair. I swear I can't stand that girl!*

Failing to see the true inner as well as outer beauty she honestly possessed, the visibly thick

Tami kicked what she looked upon as her badge of dishonor or a second-place trophy. The dress with a broken zipper landed clear across the room. Not quite done with her tantrum, she threw her maid of honor bouquet against the wall while rolling her eyes.

Possessing a fiery attitude that could be easily divided among ten angry black women, Tami stood in front of her full-length mirror. Mentally stressed, she snatched the multitudes of hairpins out of her once perfect French roll. Pouting, lace bra and panties only, the irate female stared straight ahead, second-guessing her life in general.

Why me of all people? I'm a good person. Damn, I deserve happiness too. It's not fair! Ever since we were kids it ain't been fair around here. She's always had to be the one getting her way.

"Tami, why would you eat all that ice cream?" Mr. Lewis yelled, snatching the cone from his Tami's tiny hands. "I told you to save some for my little princess! But you are always so hardheaded with your big, greedy self."

"But please, Daddy." Tami stood with tears streaming down her face. "Mommy said it was all mine. She said so."

"Look, girl, I don't know how many times I have to tell you, your mother don't run anything around here. It's about time you and she both learned that." With evil intentions toward Tami, he handed the remaining portion to her younger sibling, who happily accepted. "Besides, you're way too fat anyway. You need to go run around a park instead of chasing behind an ice cream truck. Look at how small and pretty your sister is. You need to be a little more like her."

No matter how many times Tami was talked down to, humiliated, berated, or forced to play second fiddle to her stepfather's biological daughter, she tried being strong. The fact that her mother married her stepdad when she was barely one year old meant absolutely nothing to him. He still hadn't grown any sort of true attachment to her. No matter how hard she'd try to initiate conversation or call herself trying to get close to him like most daughters did with their fathers, he was not receptive. He would use that as a reason to mentally abuse her more.

Never having any true knowledge of her real dad, Tami was told he'd abandoned her and her mother early on. She was led to believe that her stepfather was some sort of a hero who swooped *in and saved the day, making an honest woman out of her mother. Maybe to others he was indeed that, but not to her. He was the original source of her resentment of Tori, the little bitch that could do no wrong. In Tami's small world, they were both monsters she wished would just go away.*

Depressed, the sister to the perfect bride wanted to swallow a handful of sleeping pills, just to ruin Tori and Vance's night. She spitefully snatched the always present bottle off her nightstand. However, the way her luck was going, Tami felt she might actually mess around and die from an overdose, trying to seek attention. Instead, the troubled female dropped the bottle, reaching for her journal. In tears, she climbed in the bed, jotting down her vengeful frustrations as the therapist at the free mental health clinic suggested she do. Line by line she detailed her overwhelming hate and resentment not only for Tori, but her parents as well.

CHAPTER TWO

Oh my God! What in the hell is going on? Am I dreaming or what? Tami fought like hell to open her red eyes, still puffy from the night before. *Oh, shit! Is that Mommy's voice I hear?*

Loud, piercing screams from her mother's normally calm voice snatched her out of a sexually charged fantasy starring her sister's new husband. Quickly gathering her thoughts, Tami kicked the sheet and thin blanket off her legs and feet. Jumping out of the bed, she stumbled over her torn bridesmaid dress while slipping on a pair of old, stained jogging pants.

Damn, what in the hell is going on around here?

Hearing her mom yell out once more, she pulled a T-shirt over her head and swung her bedroom door wide open. Seconds after stepping in the hallway, the bewildered daughter was met with her stepfather half dressed, running down the stairs as if the house were on fire.

Trailing behind him like a lost child, she wiped sleep out of the corner of each eye. Now fully awake, seeing him with wallet and house keys in hand, Tami's curiosity increasingly grew.

"Daddy, what's going on? Why was Mommy yelling? What's happening? What's wrong?"

"Just hurry up, Tami! Hurry up and get dressed!" he demanded, stuffing his wallet into his rear pocket. Grabbing a pair of shoes from the front closet, he lifted up, turning to face her. "Look, girl, your mom is already out in the car waiting. You have to drive your own and meet us down there. So like I said, hurry up and put on some damn clothes. We have to go!"

Dumbfounded, Tami was still in search of what had her parents in such an uproar. "Down where? Daddy, what's going on? Please slow down and tell me what's the matter."

Now also panicked but not knowing why, Tami raced out to the driveway to question her mother. Finding her shaking with a face soaked with tears, Tami wasted no more time. "Mommy, please, what's going on? Tell me please," she begged, watching her father rush off the porch, trying to button his shirt. "Why were you screaming like that and where are you two going? Please tell me."

***

Small bits of gravel slid in between Tami's manicured toes as she slowly strolled barefoot back up the driveway. Knowing she should've been moving faster, like her parents, she was now also in shock.

Wow, sweet Jesus, I can't believe this. It's like I'm having a dream and a nightmare at the same time. If I am having a dream, I hope I stay asleep forever!

In the midst of all the shouting, yelling, and questions, she'd not once thought about where Tori and Vance were after the abrupt disruption of her morning sleep. She'd not noticed her sister's bedroom door was wide open and their luggage, left by the front entryway the night before, was gone. After hearing her mother's sorrowful voice echo throughout the house, Tami was totally thrown off her square.

Her main objective at that point was to find out the source of her mom's pain. Less than twenty-four hours ago, her parents were all smiles and handshakes at her baby sister's wedding; now this. Tami was at a loss for words as her thoughts raced through her mind.

I gotta get myself together. This is crazy. I mean really crazy.

Walking through the eerily silent house for the first time in years, she stared at the framed elementary-age picture of herself and Tori that sat proudly displayed on the mantle.

I gotta get some clothes on and meet Mommy and Daddy. Oh my God! Tori and Vance!

Tami's body trembled as she held on to the handrail, climbing the stairs. Before going to get dressed, she solemnly paused at Tori's room. Standing in the doorway, she couldn't believe what her mother had just told her.

Okay, Tori, that's a personal blessing from God Himself, but Vance? Not him of all people. He doesn't deserve it. He's just a confused brother.

Still moving at her own pace, it was like she was still asleep or hadn't heard correctly. This was an emergency, and Tami was moving with a casual attitude. Taking a deep breath, she went over to her sister's twin bed. The reality of what was told to her in the driveway was starting to sink in. Lifting the single pillow off the bed, Tami smashed it to her face, taking a long whiff of what she knew was Vance's signature cologne.

Damn, boy. This is so messed up. I wish you were here with me right now, kissing me and holding me like you did that no-good Tori last night.

With no guilt about the family turmoil that was going on, she slipped the case off the pillow and left her sister's room. After placing it in the lower drawer of her dresser, Tami threw on a clean tracksuit. Taking her time, brushing her teeth then washing her face, Tami finally texted her mother, informing her she was on the way.

"Tami, hey, we're over here." Mr. Lewis signaled to his stepdaughter from across the waiting room area. Consoling his hysterical wife, he gently rubbed her shoulder, reassuring her everything would be fine.

"Mommy, Daddy, I got down here as soon as I could," Tami easily lied, knowing she'd stopped at McDonald's for two Egg McMuffins and a small coffee. "What are the doctors saying? Is Vance going to be okay? Is Tori still alive? What's the update on the situation?"

Her parents' mood was obviously solemn. The unexpected, tragic call received about their youngest daughter and new son-in-law's car accident had taken an immediate toll. Tami's demeanor, on the other hand, was sinisterly indifferent. Getting the impression her bitter-filled prayers on the drive to the emergency trauma room had indeed been answered by God Himself, she looked into their worried faces, searching for clues. Her one hope and constant desire was for Tori to be removed from her life once and for all. Not temporarily, like when she'd go away to summer camp, spend the weekends at some of her equally-as-shallow friends' homes, or get taken on some impromptu shopping spree courtesy of her father. Tami wanted her sister erased from the face of the earth.

"Oh my God," her mother cried out as the tears poured from her eyes. She was frantic not knowing what the immediate future held for her beloved youngest daughter.

"Tell me, Mommy! What was said? What did they say? Please tell me." If their glum expressions gave any indication of what the doctor had just revealed, she knew her baby sister Tori was no more. Bracing herself to at least act as if what should be dreadful news was not a joyful event, Tami fought back the appalling urge to smile. She wanted to jump up and down and celebrate her sister's sudden demise, but she held her wicked emotions in check.

Holding several tear-soaked pieces of tissue provided by the hospital, her mother fought to regain a small bit of composure. She wanted nothing more than to tell Tami all was well. The constant caregiver since birth wanted to assure the world that Tori had walked away with nothing but small cuts, bruises, and abrasions; however, that wasn't the case.

"Baby, I don't know how to tell you, but Tori is in critical condition. They say your little sister lost a lot of blood and might have some internal injuries. They are saying that it's bad, very bad."

"Oh wow, Mommy."

Confused, her mother cut her eyes over to the double doors the doctor had disappeared through. She wished she could've followed him and changed the prognosis.

Still as cold as ever, Tami continued to act genuinely concerned about her sibling. "I don't know what to say. Have you and Daddy talked to her yet? How does she look? Is her face messed up?"

"No, Tami, we haven't. She's still unconscious they say." Her stepfather somberly intervened, answering for his emotional, weary spouse. "The doctor just informed us they're contacting a specialist and are still running needed tests. He said we can get a chance to see her shortly after that. At this point, we just have to wait and pray."

Tami let the crucial realization of her sister's current crisis roll off her back. It meant nothing to her in reality. Pressing her hand to her chest, the older sibling pretended to be relieved. Knowing she'd at least attempted to play the game, the preliminaries just for show were out of the way. It was finally time for the million-dollar question, the one that'd been burning a hole through her heart. Without fear of being too obvious, she inquired about the secret, unreciprocated love of her life.

"Well, dang, Daddy, what about Vance? What are they saying about him now? I know back at the house you said his injuries aren't that bad, so can he have visitors? Can I see him? You know he's family now too."

"Well, I just finished calling your sister's friends and Vance's best man, Courtney, so they're on their way. Plus I tried getting in contact with his aunt, but got no answer. At this point all we can do is pray for both of them. Luckily Vance's injuries weren't as severe as Tori's. I swear I'm going to sue the pants off that limousine car company!"

"Oh, all right then." She backed off her small-scale interrogation of her grieving parents. Tami's people were consumed with worry. Each failed to take notice of her overly sympathetic concern for Vance's condition and whereabouts in contrast with their daughter's. Not wanting to push her luck and be found out, Tami eased away from the waiting room area and her stepfather's rants. Being accused of any sort of inappropriate compassion for her brother-in-law was not on her agenda for the day.

Out of eyesight and ear range of her mom and dad, Tami approached a nurse sitting behind an oval desk. She was determined to get answers to her questions. Her infatuation with Vance was beyond normal. It had crept up on being considered full-blown demented to her therapist, but who was she to judge? Without so much as a small bit of compassion for Tori, her main focus was finding out where he was. She had to be by Vance's side. Embedded deep in Tami's twisted mind, she knew her sister's husband needed her in some form or fashion.

CHAPTER THREE

"I was terrified when my mother first told me what happened to you. I felt like a little piece of my soul shattered." Lowering the hospital bedrail to get closer, Tami finally felt free to speak her mind. "Oh, sweetheart, I swear to you my heart was beating so fast I thought it was going to jump right out of my chest." She nervously placed her right palm firmly against her breast. Exhaling, Tami shook off the chills. As the goose bumps prickled her skin, the drama queen lifted the thin white hospital blanket. Making sure no one was looking, she hoped to get a glimpse of Vance's "thick and long" package she'd heard her sister brag so much about. Slowly easing back the blanket, a huge smile graced her face. Licking her lips, Tami was pleasantly satisfied with the bulge resting undisturbed underneath his hospital gown. Resisting the urge to at least touch it, she instead pulled the covers back up to his chest.

"Excuse me. I just need to check the patient's chart." The nurse peeked inside just as Tami was adjusting his pillow.

No sooner had the nurse returned the cream-colored folder to the door slot than the disillusioned female was back at it. Sympathetically examining the small bruises and abrasions scattered about his face, her declarations of love and loyalty continued. "You know, bae, when Mom told me the caller said your injuries weren't considered life-threatening, I was relived, but I was still terrified just the same. Hell, I still don't know the entire story, but I can bet it was your fake-ass wife's fault. She was probably yelling at the driver, trying to convince him he was going the wrong way or something. You know Tori's been a true bitch since birth. Why didn't you just pick me from jump?" Tami leaned in closer, kissing his cheek. Using her left hand, she gently stroked the side of Vance's jaw line.

"Oh my God, Tami! What in the hell? Hell, naw!"

Startled by the thunderous tone of a man's voice, Tami stumbled backward. In hopes of avoiding knocking over Vance's IV, she reached for the wall. Face to face with what seemed to be a sea of royal purple and gold, her chills instantly turned to shame. Guilt from kissing her sister's husband consumed her thoughts as she struggled to speak.

"Oh, hey, Courtney," Tami greeted Vance's frat brother, who'd just rushed into the room.

Courtney was dressed in a tight-fitting T-shirt. With camouflage pants and black combat boots, he looked more like he was going to a Greek step show than coming to check on his best friend. "Wow, girl! What happened to my boy? Your parents told me it was a car crash, but any details? I mean, what did the driver have to say for himself? Was it on the interstate or what?"

Tami was bombarded with question after question about Vance's well-being and what had caused the accident. Glad they were about that and nothing that might be deemed inappropriate, she took a deep breath. Tami took great comfort in realizing her secret crush had not been revealed. She'd not been discovered hovering over the semi-conscious, drugged patient, and all was well.

"Well, the nurse told me there appeared to be no internal injuries. From what they could tell, my sister got the worst of it. They said besides the cuts on his face, the only thing of major concern is his legs. They both seem to be pretty badly banged up."

Panicked and bewildered, Courtney was now standing shoulder to shoulder with Tami. "Oh, hell naw. His legs? What's wrong with them? Please don't tell me he can't move them! Please don't tell me that!"

Once again lifting the blanket, Tami aided him in seeing the multitudes of bandages and thick cream ointment that covered both Vance's legs. "No, Courtney, calm down. They don't think it's any type of spinal damage. There's just a series of breaks in his bones. His right leg is much worse than the other, but other than that he's good."

Patting his frat brother on the shoulder, Courtney couldn't believe what was going down. Less than twenty-four hours prior, he was holding the entrusted rings at his best friend's wedding; now this tragedy. "Dang, Tami girl, that reminds me. I got so caught up in seeing him like this, I almost forgot. Your parents ask me to tell you your sister is about to go to surgery and you can see her for a few moments before they take her down."

"Oh, yeah." Tami seemed unbothered by what he'd just said. Her main focus was still on Vance, but she didn't want to appear so obvious. Although she knew it'd be hard to see Tori and not burst out laughing at her misfortune, Tami put on her game face. "Well, since you're here with him, I'ma go check on Mom and the old man. They're probably both falling apart right about now."

"That's cool. I tried to get in touch with Vance's auntie and two cousins to tell them what happened, but no one picked up. I'll try to get back with them later."

"I know, Courtney. My stepdad tried as well." Tami stared at a helpless Vance from the doorway. "Maybe one of us should try again before they do any more procedures on him and see what they think."

After finishing up several texts to other frat brothers, Courtney reminded Vance's new sister-in-law that besides those three family members, his fellow Que was on his own. "Tami, now you know Vance people aren't that stable in the money department. He was the one who had to finance their trip here. So you know nine outta ten times they can't afford to hop back on another flight just like that."

"Yeah, you're right." Tami pretended to be sad, when all along she was feeling blessed that there was a strong possibility Vance would be all hers—at least if her little sister succumbed to her injuries or one of the surgeons was having a bad day.

CHAPTER FOUR

It had been a dreary and grueling two weeks of operations after operations, not only for her sister, but Vance as well. After the first exploratory procedure, it was discovered Tori was worse off than initially believed. Knowing she was in great pain, they put her on heavy doses of morphine along with several other medications. Tori suffered brutal damage to her upper torso. Having been ejected out the rear window when the Town Car flipped over, she was lucky to be alive. Both lungs had small puncture wounds and leaked fluid. Reading the results of the emergency CT scan, doctors also discovered bleeding near the brain. Immediately the decision was made to place Tori in a medically induced coma. Certainly the bruises on her face, hard to look at, would heal; however, her having any type of normal life after this hospital stay was not at all something to be optimistic about.

With her father, mother, and a slew of happy-go-lucky friends marching in and out of her hospital room, Tori would not be alone. Tori's husband was not as fortunate as she was. His family could not be by his side. Besides Vance's frat brothers, who all had nine-to-fives and families of their own to deal with, Tami was the one person who unconditionally stepped up to the plate. She would be his designated caregiver and was happy to do so. Proving to her mother as well as the doctors on staff that she was capable of aiding her ailing brother-in-law, Tami grinned, content with the opportunity.

Conniving in her intentions, she turned the top deadbolt on the suburban condo Vance and her little sister shared. Reaching down, she swooped the mail off the floor, sticking it into her purse. Tossing the keys on the dining area table, she took a quick assessment of the one-bedroom apartment. Slowly walking past a bookshelf, Tami causally knocked over each and every snapshot of the "faithfully in love" couple. Letting a few drop to the plush carpet, deep in her emotions she had no problem whatsoever stepping on them.

Heading into the kitchen, Tami swung the refrigeration door open in hopes of grabbing a quick snack. Met by nothing but a jug of water, a few granola protein bars, a stick of butter, and an aging orange, she was peeved.

I should've known that uppity, lightweight bitch don't do no cooking for her man. But it ain't no thang. When Vance gets over Momma's, I'ma keep him fed! I'ma make him feel all the way at home.

Ignoring the fact that her sister was still knocking at death's door, Tami stayed in a vindictive state of mind.

Per Vance's instructions and wishes, she removed a small duffle bag from the top of the hallway closet. As his cosmetics and daily grooming aids were packed in their now missing luggage, Tami only had to gather undergarments, T-shirts, and a few pairs of track pants.

The moment she stepped into the bedroom, her anger grew. Every bit of her soul told her that should be the room she and her beloved Vance shared. Tami rubbed her hands together to try to regain her train of thought.

Glancing over at the perfectly made bed made the mentally drained sister practically sick to her stomach. Not caring what side Vance slept on, she fell back onto the mattress. Snatching one of the pillows, she took in the aroma. It smelled of jasmine and sunflowers. Without hesitation, she threw it across the room, knowing who it belonged to. Taking the other, she followed the same procedure as the first. Closing her eyes, a smile of satisfaction graced her face as Vance's signature scent filled her nostrils.

Caught up in the moment, she pulled the covers back. Tami then crawled underneath them, fully dressed, shoes still on. Surrounded with the scent of him, she eased her hand in between her legs. Before she knew it, Tami had gone as far as pushing her track pants down to her knees. Moving her panties to the side, she squirmed with thoughts of Vance's hands being all over her.

Minutes later, with wet fingers, Tami snapped back into reality. Turning her head to the side, she saw the digital clock was blinking in her face. Time was ticking and she had to pick her adored brother-in-law up from the hospital. Shortly he'd be released and in her capable care. All would be good in the universe.

Knowing she was the only one with keys, her attitude was one of happiness. Having total access to their personal property, Tami knew she could return anytime she'd like to partake in more of the same foolishness. Deciding not to even wash her sticky hand, she stood to her feet. Wiping it on the end of the blanket, she smirked. Adjusting her clothes, Tami caught her breath then fixed her hair. Walking to the other side of the bed, she then evilly hawked in the area she assumed baby sis rested her head. Jealously and hatred for her bloodline had taken over, consuming Tami's entire mind.

Standing in front of the dresser, she used her forearm to clear everything off the top that obviously belonged to her "competition." With the keen skills of a detective, she searched through the dark oak dresser. Eager to please, Tami quickly retrieved every item her sister's husband requested. She wanted to steal some of her sister's lingerie sets, but knew it'd be damn near impossible for her to fit half of a breast or a tiny portion of her lower butt cheek in any of them. Instead, she threw them across the room, landing them near the place Tori's discarded pillow rested.

After grabbing a few of Vance's shirts that she wanted to sleep in, along with his needed belongings, she zipped up the duffle bag. Just to get her mind right, Tami took one more whiff of his pillow before heading toward the front door. After a fast stop by Walmart, then the pharmacy, she'd be hospital-bound to get her imaginary man.

"As I was saying, it's indeed a happy day for you since you are going home." The doctor stared down at his chart before looking up. "I know it's bittersweet because your lovely wife won't be accompanying you, but all in God's time."

Vance's overall state of mind was not yet at a hundred. Disheartened, he wondered why the driver from the limousine company they'd used the day of the wedding had taken the shortcut route he did in the first place. Vance's impromptu mood swings could only be controlled by a pre-

scription of antidepressants the doctor handed to
Tami.

"Look, I know I should be happy, Doc. And I
also know I'm blessed. It could've been so much
worse on both our parts, but I'm good. And I'm
glad the love of my life is still alive, still fighting."

"Yeah, she still hanging in there fighting,"
Tami sarcastically mumbled underneath her
breath, reaching out for Vance's arm.

*Still cursing us with her presence on this
earth.*

With his right leg broken in three places and
his left extremely sore, Vance grimaced while
accepting Tami's help. Making the agonizing
transition from the hospital bed to the wheelchair caused the grown man's eyes to water,
but being a soldier, he fought through the pain.
Getting as comfortable as possible, he thanked
the entire staff for their compassion and care,
physically and mentally. Each knew of his wife's
dire medical condition and sympathized with
his ongoing grief. Besides a handful of his frat
brothers barking from time to time, attempting
to keep his spirits up, Tami, his sister-in-law,
was the only constant light throughout the dark
tragedy he was facing.

Vance, doped up on pain meds most of the
day, had several dreams with visions of Tami.
The cloudy-minded dreams of her touching his

manhood, holding his hand, and kissing his lips seemed more real at times than he cared to admit. He knew they couldn't be reality. Knowing his sister-in-law was not that type of person, he could only attribute the inappropriate hallucinations to the drugs. Vance felt sheer disgust for even imagining such actions from a female who clearly wasn't his type, being his wife's sister or not.

As Tami helped him get dressed, he felt more and more ashamed of his thoughts. Tami was a champion in his eyes, the real MVP. Whether it was her bringing him a warm washcloth for his face or pushing his wheelchair to therapy, she was there. When it came to cleaning the gash in the side of his head or bringing him a bedpan, his wife's sister was on point. Even when he suggested hooking her up with his best friend Courtney, Tami adamantly refused, claiming the family needed all her spare time and nothing else mattered. Vance, heavily medicated most of the day, had no worldly idea the devoted caregiver wasn't including his comatose wife or his in-laws in her twisted equation or definition of family.

Some of the more attentive hospital staff took notice of Tami's strange devotion to Vance while hardly ever going two floors up to visit her younger sibling. Clearly, it wasn't their place or in their best interest to openly speak on it; however, they noticed it just the same. Tami had given several of the more attractive nurses' aides the serious side eye on more than one occasion for showing Vance extra care. And moreover, no one wanted to dare run the risk of losing their job over the next female's husband.

Waiting for the elevator, Tami placed Vance's discharge papers and prescribed medications in her purse alongside of his and Tori's mail that she'd clipped earlier. Slightly agitated because he'd corrected her in hitting the top button instead of the lower, she tried not pouting.

Each time over the past few days that Vance had been allowed to leave his floor and visit Tori, Tami did as she was asked, pushing his wheelchair. Although she took no real joy in delivering the man she believed should've been her husband to his wife, the deranged plus-size diva sucked it up, knowing the evening and night would soon belong exclusively to her.

CHAPTER FIVE

"Is everything okay for you in here? We tried to transform it from just the den to a place you can heal in properly." Mr. Lewis was more than happy to welcome his new son-in-law into their home. He knew Vance had no family in state and could not afford to have his elderly aunt relocate to try to take care of him. "We would've put you in Tori's old bedroom, but those stairs would be too much considering the cast on your leg, especially with all the various doctors' appointments you have coming up."

Having been sitting in an upward position by his injured wife's side for at least thirty minutes, Vance's lower back was throbbing. Coupled with the bumpy ride home from the hospital, Vance was weary and out of sorts. Normally in great physical condition, the former captain of the football team yearned for nothing more than to lie down in the rented hospital bed. He didn't just want his medicine; he needed it. Vance wasn't accustomed to taking even a mere Tylenol for a headache, but this pain he'd been experiencing since the accident was excruciating.

"Wow, he's good. I'll get him all settled in. Don't worry about him." Tami escorted her stepfather out of the den and into the living room. "I told you and Mom not to concern yourselves with Vance. I know you two have enough on your hands with Tori. I know the insurance company is fighting her coverage. I heard you guys talking about it."

"Yes, that's true, but—"

"But nothing, Dad. I got Vance. He's family now. I'm gonna look out for him." Tami sarcastically grinned. "After all, it's the least I can do for my sister. I mean, if my husband was ill and I wasn't able, I know she'd do it for me."

It was no secret that Mr. Lewis didn't love both his daughters equally. He never got over the fact that Tami was tragically a product of rape. As the years went by, he tried to soften up and not play favoritism. Even though he'd never speak it out loud, he knew Tami seemed to be miserable more times than not, especially when Tori was around. But now, since this tragedy, he felt it was time he spoke up.

"Listen, Tami, I know you must be feeling some sort of guilt for not being as close to your sister as you should have been. I get that."

"Say what now?" Tami loudly puzzled. Not wanting Vance to overhear her family's dirty laundry being aired, she made sure the den door was closed.

"Yes, isn't that why you are doing so much for her husband? Kinda a way of making amends to your little sister. You know life is too short for you to always be bitter toward Tori because she's so pretty."

"Bitter? Me? Are you serious?" Tami rolled her eyes and waved her hand, dismissing her stepfather's outlandish statement.

"Yes, Tami." Mr. Lewis sat down in his favorite chair. Resting before he had to pick his wife up from the hospital, he continued to read his wife's firstborn. "Your mother and I saw the way you were behaving at your sister's wedding—and after we begged her to let you be her maid of honor. She felt you were a little too plump for the style of dress she picked out, but your mother insisted."

"Begged? Insisted?" Tami grew more heated hearing each hurtful word escape her stepfather's old lips. "And I'm plump, huh? That's code word for fat, right? Y'all, my own family, calling me fat?"

"I didn't mean it like that. It's just if maybe you dropped a few pounds you could get you a husband like your sister did." His words cut like a knife, and Tami waited for the one-line statement she'd grown accustomed to hearing. Seconds later, as if on cue, there it was: "You have such a pretty face."

Tami was insulted. What colossal nerve her mother's husband had. How dare he think her eagerness to care for Vance was based solely on that bony, anorexic daughter of his? Resisting the urge, she wanted to run up in his face and shout out, "Negro, please!" Then tell him not to play himself.

With her hands planted firmly on her hips, it took everything in Tami's soul not to let her misguided pappy in on her wicked true intentions. Her stepdad needed not feel sorry for her. She would indeed have a husband soon: Tori's.

Tami's calculated scheme of snatching her sister's man right from under their noses was about to hatch, but instead of revealing her ulterior motive, Tami pumped her brakes, calming all the way down. She'd dealt with her parents her entire life. The pair acting as if the sun would rise and shine based on Tori's command was nothing new. The only major difference between now and then was that she was going to win and Tori, already close to death, was going to lose. It was simple as that, so there was no need to argue. Tami just smiled at her stepfather's ignorance of truth and walked away.

"Hey, sis." Vance was almost too weak to speak but managed to push the words out. "Is everything okay between you and the old man?"

Tami wasn't sure what he'd overheard her stepfather say, and she tried to brush it off. "Yeah, Vance. Don't worry about it. You know how he gets."

"Are you sure? Because I don't want to become a burden to anyone. Courtney said I could crash at his apartment if I really needed to. Or maybe I can get someone to stay with me at my condo."

Tami was pissed that her stepdad had made her future husband feel some sort of way. There was no way in hell she was going to let Vance do any of the things he mentioned, unless of course she was the person staying out at the condo with him. "Listen, Vance, don't talk crazy. I got you. We got you. I told you that the first day after the accident. You need to focus on getting better."

"I know, Tami. And trust me, I'm mad thankful." Vance took off his T-shirt, showing his rich brown skin and Omega Psi Phi chest and arm tattoos. "I'm glad I got you and your entire family in my life. The only thing I need now is for your sister to get better. I swear to God I love Tori."

Hearing the man of her dreams confess his love for another woman only added fuel to the scorching fire her father initially sparked. Tami hated to hear Tori's name roll off Vance's perfectly shaped lips. Why did he have to ruin their special moments speaking about her sister, his wife? It was bad enough she had to watch him break down in tears earlier when saying good-bye to the mangled little bitch, and now this unwanted declaration.

Feeling a wave of intense rage coming on, Tami fought to be as pleasant as she could when handing Vance his meds and a glass of juice. Making sure he was good, she took his clothes off the edge of the bed. Without smelling them, as she'd grown accustomed to doing over the past week or so, she placed them in a chair in the far corner of the room. With a serious attitude on the verge of showing up and showing out, Tami knew she needed some alone time before her true, craze-minded colors revealed themselves for Vance to bear witness to. Leaving the den, she peeped in the living room, taking notice that her opinionated father had dozed off.

I wish that ancient wannabe black Dr. Phil would go to sleep for good, him and that

*no-spleen-having wife of his. Shit! I'm sick of
everybody in this entire damn house! Even
Vance acting out, keep whining about Tori!
I swear one day I'm gonna mess around and
snap!*

Heading upstairs, Tami struggled not to be
resentful toward her man, but it was hard. She'd
been doing everything in her power to keep his
spirits upbeat, yet it seemed at each and every
turn, he was bringing up the future—the future
that didn't include her and him as a unit. By the
time she got in front of her younger sister's door,
Tami was damn near in tears. She hadn't been to
the free clinic in weeks and had yet to write down
any of her tainted emotions as the therapist had
suggested. Finding it hard to swallow, she felt
herself getting out of control. Her heart raced.
Stepping across the threshold, mad at the world,
she closed the door behind her.

Slowly turning in a complete circle, Tami
paused. Staring at her sister's beloved auto-
graphed poster of Usher, she wasted no time
snatching it off the rear of the door and ripping
it to shreds. Behaving as if she were a small
child having a temper tantrum, Tami then took
the time to remove each of Tori's awards and
certificates off the wall, out of the frames,
and then proceeded to do the same to them as
she had done to the poster.

Finally, after breaking the arms off every cheerleading trophy on the shelf, Tami was done. She was mentally drained and physically ready to tap out. Balled up in the fetal position, she fought to catch her breath. Her face was filled with multitudes of tears.

After what seemed like an eternity, the tormented, older, plus-size daughter heard her father calling her from the bottom of the stairs. Shaking herself out of the dark zone she'd slipped into, Tami crawled over to the door. Reaching her hand up, she twisted the knob, opening the door.

"Tami," her dad yelled out once more, not receiving an answer the first time. "Do you hear me calling you?"

"Yes, Dad. What's wrong?" She prayed he couldn't tell her voice was temporarily cracking from crying.

"Nothing at all. Your mother just called and wants me to pick her up from visiting your sister. She wants me to run her by the grocery store too."

"Oh, okay then."

"Well, I just wanted you to know I was leaving. I just checked in on Vance and he's 'sleep."

Tami wanted to yell down the stairs at her stepfather. She wanted him to leave Vance the hell alone, and as far as she was concerned, he could pass the message along to his wife to do the same. Yet she didn't want or need any more confrontation in the already chaotic household. Moreover, as she looked back over her shoulder at the awful mess she'd made by maliciously destroying Tori's most beloved childhood possessions, she knew it wouldn't be a good idea for her dad to come upstairs.

Listening for him to leave then pull out of the driveway, Tami went downstairs to get a plastic bag. Her plan was to clean up the mess, toss the bag in the trunk of her car, and discard it into one of her neighbors' garbage cans, preferably a few blocks down. Wanting to complete the mission she was on before her parents returned, Tami was sidetracked by her empty stomach. Greedily she took the time out to fix herself a small snack. As she passed the closed den door, plate in hand, she could easily hear the sounds of Vance snoring. Wanting nothing more than to go climb up in the bed next to him and take a nap, she opted to sit on the lower stair and eat so she could be at least somewhat close. Each chew Tami took seemed to ease the tension and stress her father had caused.

CHAPTER SIX

Three days had flown by. After a few rough patches, Tami and Vance had fallen into somewhat of a regular routine. She knew what time her man would turn over to yawn and what time he needed to take his first piss of the day. Like a loyal solider on night duty, Tami was there for his every wish, want, or desire.

With her mother spending the majority of her time at the hospital and her father at work, Tami and Vance spent a lot of quality time alone. Avoiding any unwanted conversation pertaining to her sister, she made sure Vance's days were occupied. Helping him with his daily required exercise, she allowed her hands to roam and explore her brother-in-law's body on the sly as much as possible. If she thought he'd felt any sort of way, she was wise enough not to suddenly stop dead in her tracks, but continue, playing it off like she meant no harm. If she didn't make a big deal about it, neither would he. He'd just take it as a mistake because they were in such close quarters in the den.

Entering the family room, breakfast tray in hand, she smiled at Vance, who'd managed to prop himself up in bed.

"Hey now. Good morning, sleepyhead. I've got you some scrambled eggs just the way you like them. And wow, I see you taking matters into your own hands."

"Yeah, sis, I need to try to do more things on my own. The stronger I get, the quicker I can be out your hair."

"Shut up, boy. You know I got you covered. We good! Now get ready to eat this grub."

"Damn, Tami, I ain't bullshittin'. You're the best. You gonna make some man a good-ass wife one day." He returned her bright smile as he rubbed his growing beard.

Yeah, your wife, she humored herself temporarily, placing the tray down on the coffee table. "Well, that day is not today. Today is feeding your silly self, then helping you wash up. Now let me get you the extra pillow so you can be more comfortable and stop talking out the side of your neck."

Vance never liked to play matchmaker, but he and Tami had grown to become somewhat close since the near fatal accident. He wanted her to be as happy as he and Tori were; at least, before the coma. She deserved that much for all the time she was sacrificing to help him.

Vance had never once thought about hooking any of his frat brothers up with Tami—not because she was thick-boned, but because his wife had claimed her older sister was no more than a jealous-hearted bug who stayed angry at the world. However, if that assessment of her character was indeed true, he'd yet to see that flaw. She was being 100 percent official with him, and that's all that mattered to him in life: who has your back when you're down and out.

"Tami, I'm telling you Courtney likes you. He told me just last night when he stopped by. My boy is a good dude, and a Que man at that. You better jump on him. He's a good catch, as y'all women say."

Yeah, he might be a good dude, but he's not you.

She dismissed what he was saying and counteracted by joking. "Now look, Vance. Stop trying to pawn me off on Courtney's crazy, ten times a day good-barking ass. He ain't right in the head and you know that. And I already told you I'm focused on helping the family right now. Forget a man—especially Courtney."

"All right, sis, I'll get off your back . . . for now." He winked his left eye and smirked. "I'm done campaigning for my homeboy, but everybody is human and needs some sort of love.

God ain't put us here to be alone, and you ain't no exception to the rule. You're a strong black woman, that's obvious, and you deserve a good man. Now don't let me find out you one of those power-to-the-people females who feels she don't need no guy to complete her. A damn foot soldier in Oprah's army!"

"Naw, naw, Vance. I'm far from that, sweetie. It's just I've got other priorities right now; that's all. Family looks out for family."

For the first time since she and her sister met him, Vance appeared to be seeing her in a different light. It was like she was a real down-to-earth woman and not just Tori's older, fat, bitter sister. Tami was overjoyed, feeling as if her outrageous plan might actually work. The longer Vance was out of commission and relying on her, the greater chance she'd have of transforming her demented dream into a reality.

Secretly doubling up his already strong dosage of meds, his trusted caregiver crushed not one but two extra pills up in his orange juice. She knew how frisky she could be with one extra pill, so with two the sky would be the limit. Both her parents were gone, and she was feeling herself, especially after Vance's compliments. With unreserved satisfaction, Tami grew hot and bothered watching him drink the potent mixture.

***

Is it my imagination, or is this girl rubbing on my back longer than usual? Did she just put the warm washcloth down near my thang? Aww damn, are those her fingernails that feel like sharp, tiny knives scratching my moist skin? Shit, I know I must be tripping. Why is she pressing her breast on my shoulder? Oh my God, I feel myself getting hard. Damn, I miss getting pussy on the regular! Naw, man, stay focused. Get it together.

Vance was fighting like hell to stay coherent. It was like a dark cloud suddenly appeared in his mind, making him dizzy. No matter how hard he tried to focus as Tami was giving him a light sponge bath, he couldn't. One minute they were joking around; the next he was having sexually charged hallucinations.

It had hit him hard right after he finished his breakfast. Shortly after his sister-in-law removed the tray from in front of him, he felt lightheaded. By the time he finished drinking his juice all the way down, he started to feel drunk. It was as if he'd consumed too many red cups of beer at one of their wild frat parties. Now his body was telling him one thing as his manhood started to stiffen almost involuntarily from Tami's seemingly seductive strokes: *get some ass.*

Vance knew his wife's older sibling truly meant nothing sensual about the way she was touching him. She was only trying to help him wash the parts he couldn't reach and tend to changing his bandages, but Vance was a man. He was a man who'd been away from the warmth of his woman's embrace for weeks. Unknowingly with the aid of Tami, his sexual senses were heightened, and Vance was ready to damn near explode.

"Hey, sweetie, are you okay? You seem a little out of it." Tami eased her plus-size body around in front of Vance, placing both palms on his chest. "You might need to lie back and catch your breath." She copped a feel, knowing that if it was like the countless other times she'd overmedicated him, he wouldn't remember what was what within a few hours' time.

"Ummm, you might be right. My heart feels like it's racing." Vance allowed his upper body weight to drop down into the mattress. Under the influence of the prescription drugs, he had no shame; his dick was standing up at full attention. He wanted to adjust it and make it lie down, but he couldn't seem to lift his arms. They both felt numb and extremely heavy. The thin track pants he was wearing made it possible to see not only to see the ridge around the head of his pole, but a few drops of pre cum seeping out of the tip.

Not one bit concerned about her brother-in-law's health, Tami picked up the washcloth. After submerging it into the still warm bowl of water, she rubbed it on his stomach in a slow, circular motion. Watching his manhood twitch from her "accidental" brushes, she got chills.

Taking a quick glance into Vance's face, she saw his eyes closed. His lips were moving as if he was trying to say something, but no words were coming out. Brazen, wanting nothing more than to grip what belonged to her despised sister, Tami pushed the envelope. Allowing her fingertips to slip underneath the top of his track pants, she trembled with anticipation. Looking up one last time before she overstepped her self-imposed boundaries, she became irritated when she heard him mumbling Tori's ratchet name.

Listening to him moan out for that selfish, bony bitch made Tami infuriated and cocky. That was it. She was done. She'd had enough of running around like Vance's personal slave and getting no reward for her loyal service. She'd put her entire life, as simple as it was, on hold for him. Now she would get her just desserts. He owed her that much and more.

Easing down the thin track pants, she grabbed a hold of Vance's prized possession with both hands. Feeling his body slightly jerk from her strong grip, Tami knew she was doing something right.

After Tami slowly stroked his pole several times, Vance grew harder and Tori's name got louder. The combination of those two factors created the perfect storm for the jealous sibling. Parting her lips, she eagerly lowered her head downward. Taking a deep breath, Tami anxiously took her brother-in-law's blessing deep in her mouth.

CHAPTER SEVEN

"Where have you been?" The therapist at the free mental clinic settled down in her chair. She hadn't seen or heard from Tami in weeks and was genuinely concerned. "I read in the paper about your sister and her husband. How are you handling that?"

"I'm doing well. I've just been extremely busy, considering." Tami locked her fingers together, biting the corner of her lower lip. Trying her best not to make eye contact, she nervously stared out the window into the busy parking lot.

"Okay, Tami, well, I'm glad you stopped by. You did cross my mind the other day. Please give me an update on your daily situations, both good and bad."

Tami was stressed and prayed it didn't show. Her conscience was eating her up alive; however, she fought it tooth and nail. The demons residing in her head were wide awake most of the time. They were on both sides of her mind, encouraging bullshit. It was bad enough she'd wished death upon her skinny-tailed sister on a daily basis, but now she was keeping Vance so drugged up that even the doctors couldn't get a grip on his constant blackouts and unexplained delusions he claimed to have on the regular. Counting the amount of pills in the various prescriptions he had left, she'd started crushing up some of her own depression medications, Tylenol PMs mixed with a few extra-strength sleeping pills, and a handful of Norcos she'd bought off the street.

In a matter of days, Tami had catapulted from being a mere semi-desperate, slightly overweight, scheming female wanting just a small bit of attention from a man to an all-out overbearing, no-holds-barred, coldhearted bitch. She didn't care what the unmeasured combination of medications could possibly do to Vance physically or mentally in the long run. The outcome of that was not her main focus, not now. Tami's agenda consisted of having as much physical contact with her sister's ailing husband as she saw fit.

Not naïve, she knew she was living on borrowed time. Every single day offered new possibility of the doctors discovering that he was being unknowingly drugged. No doubt

Tami didn't want Vance to discover that he'd been sexually taken advantage of or, far worse, Tori actually getting better and her new man wanting to flee to her bedside. God forbid the thought of her not being able to lick on her man's good-good any longer. If that happened, she might go all the way crazy.

She was already on the edge of insanity with her unhealthy attachment to him. Tami was all the way gone and she knew it. Living in a dream world, she'd unbelievably turned her simple life into their fabulous life, as if they were a happy couple in love. At this point, the devious daughter would stab her own mother in the back twice and shove her father down a flight of stairs face first if they got in her way.

However, she couldn't reveal her true, insecure, low self-esteem colors to the nosy therapist who wanted to dive deep into the inner crevices of her business. What was she going to do, confess the truth? That she'd ruthlessly prayed for the Almighty to take her younger sister from the land of the living and He'd come close to answering her demented prayers? That she'd been putting on an act worthy of an Academy Award pretending she gave a rat's ass if Tori ever woke up again from the coma she was in? Oh yeah, damn, and to place the final nail in the coffin, she was not only wishing she could be with a man just like her sister's husband, but she was indeed with him in every sense of the word. How could she look this prim, proper, college-educated woman in her face and actually say the words, "I've been keeping my brother-in-law Vance doped up high as a kite, sucking his dick nightly, and riding the pole every morning"? Tami couldn't dare do that; of course not. She might be looked upon as being crazy, but she was far from a fool.

Instead, the drama queen took a deep breath and did what she felt was best: lied. "I've been trying to take it easy. And yes, before you ask me, I've been writing in my journal instead of outwardly venting. My sister and entire family are going through it, as you know, so I'm just trying to help out where I can."

"So you want me to take you up to visit with Tori for a little while? No problem. I got you." Helping Vance get comfortable in his wheelchair, Tami grudgingly pushed him the short distance between the orthopedic specialist's office located on the lower level of the hospital and the two sets of red-door elevators.

As they stood there making small talk, Vance informed his sister-in-law of his good news. The

X-rays taken showed at least two of the three breaks in his leg were healing at a rapid pace. The once strong, independent man announced that before they knew it, he'd be able to get around on crutches and go home to his condo.

Hearing his update and desires made Tami's heart skip a beat. Immediately she felt sick to her stomach. Leaning against the wall to fully take in what he'd just said, her mind trailed off. Exercising some of the coping skills the therapist had just taught her, Tami closed her eyes while counting backward from twenty by threes in hopes of calming her nerves and the onset of an anxiety attack. Midway through, luckily, it worked. Just like that, it dawned on her that if she could only find a way to slow down his healing progress, he'd remain her medicated sex toy. Keeping him spaced out half the time had been hindering his mental capabilities, but now she'd have to refocus on further handicapping his physical well-being. The dick was much too good to give up on without a fight.

Interrupted by the chiming sounds of the elevator doors sliding open, Tami quickly regained her senses. She waited for a few doctors and other visitors to step out, then she wheeled Vance inside and pushed the appropriate button. They were soon on their floor.

Used to all the suspicious stares and judgmental glances of a handful of nurses' aides,
Tami held her head high as they passed the
nurses' station. Overweight or not, she always
had pride, and now that she was sneak-banging
her brother-in-law on the regular, Tami felt
untouchable. She was on top of the world. The
thick-boned beauty didn't care about them
whispering about her not spending time by her
little sister's bedside like her parents, friends,
and, of course, her husband had been doing. So
what they if wanted to start rumors of why she
and Vance seemed so close? To hell with them
all, was her overall attitude. Who were they to
question who, what, or why she did the things
she did? If Vance or her parents ain't speak
on it, then why should some salty, shit-wiping
strangers?

"Baby, I love you so much. I've been missing
you being by my side. I miss us laughing and
joking like we used to do. My life isn't the same
without you by my side." Vance's eyes filled
with tears as he laid his head down at the side
of Tori's hospital bed. With his mother-in-law
and Tami right outside the door, he still had no
shame whatsoever expressing himself. It was

no great secret. He wanted the world to know how he felt.

"I'm so sorry I wasn't able to protect you. You're my wife, and here you are fighting to get better, and I'm sitting on my ass in this wheelchair."

Tami tried her best to focus in on her mother and the things she was saying. What they would have for dinner; what her stepfather had done or said at work; the doctor's recent prognosis, and if the mailman had been delivering their mail on time topped Mrs. Lewis's conversation with her daughter.

Unfortunately, Vance's voice was trumping all of that. Tami's heart burned with fury as she ear hustled most of what her man was saying to his wife.

How dare he act as if he is so damn miserable being with me? Not only do I cook special food for his ass, put up with his barking, bring him his meds, but I bathe him and fuck him too! What else can a man want?

Tami fought not to rush in her sister's room and knock Vance out of his wheelchair and onto the floor. The demons embedded deep inside of her head were calling out for her to yank Tori up by her neck, snatch all the tubes out of her arms, and throw the machine that was keeping her alive out the window.

*This can't keep going on. I won't allow it.
I've put too much time in with getting him
better just for this little bitch to still have
him under her no-good spell.*

"Tami, do you hear me talking to you?"

Brought back to her right mind, Tami answered
her mother. "Yeah, I hear you—some more madness about Daddy and how he clowning again at
work."

"Well, come over here. I want to write down a
list of things I want you to pick up for your sister
to make her feel more comfortable."

"Pick up?" Tami puzzled, taking a few steps
backward. "What kinda stuff she need? She's not
about to go anywhere, is she? Is it something
that I'm missing? Something you wanna tell
me?"

"No, Tami, and stop acting so overly dramatic
all the time. I want some nail polish and a new
brush. You know your sister would act a fool if
she woke up and seen how she's been looking."

*This bitch as crazy and disrespectful as
Vance, who's in there crying the blues. Why in
the fuck they acting as if that tramp in there is
so special? What's next? A marching band, her
own stylist, maybe her own personal chef when
she wakes up! Shit, I wish she'd stop lingering
and die already. That way she can set Vance
free once and for all.*

Pretending to remember the many frivolous items her mother wanted, Tami was happy when a small group of doctors appeared, needing to perform a gang of tests. Vance had to thankfully cut his visit short. Shortly after him saying his temporary good-byes, the pair was back in the elevator, heading toward valet parking.

Vance was strangely silent. Tami could tell her brother-in-law turned secret lover had a lot on his mind. She wanted to ease his pain and convince him everything was going to be okay, but she just couldn't force herself to act as if she gave a damn. She had bigger fish to fry, keeping in the rear of her head the news about his legs healing. She had to stay on her game plan. Tonight she was gonna go all out and drug him up on an even more powerful mixture of pills. After all the time and energy she put into dealing with Vance, there was no way she was gonna allow his actually getting better to get in her way. Forget Tori. He was now hers, like he should've been in the first place, and tonight he'd know it.

CHAPTER EIGHT

Vance was exhausted. He'd had a long day, first being overjoyed hearing about his health improvements then being emotionally brought down seeing his beloved wife was getting no better. He wanted nothing more than to finish the dinner his loyal sister-in-law had prepared, take his meds for the night, and go straight to sleep.

He prayed the new medication the doctor prescribed would help him with the almost nightly hallucinations and dreams he was having starring Tami. Vance knew she'd proven herself to be nothing but good to him and a stand-up sister-in-law. He couldn't ask for a better caregiver who, he knew, truly had his back. Tami had kept it a hundred with him from the beginning of this nightmare. He knew she didn't deserve all the nasty, disrespectful things he was doing to her in his nightly dreams. He couldn't seem to help what he knew were side effects of the strong, but much-needed, meds he was taking.

"So you're all good right?" Tami stood up, taking the tray of dirty dishes out of the room. "I'ma get you a glass of water and your pills. I was going to help you wash up, but if you don't mind, I'd rather wait until the morning. I'm kinda tired."

"Hell naw, I don't mind," Vance replied, seconds away from having made the same announcement. "I'm out of it myself. After I take my hookup, I'm going straight to sleep. I'm not even gonna turn the television on."

Tami nervously paced the floor of her bedroom. Knowing her stepfather was out of town at a conference and her mother was knocked out, she knew tonight was the night. Since the moment Vance revealed what the doctor told him about his leg and how anxious he seemed to get back home to his own condo, she'd been scheming. She'd gone too far all the way around to let him go just like that. As far as Tami was concerned, her sister's husband belonged to her, even if he didn't know it yet. She knew what his manhood felt like as well as tasted like and was not ready to give up those feelings.

Standing naked in front of the mirror, she tried gathering not only her thoughts but her nerve as well. Taking a brush, she made sure her hair was off her face and in a ponytail. Rubbing two palms of baby lotion on her entire body, she felt her inners start to get moist. Imagining Vance was really returning the favor for all the many nights she'd sucked him off while he was in his drug-induced zones, her fingers worked their magic with her box. Knowing she was at the brink of explosion, Tami stopped short, wanting to save everything she had for Vance.

With a bathrobe on just in case her mother was to wake up, Tami slowly crept by her parents' closed bedroom door. Each foot that touched the steps was leading her to her true destiny: her sister's husband. It was eerily quiet throughout the lower level of the house.

Barely hearing the sounds of a few passing cars, Tami stood motionless outside the den. Pressing her ear close against the door, the low-key sexual predator placed her hand on the knob. Making as little noise as possible, she eased the door open.

Poking her head inside the room, Tami saw the back of Vance's head lying on the pillow. Taking a deep breath, she stepped all the way across the threshold. Tonight was going to be her night. Listening to him snoring, she prayed her plan would work. Tiptoeing by the end table, she immediately noticed not only had he drunk all the water, but he'd taken not only his dosage for the evening, but somehow the three tiny red and blue pills he was told to take in the middle of the night. Combine those medications with the pills Tami had crushed up in his dinner, and Vance would definitely be out for the count.

"It's just gonna be me and you, baby, like it was meant to be from the very start. It's no need for you to leave me and go back to that condo. I've got everything that you need right here," Tami seductively whispered in his ear. "I don't know why you've been wasting your time with my sister when you can have all of this."

Reaching over, she raised Vance's hand, placing it on her full-figured breast. Covering his hand with hers, she moved both their hands in a circular motion. Moments later her nipples hardened. Closing her eyes, Tami was caught in the trance of what she believed to be her brother-in-law's voluntary touch. Licking her lips, Tami was caught off guard when she surprisingly saw she was no longer in control of his hand. Vance's movement had increased, along with the strong grip of his fingers diving deep into her skin.

"Oh, yeah," he moaned out, wanting more. "Bring that ass closer. Let daddy touch and feel all of you."

Vance had mumbled things like that before when Tami had him under the influence and was doing her thang, but this time was different, much different. His tone wasn't groggy as usual, and his eyes were wide open. Still caressing her breast, Vance used his free hand to go underneath Tami's robe. Intent on finding her box, he let his hand roam until the heated zone was found. One finger then two found their home in the warm moisture.

She was lost. Her predatory demeanor changed quickly to that of prey. As her knees grew weak, Tami's thick legs started to buckle. Although it was dark in the den, she felt like she was seeing stars.

This can't be. I know this isn't really happening. Tami was totally confused. She knew she hadn't taken her own depression and anxiety medicine in over a week because she was slipping it to Vance, but this had to be a dream turned to reality. The man she'd been slowly overmedicating for weeks to take advantage of had somehow flipped the script. He was now in control, having her want to practically climb the walls.

His hands are all over me. Oh my God, he's looking dead at me! Oh my God, is he about to kiss me in the mouth, for real?

The mutual moaning and groaning continued. Each one of them seemingly took turns as the room grew hotter. The more Tami's body would jerk, the more Vance would attempt to gyrate his strong hips. Restricted from total movement by the cast on his leg, Vance pulled an overweight Tami as close as he possibly could. After a few moments of what Tami thought were gifts from God, Vance's body jerked twice more as he embraced her tightly.

Just like that, as fast as it had begun, Vance pulled away. Closing his eyes, he laid his head down into the pillow. Wasting no time, he was fast asleep, snoring. Tami was left speechless and confused as to what had taken place. With her robe now on the floor of the den, she was frozen as her love box dripped down her voluptuous inner thighs.

Morning came, and Tami was just as shocked as she had been the night before. Lying in her bed, she didn't know what to do or what to say next. Vance had totally flipped the script. Out of all the nights she'd done what she did, he was never this alert. Knowing for sure he'd taken all his meds, plus the extra ones, on top of the medication that was crushed in his food, it was a miracle he was even coherent enough to mutter his own first name, let alone remember it.

Now she had to get dressed and go downstairs and face the man she'd been secretly worshiping for over a year: her sister's husband, the same man who had his hand deep up in her snatch only a few hours earlier. She couldn't avoid him. At this point, as the weeks before, Tami knew she was Vance's everything. She understood he relied on her not only for breakfast, lunch, and dinner, but for his meds, to help him bathe his body, and for transportation if need be. There'd be no hiding in her bedroom. She had to face him and let the chips fall where they may.

CHAPTER NINE

"Yes, Mrs. Lewis, it's true," the caller reaffirmed.

"Oh my God! Please tell me God has answered my prayers. What does it all mean?"

The doctor was ecstatic. Delivering the news that would give a household full of concerned family members and friends that much-needed hope to stay vigilant in their prayers. "Yes, she opened her eyes briefly. And our monitors also show a small bit of brain activity."

Mrs. Lewis couldn't believe her ears. Jumping out of bed, she praised God. Not being able to share the good news with her husband, who was out of town as usual, she darted across the hall. Without knocking, she burst into Tami's domain. After giving her Tori's medical update, the exuberant mother ran down the stairs to let the now most important person in her daughter's life, her husband, in on the happiness.

***

This worrisome-ass little bitch! Why don't she die already? It's like she sensed Vance slipping away and won't let him go. I know he wants to be with me deep down inside. Last night proved that. Even through the influence of all the drugs, he was looking dead at me. He called out my name as I was climaxing. He did that. I know I'm not crazy.

Tami's mind raced as she took her time drying off after callously taking an extra-long shower. In no great hurry to get dressed, the vindictive sister defied her mother's wishes to just throw on any old thing, get Vance in the car, and for them to meet her down at the hospital.

I'll get there when I get there. Last time I rushed down to that place, God left me hanging in a major way. He allowed that bitch, Daddy's little angel, to live. Well, fuck that. I'ma get myself all the way together, then leave!

Tami was in no huge rush to come face to face with the love of her life, but she could stall no more.

In the midst of all the excitement Vance was feeling, he and Tami hardly got a chance to say more than two words to each other pertaining to the events of the night before. When she first entered the den, he was trying to finish up with a small breakfast tray his mother-in-law had prepared before running off to the hospital. In the midst of trying to get his own self together, he even failed to make direct eye contact, leaving Tami even more bewildered about his brazen actions.

As the two of them drove en route to the hospital, Vance stayed on his cell, reaching out not only to his best friend and frat brother, Courtney, but his elderly aunt as well. Tami wanted to snatch his cell phone out of his hands and throw it out the window. She wanted to yell out that she was on the other side of the fence of recovery and hoped her little sister had shaken hands with the devil. Yet it seemed as if she'd have no such luck, not today.

Pulling up into valet as they'd done so many times since Vance was released, they were greeted by the attendant who knew them both by name. Sensing they'd received some good news about their loved one, he shook Vance's hand, telling him that he was praying for the entire family. Tami, of course, fumed. Knowing that Vance would have to at least end all his exuberant cell conversations when the doors of the elevator closed, she hoped she'd at least have an opportunity to gauge his mindset. However, just as luck would have it, one of Vance's orthopedic surgeons was already on the elevator heading upstairs. He'd been called in to look over some other bone-mangled patient's X-rays. Engulfed in a conversation about how Vance's leg had been healing since he last saw him, they spoke until Tami announced they were at Tori's floor.

Gripping the black foam handles of the wheelchair, Tami pushed Vance off the elevator and down the long hallway. Ignoring the once-again prying and judgmental glances of a few of the nurses' aides, Tami still stood tall. She held on to her pride, knowing that even if her conniving sister had miraculously snapped out of it and was at 100 percent, she still won. Tami knew she'd still live in the celebration that she'd had Vance the way she wanted him on more than one occasion. And no matter how much Vance seemed to want to ignore or play dumb about what happened the night before, he wanted her just as much; at least, in that one small moment of time.

"Here comes her husband right now! You can tell him the update on my daughter." Mrs. Lewis raised her arm, bringing the doctor's attention to an oncoming Vance. "He will want you to explain it to him just as you did to me."

After hearing that, in most cases, a lot of coma-induced patients open their eyes from time to time, there was a major setback in the joy Vance had been feeling since his mother-in-law gave him the update. The only good thing he felt they'd told him was that there was indeed some activity going on in her brain. Tori had several small blood clots the doctors were extremely concerned about, but they assured Vance at this point they were stable. They told Vance, his mother-in-law, and a secretly elated Tami that even though Tori was moving definitely in the right direction, she was not out of the woods.

Vance felt defeated and it showed. Still showing signs of the various medications in his blood system, he slumped over toward the side of his wheelchair. Being comforted by Mrs. Lewis, he wanted to cry. Making his way to his wife's bedside, he reached over, touching her hand. Although the hospital climate was not cold, her tiny hand felt cool to the touch, reminding him of the way his deceased mother's hand felt over ten years ago. Vance finally broke all the way down.

Alarmed by the loud sounds of his sobs, Mrs. Lewis rushed to his side, wrapping her arms around him. Tami, on the other hand, was disgusted.

After what we did last night and every other damn night, he in there crying his head off like a damn fool! I swear I wish this little bitch would just die already and get the fuck out of our way! I hate feeling like I wanna slap the hell outta Vance's dumb ass! I swear I do. Listen to this fool in there acting like Tori the last woman on earth, and my mother fake ass in there facilitating that bullshit. She don't never put her arms around me when that rotten-ass husband of hers gets to going on me! After all these years, she still just acts like she's so scared of him leaving her.

Not in the mood to be a part of her mother and Vance's pity party, Tami walked away from the doorway of her sister's room. Caught up in her own selfish emotions, she was staring straight ahead. Making it only a few yards down, she was shaken out of her heated trance by the piercing sounds and alerts being announced over the intercom system. With all the available doctors and nurses rushing to lend assistance to the emergency at hand, it seemed like chaos.

Tami wanted to feel sorry for whoever was in room 219 who was in such dire straits, but her own problems trumped that waste of concern for a stranger. Instead, she saw an opportunity to take advantage of the pandemonium.

Taking notice that a nurse had temporarily left the medicine cart unattended, Tami seized the moment to empty as many of the three, four, five, and in some cases six different-colored pills from the small white paper cups as she could into her purse. Satisfied she'd stolen what she'd need to get Vance back all the way ripe for her sexual desires, she pushed the elevator button.

Fuck my damn fake mother not giving a shit about me, Vance's pussy-whipped dumb self, and Tori's half-dead ass. I'm going to get me something to eat, count these pills up I just got, and let them all three do what they do!

The ride home was more silent than coming. Vance was still teary-eyed after crying at Tori's bedside all afternoon. Hoping to get better news, he was obviously hurt. He'd barely eaten breakfast, not had lunch, and was running out of gas. Still having to take his prescribed meds, Vance was feeling the true side effects, and needless to say it was nothing nice. Leaning his head over on the car window, he didn't mutter a single solitary word the entire ride.

Tami was still pissed, having seen him behave the way he did about his wife, her sister. She knew in the back of her mind that was a normal reaction that most men would have after hearing bad news about their spouse, but so what? She didn't want to have a ringside seat to what she felt was the ultimate betrayal to the seemingly mutual sexual encounter they'd had the night before.

But, no, she was somewhat thankful. Vance's action earlier was her third wake-up call. First there was the doctor informing Vance that his leg was healing faster than expected. Then Vance was making constant comments about wanting to leave her parents' house and return to his own condo; and now this bullshit, lastly, the display of weakness he'd just shown at the hospital for a female Tami knew was not worthy of his devotion. No, she knew what she had to do. She had a plan the night before, but Vance doing what he'd done threw her off. Tonight Tami swore to herself she'd be more focused. Tonight she'd win.

CHAPTER TEN

Tami helped Vance out of the car and into the house. After getting him situated in the den, she went upstairs to gather her thoughts. Lying down across the bed, before she knew it, she fell asleep and started to dream.

"Okay, birthday girl, please go upstairs and tell your little sister that dinner is ready," Mrs. Lewis said while removing the last piece of chicken from the fiery hot grease. "Your father will be home soon, so we can eat then cut the cake he's bringing you."

Tami turned up her nose. "You mean Tori's father, don't you?"

"Listen, baby, please don't start that again; especially today of all days. You need to enjoy your birthday and not act so mean-spirited all the time."

"Mommy, you know he doesn't like me, and sometimes you act like you don't either." Tami pouted, feeling as if every word she spoke was gospel.

"Baby doll, don't say that." Mrs. Lewis turned to face her eldest. Wiping her hands on her apron, she reassured Tami that she was indeed loved by not only her, but Tori and her husband as well. "We all love you. We're a family. That's why Mommy cooked you this good birthday meal."

"Then why does Daddy treat me so mean? It's not fair. I always get in trouble even when it's Tori's fault." Tami's pudgy face was full of resentment as her empty stomach growled.

Having answered enough questions, Mrs. Lewis finally commanded an inquisitive Tami to go and do as she was told. Once upstairs, Tami looked in her little sister's room, but she was nowhere to be found. Knowing Tori would sometimes go into her bedroom and mess with her toys and stuffed animals, Tami rolled her eyes as she marched down the hallway. Poking her head inside the room in hopes of catching her sibling in the act, Tami once again came up empty. Tori was not in there either. Frustrated, she started calling out her sister's name. Tami hated that she was such a busybody and prayed she'd hadn't gotten into anything.

Finally hearing noise coming from their parents' room, Tami hoped for the best but *prepared herself for the worst. Of course, with her luck, Tami found Tori sitting at the small desk in the corner of the room. With an ink pen in hand, Tori was creating one of her refrigerator-ready masterpieces. Using her father's important papers as her canvas, she happily drew away.*

Tami was speechless. Grabbing the pen out of her hand, she tossed it to the side. Staring first at the documents that were ruined then at Tori's face that had just as much ink on it as did the papers, Tami frowned.

"Hurry up and come downstairs. Your father is pulling up in the driveway."

Hearing her mother's voice even mention her stepfather caused Tami to panic. She knew he would be mad, but hopefully this time it'd be at his beloved Tori, who'd created such a mess and destroyed his work. Taking her little sister by the hand, Tami led her down the hallway. Reaching the top of the stairs, Tami heard the front door close. Seconds later, her mother was fussing about the cake being chocolate instead of yellow, which was Tami's favorite as requested.

"What damn difference does it make if it was every flavor in the world? You know like I know Tami will eat everything you put in front of her and anything she can put her hands on."

By the time the sisters got to the bottom step, Tami was damn near in tears having to yet again listen to her stepfather talk about her so cruelly, especially today of all days.

"Mommy." Tami led Tori into the kitchen where their parents were standing, still arguing. "You need to clean Tori's face and hands with something."

Immediately what should've been an evening filled with cake, ice cream, presents, and songs of "Happy Birthday" turned into another evening of verbal and mental abuse at the hands of both parents. Not only was Tami completely blamed for not watching her little sister, but she was sent upstairs to her room having none of the special dinner her mother had prepared in her honor. To add further insult, she didn't even get a chance to see the cake, wrong flavor or not.

Balled up in the bed, Tami sobbed, still overhearing her stepfather rage about how fat and lazy she was. Tori, who kickstarted all the chaos in the first place, not only got to eat Tami's favorite chicken wings, but she got to cut her older sister's birthday cake as well.

Standing in the doorway of her sister's bedroom, Tori repeatedly chanted what her father had just stated: "Fat girls like Tami don't need cake anyway!"

"Tami, please wake up." Mrs. Lewis knocked at the closed door. "I forgot to stop by the store after I left the hospital. Your father will be home later this evening and there is none of his favorite soda left, so I need you to run and get him some. You know how he gets without his cola."

Tami was glad to be back to reality and out of the nightmare of her childhood. Over the years, things hadn't changed much in the way her family treated her, but she found small ways to get revenge. Sure, she'd get out of her bed to go get soda for her disrespectful stepdad, but Tami would make sure to shake up each and every bottle so it'd explode.

Fuck him. Tami thought about her dream as she left out the front door, jumping in her car. *Him and Tori both.*

CHAPTER ELEVEN

Tami's stepfather had returned from his trip. He and his wife wasted no time going to be by Tori's bedside. Mr. Lewis knew everything the doctors had said as far as his daughter's condition. Even though some of it seemed somber, he never would give up hope that his little princess would somehow pull through.

With them gone, Tami finally found the inner courage to go in the den and ask Vance what he wanted her to prepare for dinner. Without lifting his head, he replied that he was not hungry and wanted to just skip eating anything for the evening. Knowing that would not be a good idea, especially for what she had planned, Tami advised him differently.

"Look, Vance, I know you don't like what you heard today, but you have to eat to keep your strength up."

"Yeah, I know, but I just ain't feeling any food right about now." Vance glanced over at Tami, barely acknowledging her existence.

"Well, I'm going to fix something anyway. You can't take your medicine on an empty stomach."

Thirty minutes later, Tami brought the food tray into the dark den. Flipping on the light switch, she coaxed Vance to get up and try not to be so depressed. Adjusting the pillows behind his back, she assisted him in sitting upright. Placing the tray in front of him, Tami clicked on the television to try to take his mind off Tori. Still having said nothing about what had taken place the night before between them, Tami could only believe Vance had indeed been out of it, eyes wide open and all.

Knowing that if all went as planned the two of them would go even further, the deranged, focused female left the room. Standing outside the doorway, she smiled, knowing her naïve brother-in-law was only a few short yards away, consuming a few of the pills she'd stolen off the nurse's cart earlier.

After doing a Google pill search, Tami happily discovered several of the tablets would cause extreme dizziness and hallucinations if not taken in proper intervals. It was also advised that they should not be consumed in conjunction with other medications without a doctor's advice.

Hearing the fork scrape the plate and the sound of the glass of juice being drunk, Tami grew more elated. She'd play Candy Crush another thirty or so minutes before going back into the den to hopefully gloat at her accomplishment of slowly poisoning her sister's husband. Tami was doing the devil's work and couldn't care less as long as she got what she wanted, which was Vance.

Submerging her thick body in the hot water, Tami welcomed the comforting warmth the tub was providing. Laying her head back, she immediately got caught up in thoughts of what her life would and could be like as soon as Tori was dead and Vance was all hers. Her life would be perfect. She could move out of her parents' house and finally tell her cruel stepfather to kiss her ass in three places.

Allowing her arms to relax down at her sides, a constantly conniving Tami made her fingertips move, causing small ripples in the water to shift the multitudes of bubbles. Her parents and Vance may have taken what the doctors said as a small setback in Tori's recovery, but not Tami. She gladly accepted the update as what it was: a true gift and blessing.

Tami had been teased her entire life for being overweight, especially by her bony sister, but like the saying goes, God don't like ugly. Tori was the ugliest pretty girl Tami knew. However, tonight would be revenge for all the teasing and constant ridicule about her being fat. Feeling smug, Tami enjoyed the rest of her bath knowing what the rest of the evening held.

"I gotta stop taking all these damn pills," Vance angrily mumbled as he raised the glass of juice to his lips. "I know I'm in pain and all, but it's like I'm addicted to these bad boys or something. I feel like I'm straight turning into some sort of back alley junkie needing a fix. What I might need to do is get out this den and maybe back to my condo. Besides, I'm thinking things about Tami's big ass that ain't even funny or natural anymore to be thinking about your sister-in-law. I need to hurry up and call my boy Courtney and see what the hell he thinks." Rubbing at the cast on his leg, he found some peace knowing that the doctor said the breaks in his bones were healing nicely and they might be able to make the white plaster tomb much smaller. If that was to happen, Vance knew that no matter if Courtney or anyone else advised against it, when it came down to it, he was going home.

CHAPTER TWELVE

It was well after midnight and the entire Lewis household was asleep, except for Tami. Having bouts of insomnia and late-night binge eating since she was a young teenager, she reached over to her nightstand. Opening the lower drawer, she pulled out a small package of cookies and a honey bun. After devouring them, Tami got out of bed and went to the closet. Pulling down a shoebox off the top shelf, she walked it back over to her bed. Climbing back underneath the thin blanket, hell bent on satisfying the hungry monster that lived within, Tami eagerly removed the top. Excitedly she searched through the huge amount of candy that filled the box to the rim. Empty wrappers were discarded to the floor no sooner than she ripped them off the sugary treats.

After some time, Tami finally had her need under control. Making her feel as if she were drunk, high, and hyped all at the same time, the sugar rush had her gone. It had her geeked to go downstairs and get it going with her man.

He knows he wants all this right here.

Tami stood at the door to the den, caressing her own breast. Licking her lips, she knew that she was seconds away from giving Vance the ultimate thrill of a lifetime. He would know what it felt like to have his manhood buried in her inners until he busted a nut. She'd ridden him the best she could considering the small twin-sized hospital bed and the size of their bodies, but this was going to be different. Tami had her mind made up that no matter what she was going to go all out. She was going to feel his hot sperm shoot up in her pussy even if he woke up out of his drugged trance and tried to protest. The awful sister had put in a lot of work trying to get Tori's husband to love her like she loved him.

Reaching her hand downward, Tami slowly turned the knob. Not caring if Vance was all the way asleep or not, she came inside the den, shutting the door behind her. As usual his back was to her. Taking a deep breath, she eased by the coffee table, going to the other side of the room. Now standing directly in front of a shirtless Vance, she heard the light sounds of him breathing. Baffled as to why he wasn't snoring loud like he normally did, Tami waved her hand across his face. After double checking, she realized he was asleep.

Dropping her white fluffy robe to the floor, she stood stark naked. Anxious to get what she came for, Tami placed one hand on Vance's shoulder and the other on his hip. Using a small amount of strength, she pushed him all the way over on his back. Marveling at his muscles, she traced the outline with her fingers. Vance still had yet to wake up. Tami was elated knowing the combination of pills she'd crushed up in his food was working.

Lifting one leg up, she placed her knee on the side of the mattress. Pressing the palm of her hand on the wall, the plus-size vixen raised the other leg, straddling Vance's body. With barely enough room in the hospital-rented bed for him, Tami adjusted both knees the best she could.

Leaning forward, she kissed him on his neck. The taste of his skin was always like vanilla ice cream. Licking it like a cone with double scoops, Tami used one hand to reach down in between his legs. Grabbing a hold of his fast-hardening manhood, she stroked it up and down, first fast then slow. Vance moaned out Tori's name, throwing Tami off. Initially she got infuriated, but that still didn't stop her from rocking her wide hips after sticking his pole inside of her.

The more she slowly grinded, the more Vance called out his wife's name.

Before Tami knew what was happening, her brother-in-law had both his hands tightly gripping each butt cheek. As he applied pressure, Tami felt his pelvis rise, matching her movement for movement. Bringing her lips down to his, she became lost in emotion as Vance's tongue darted in and out of his mouth and into hers. Tami welcomed every touch as did he. She wanted to scream out his name but didn't want to risk waking her parents or startling Vance out of the zone he was so deep in.

Before she knew it, Tami felt like he'd used every bit of strength he had within to jerk her body forward and whisper his wife's name in her ear once more. The force of the rough series of movements made her explode and climax, as well as Vance. Tori's older sister could feel the warm stream of nut shoot up in her.

Now out of breath, Tami didn't say a word. Vance let go of her hips and exhaled. Climbing off of him, Tami reached down, picking up her robe. Tiptoeing back to the other side of the den, the morally corrupt female left out the door just as quietly as she'd entered, acting as if she'd done no wrong.

CHAPTER THIRTEEN

Morning came and as always after you do dirt, you have to take the walk of shame. Tami, although deliberate in everything she'd initiated and participated in the night before, was no great exception to the rule. She was more than happy to jump Vance's bones, but to come face to face with him was an altogether different thing. Climbing out of the bed, she threw on her robe and took a deep breath. Thinking she was hearing voices coming from downstairs, she knew it would only be a matter of time before the entire house was up and moving about. No sooner than Tami opened her bedroom door to attempt to go to the bathroom, she was strangely met by Courtney, Vance's frat brother, coming out.

"Hey, girl, good morning," he spoke in his deep tone, trying to be extra seductive.

"Oh my God, Courtney? What in the hell?" She was bewildered by him being the first person she saw at this time of the day. She thought maybe she was dreaming or seeing things. Wiping the sleep out of the corners of each eye, she looked toward the hall window, seeing if the sun was even fully up yet. "What are you doing here? And damn, what time is it?"

Courtney smiled, hoping to get a small glimpse of what she was working with underneath her robe. "It's time to give a brother a chance to take you out. You down with that or what? I got an extra pair of handcuffs out in my car. I mean, if you down for that type of freaky behavior."

"Oh my God, give that shit a rest already," she protested, trying to hold her pee. "You doing too much for me. Now, like I just asked, why are you here so damn early? What's going on? And where's Vance?"

Courtney sensed Tami was still not in the mood to entertain going out with him, so he let it go for the time being. He always thought she was cute, but slowly sweating her was playing itself out quick. "Look, girl, I'm just here to pick up my boy and his stuff. Ain't nobody trying to marry your pretty self. I was just trying to go out and have a few laughs."

"Pick your boy up?" Tami was confused, still holding her urine. "What you mean pick him up? I'm confused."

"Yeah, I guess he's on some old grownup bullshit thinking he can take care of himself. He texted me this morning saying he needed a ride out to his condo, so here the hell I am. I don't know how he gonna get around way out there, but so be it. His wish is my command."

Tami couldn't take it anymore. She was two seconds away from urinating on herself. Wasting no more time, she darted into the bathroom. Sitting on the toilet, she grew more confused over what Courtney had just said.

What the heck is really going on? Vance is leaving? Naw, it must be a mistake. He can't take care of himself. He needs me. I hope it's not because of what we did last night. I mean, he acted like he was with it. Oh my God, I can't believe he's leaving. Just like that.

Barely wiping herself, Tami forgot to even flush the toilet before running back out into the hallway that was now luckily empty. Going to the edge of the stairs, she stood there motionless. Eavesdropping on what was being said, she hung on every single word. Her mother, of course, was totally against her new son-in-law leaving the convenience of being in the household. Telling him that Tori would want him to stay as long as he was still healing, she meant it. Mrs. Lewis also expressed how much comfort it brought to her as well to have him so close. Vance was humble, just saying he didn't want to overstay his welcome.

Mr. Lewis made his opinion known as well, explaining that he wanted him to stay, especially since he was spending so much time traveling lately, but he definitely understood a man wanting to have his privacy and be the king of his own castle.

"Son, I want you to know that this is always your home. You're always welcome here at any time. And if you get out there and change your mind, you just give me a call and I'll come and pick you up personally. The day you married my princess was the day you became a real man in my eyes. We family."

As Courtney returned from taking the last duffle bag of Vance's belongings out to his car, Mrs. Lewis yelled up the stairs to her eldest daughter. "Tami, come down here!"

Acting as if she hadn't heard her, Tami leaned back into the shadows. Almost stumbling into a small bookshelf, she caught her balance. Hitting her small toe, Tami kept her composure and sucked it up. She didn't yell or make a sound. She didn't want to be discovered lurking around like she had something to hide. After her mother called her name once more, Tami knew she had to answer before her mom, her stepfather, or, worse than that, Courtney came up the stairs to see where she was.

"Yes, Mom, I heard you. I was in the bathroom," Tami lied, yelling back down. "What is it?"

"Well, come down here and bring Vance's house keys and say good-bye."

"Huh? Oh, okay then, give me a minute. I have to get dressed."

"You don't have to get dressed to give this man his keys and say good-bye. Now, come on down, silly. Vance is family. He doesn't care what you look like."

Returning to her bedroom, Tami was panicked. The room felt like it was spinning. Her heart started to race. She couldn't believe he was leaving. They'd just had such great sex; now he was out, just like that. No warning or anything.

Racking her brain, she couldn't remember exactly how she'd left the condo when last out there. Did she leave the bed unmade? Did she leave some opened mail on the table after reading it? Was a pair of Vance's boxers she was smelling still near the bathtub? How would she keep him overmedicated and keep having her way with him? Tami's mind was in a tailspin. She had to think quickly. She had to find a way to stall.

"Tami, please hurry up with those keys. Vance has to stop by the hospital first and talk to some of Tori's doctors about some possible new treatments." Mrs. Lewis's voice seemed to get louder and more serious, especially when her youngest child was involved.

Yes, that's it!

"Mom, I can't find where I put them at right now. It's been so long since I've been out there. Just have Vance go ahead down to the hospital and I will meet him down there with the keys. That way he won't be held up. Is that okay?"

"I bet if it was some cookies, candy, or a cheeseburger she'd know where to find them at real quick," Tami's stepfather cruelly spoke, trying to be funny; but no one laughed.

Not even bothering to go down the stairs and say her farewells to their houseguest, Tami rushed to get dressed. There was no time to waste. Things had spiraled out of control fast. She had to drive way out to the condo, clean up any traces of her weird obsession with Vance, and drive back to the hospital before he finished up his meeting.

Throwing on an old pair of track pants and a soiled T-shirt, she ran out the door. She was on a mission and her not being labeled as crazy and the family whore depended on her completing that mission. Roaring out of the driveway, she prayed every mile of the way.

Relieved she'd made it out to the condo in record time, Tami stuck the key in the door and went to work. Not expecting Vance or anyone else for that matter to come to the place anytime soon, she grabbed two plastic bags. Stuffing in the bag all of Vance's T-shirts and underwear she'd been lounging in while she was over there, she ran out to the car, tossing the bag in her trunk. Tami was glad she'd dodged the bullet of him and Courtney coming in to find the inexplicable and out-of-place items. She wiped the sweat from her head.

Taking all the mail, open or not, she placed it in her purse. Next the out-of-sorts Tami bolted into the bedroom to make up the bed she'd masturbated in and to pick up all of her sister's lingerie she'd thrown all across the room. After spending a good forty-five minutes or so making sure the condo was in the exact same condition it was in when she'd first entered it to get Vance's requested items, Tami was ready to say farewell to her private getaway.

Taking one of Vance's plain white T-shirts out of the closet, Tami took off the already dirty and now sweaty one she was wearing and threw it in her purse on top of the mail. Pulling his down over her head made her feel like she was wearing his letterman jacket and was still "his girl."

After making sure the double lock was on, she jumped back in her vehicle, heading to the hospital. Once again breaking every law in the book, she swerved in and out of traffic, having no regard for the next person driving.

With the situation at the condo handled, she could think more clearly. Now focused strictly on Vance, maybe she could get some answers from her brother-in-law and unknowing sex buddy about his impromptu departure.

CHAPTER FOURTEEN

Driving up to valet, Tami anxiously awaited her turn in line. Tapping her fingers on the steering wheel, she fought like hell not to just jump out of her car where it was and leave it running. If someone stole it, oh well, she'd deal with that later. At least she'd get to Vance quicker.

Finally next in line, she snatched her purse off the passenger seat and leaped out of the car before coming to a full stop. Practically knocking the attendant over, she ran to the revolving doors, almost getting the handle of her purse caught. Pushing the elevator button repeatedly, paranoid, she believed the gods had been working against her since this morning. Staring up at the small digital red numbers indicating the floor the elevator was on, she grew more impatient.

When the doors finally opened, Tami rudely didn't wait for anyone to get off; she just brushed past them, acting as if she were the only human being on earth. Completely self-absorbed in her own problems, she offered no "excuse me's" or apologies to one person. Right about now, as far as Tami was concerned, no one mattered except for Vance.

The elevator seemed to stop at every single floor, making her grow even more agitated. When a nurse held the door open for an elderly lady in a wheelchair, Tami wanted to explode, yet she knew she couldn't.

Stepping off on Tori's floor, as fate would have it, she was once again met by Courtney. He was on his way down to the cafeteria to get himself a cup of coffee, because Vance was still in the meeting with several specialists.

"Hey now, you wanna grab a cup with me or what? No pressure. Just a friendly cup."

"Naw, Courtney, I'm good." She was strangely civil with the man she deemed as a pest. "I have some unfinished business to handle."

"All right then." He smiled as one of the big-booty nurses' aides who always gave Tami shade stepped on the elevator and grinned.

Tami ignored the female's hate and went on about her way. Feeling some sort of way, she decided to go have a long talk with her baby sister. The fact that it would be a one-sided conversation made little to no difference to Tami, who had been off her own meds for weeks. She had a gang of things she wanted to get off her chest, first one being the fact that Tori hadn't wanted her sister to be in her wedding party. After all the bullshit and ridicule Tami had put up with from her throughout the years, she didn't want her involved? Tami wanted to tell her that she wasn't at all interested in being a part of that uppity circus anyway. She wanted to tell her to kiss her wide ass twice. She wanted to smack the cow shit outta her and make her apologize for all the wrong that was done to her. Tami wanted to spit in her face but feared someone might come in.

Without any reservations, she boldly marched into Tori's room. Met with multitudes of flowers, cards, and balloons, Tami grew sick to her stomach seeing the vast amount of affection received by the sister she knew to be a class A bitch.

I swear to God I hate this tramp. Why can't everybody see her for who in the hell she really is? Are they all blind?

Standing over her bedside for the first time since the day of the wedding, she was alone with her sibling. Not knowing what to say now that they were face to face, Tami stared over at the blinking lights on the various monitors and the many tubes that were running seemingly out of every part of Tori's body. Tami always hated her sister for being so small, but now, considering all the weight she'd lost being laid up in the hospital, some small part of her felt a bit of sympathy.

Half of Tori's hair had been shaved off. The skin that was ripped off of her jaw line after being thrown out the window of the vehicle had healed somewhat, but not with the same complexion as the rest of her still bruised face. A small part of her wanted to cry, but then of course her true feelings reared their ugly head.

"So, Tori." Tami quickly transformed back into being a woman on a mission for Satan himself. "I heard through the grapevine you never wanted me to be in your wedding, huh? Word has it you thought I was much too fat to rock your ugly-ass bridesmaid dress. Wow. Well, guess what. I didn't want to be in that circus anyway. In between you and your friends prancing around and Vance and his frat brothers barking, I would've preferred staying home watching *Real Housewives from Where the Hell Ever* reruns. I should've knocked that nasty cake over and spit in the champagne fountain!"

Before she could go on with her impromptu tirade, Tami was interrupted by a nurse wanting to check on the flow of Tori's IV. After doing so, the nurse made mention to Tami that she and Tori had similar features and she could easily see that they were related. Tami knew that was a big huge lie and the nurse was just being pleasant or nosy. However, whatever her angle was, Tami wasn't in the mood for pleasantries and brushed her off as soon as she could.

"Well, have a nice day, miss. And please push the button at the side of the bed if you have any questions or concerns pertaining to your loved one."

Tami made sure the nurse was out of ear range. Peeking out into the hallway, she ducked back in the otherwise quiet hospital room and continued in on her sister. "Since we was little kids you been running around thinking you better than me. Well, guess what. You ain't shit in my eyes and never have been. You might have Daddy, Vance, and everybody else you come in contact with fooled, but I know your snake ass for who you really are."

Tami viciously dug her nails deep in Tori's forearm as she expressed her true feelings. Seething with years of built-up hatred, she fought the overwhelming urge to sock her comatose sibling dead in the face for all the wrongs she felt she'd committed against her throughout time.

"I would like nothing more than to take that pillow from under your head and smother the life outta you, but I don't have to punish you. God already did that for you being such a backstabbing bitch to me all the time. You and your friends always running around claiming that y'all stay winning. Well, guess what, Miss Perfect. Your winning streak is over. Your face is now as ugly as your personality, and as for taking Vance from me when I told you I liked him, well, I had that dick last night and every night since he came home from the hospital if I wanted it! So you tell me, Tori, who's winning now? Oh, yeah, my bad. You can't talk!" Tami was elated by her younger sister's misfortune. "I'm the boss and you taking a loss. So there! How does it feel to be on the losing end of the stick, Ms. Thang?"

Seconds later, Tami was joined in the room by Courtney and Vance. She wanted an opportunity to speak to Vance alone, but his best friend was making the feat damn near impossible. Every time she thought Courtney was going to leave to go get another cup of coffee or flirt with a nurse, he stayed posted. Seeing that her brother-in-law was completely focused on Tori and paying her absolutely no attention, Tami gave up. She finally gave the house keys to Courtney and said fuck it. Whatever was going to be would be. Her game plan had gone down without a hitch. Tami had gotten what she needed from Vance, so all was well on her end. At this point, it was a waiting game. One that she had to play.

CHAPTER FIFTEEN

Tami felt drunk with power having confessed everything she'd done to pay Tori back for a childhood that was tortured. The fact that her sister was unresponsive and in a coma did nothing to diminish the conquest that she felt she'd accomplished. To Tami it made no difference whatsoever; if Tori could hear it through whatever state of mind they had her doped up in, Tami had won. She'd snatched the victory trophy right from underneath Tori's nose. For once it felt like heaven on earth to come up on the winning side of the coin. Sure, she was confused as to why Vance just up and suddenly gave her parents his notice and moved out, but so be it. Just like she thought as she left Vance at her sister's bedside to probably start his crying, "I'm so sorry; it should be me lying in this bed" routine: *Let him go ahead and act like a clown now while Tori is clinging to life.* In the long run, Tami trusted God wasn't gonna bless the recovery of a devil.

***

Having made it home, Tami was still very much in the mood to call her family members to task for their actions of the past and their present behavior. When she was finished they'd be careful how they attempted to treat her in the future. She had enough of the backbiting and catering to Tori and her feelings. Tami was ready to step up and voice her opinion.

Chalking her newfound inner courage up to having Vance's sperm circulating through her bloodstream, Tami barged into the living room. Not caring that her stepfather was watching one of his favorite shows that he'd DVRed, the enraged and bitter Tami snatched the electrical plug out of the socket.

"Tami!"

"Yeah, what?"

"Girl, have you lost your mind or something? Plug that damn television back in right now!"

"Naw, old man. We need to get something straight once and for all." She now stood in front of the flat screen with her hands planted firmly on her wide hips. "I'm tired of the way you treat me! And guess what? Today it stops!"

"The way I treat you?" Mr. Lewis sat upright in his recliner with the remote still clutched in his hand. "And what exactly is the way I treat your big, overgrown, crybaby ass? Huh? You tell me. You got a lot of nerve in that big, hefty body of yours!"

"Seriously, do you hear yourself talking to me like that? Calling me names like I'm nothing or have no feelings. I heard what you said earlier when I was looking for Vance's keys. Why would you say some shit like that?"

"And?" He openly showed no signs of remorse. "You act like I said something that wasn't true. I mean, come on now, girl. Have you looked in the mirror lately? You could stand to lose a pound or two. I mean, correct me if I'm wrong, but I don't see any line of men beating down my front door to take your heavyweight ass out somewhere for a burger or two."

Tami's attitude only worsened hearing her stepfather not only trying to defend his verbal abuse but condone his always harsh delivery. Normally she'd retreat to her bedroom to hide and lick her wounds; however, this time the outcome was going to be much different. She was hell bent on standing her ground and beating the bully at his own game.

"So let me get this correct. You, an aging old man who has to take a little blue pill to halfway have sex with his wife, a man who absolutely is hated by his coworkers and practically despised by damn near everyone he comes in contact with, wants to always pass judgment on others. Now that behavior is rich!"

"Is that how you think you can talk to me in my own damn house, you little ungrateful bitch? No, excuse me, I mean you big ungrateful bitch!" Mr. Lewis's veins started to bulge from both temples and his nostrils flared.

Still ready to get her feelings out on the table, Tami stood strong, refusing to back down. "Yeah, see what I mean? What kind of man treats his daughter like that? Oh, but this time you can excuse me. I keep forgetting you're not my real father. You're just some ratchet man my poor, naïve mother had the misfortune to mess around with and marry. Trust me, she has my sympathies."

"Big girl, you run around here eating everything you can find, getting bigger and bigger. You stay jealous of my little princess because you wish you were her. I see it. Your mother sees it. Hell, the entire world sees it. I mean, I don't know how Vance put up with your crazy ass hovering over him so long. It must've been that medication he's on."

Mrs. Lewis heard all the commotion and rushed downstairs, trying to break up the war of words. "Please, you two, stop it," she loudly pleaded with her eldest daughter and husband.

"Naw, she came in here and started with me." Mr. Lewis was heated, stating what were the facts in his eyes. "I was watching my show and this piece of shit offspring of yours came barreling through my front door like a hurricane."

"Your husband is nothing but an old, twisted-mind bully and you know that. He got some nerve calling me a piece of shit. He's been dogging you and me out for years. The only person who matters to this asshole is his precious, perfect little Tori. That stuck-up, skinny whore can do no wrong in his eyes."

"You is damn straight she can't do any wrong," Mr. Lewis agreed while trying to lunge at Tami. "You wish your huge, overgrown self could be her. Matter of fact, I wish it was you in that accident. I swear I wish it was you over across town stuck in that damn hospital bed fighting for your life, and not my innocent baby."

"Innocent? Who, Tori? Man, fuck you!" Tami was beyond deep off into her emotions. If looks could kill, her stepfather would've been dead the first time he'd opened his mouth trying to bring her down.

"Tami, I'm begging you. Please don't talk to your father like that!" Coming in between the two, Mrs. Lewis tried once more to defuse the explosive situation from going any further.

"Father?" Tami sinisterly laughed at the mere mention of the word. "This rotten-mouthed motherfucker ain't no father of mine. My real father would never treat me like this monster has been doing throughout the years. And, Mother, how could you allow him to do so?"

Mr. Lewis felt he was being tame with his choice of words up until now, but he felt the need to step up his game. Standing on the truth as he knew it, the old, cranky man decided to fire back. Now would be the time he'd give his stepdaughter everything he'd been holding back on for years.

"You know what, Tami? You're right. I'm not your goddamn father and am sure glad that I'm not. You see, as fate would have it, your real pappy was some back alley drug-crazed junkie who supposedly raped your mother and put a baby up in her ass. See, that's probably why you're so deranged now your damn self and can't find a man to call your own like Tori. You're just like that desperate dopefiend: crazy as hell! So what I want you to do the next time you call yourself marching in my damn house and passing judgment on me and the way you claim I treat you, don't! Your bastard ass might need to take a few steps back and think about that tainted bloodline you're hatched from. Now kindly plug my television back up and get out my sight!"

The room grew eerily silent. The ugly, mean-spirited biological bombshell Mr. Lewis had dropped was a lethal blow to Tami to say the least. She couldn't believe what her ears had just heard. She couldn't seem to make sense of what he claimed to be her conception. As the room started to spin, Tami felt as if she'd been hit upside her head with a hammer, or sucker-punched in the stomach. Used to being strong and brushing off the outrageously rude comments her stepfather was known to make throughout the years, this time she felt different. This information was a game changer.

The air in the living room seemed to get thin. Tami tried to catch her breath. In pain, she looked over to her mother for some sort of denial of what her stepfather had just blurted out, yet she found none. Shamefully, the woman Tami trusted to safeguard and protect her simply lowered her head.

"Mommy, say something," she angrily demanded with huge tears forming, ready to drop. "Tell him he needs to stop lying. Tell him to take back what he said!"

After a few awkward moments, Tami's mother finally spoke. "Listen, Tami, I'm sorry, honey. What your father said is somewhat true."

"What?" Tami leaned toward the wall for support before she fell to the ground.

"Wait a minute, baby. It's not all true, but yes, I was raped and you were conceived during the attack. However, the fact that he was proven to be a drug addict has no bearing on any of the problems you've faced over time. Those demons you face are just coincidence and nothing more."

"Coincidence my black ass!" Mr. Lewis wasn't done throwing mud, seeing how he had his stepdaughter against the ropes so to speak. "Oh, yes, the hell it does. I saw a television show about the bullshit on the science channel. Yeah, it's probably hereditary in her genes, her DNA. They say the rotten apple don't fall too far from the tree. So there you have it. Tami is a nutcase like her pappy and probably her grandpappy as well."

Escaping the shocking reality that was just abruptly revealed, Tami ran up the stairs, retreating to her room. Throwing herself across the unmade bed, she buried her face into the pillow. Uncontrollably sobbing, Tami was past distraught, and her head pounded as if it were about to explode. Her plan of storming into the house and setting her stepfather straight for all the years of insults had backfired. He'd won both the battle and the war. She felt broken, as if she were about to snap.

Holding herself as tightly as she possibly could, Tami rocked back and forward in denial. She knew she wanted more direct answers from her mother concerning the monster who was allegedly her birth father, yet unstable in her current mindset, Tami didn't think she could stand to hear more of the dark secrets of the crevices of her life being brought to the light. Instead, she continued to shed tears and wish that she could disappear from life.

If she only had Vance's arms to lie in later in the night and comfort her, all would be well. However, for whatever reason, he had abandoned her. Tami was all alone and felt like she had nothing or no one on her side.

***

"Why would you tell her like that?" Mrs. Lewis couldn't believe the man she'd married all those years ago could be so mean and spiteful toward her child. She knew Tami could be a handful at times, yet that still didn't warrant him not only verbally berating the girl but revealing a dark, hidden family secret that definitely wasn't his to tell.

"What do you mean, like that? You were standing here. Didn't you hear your daughter attacking me in my own house? I was sitting here minding my own business when she brought her big, crazy ass in here."

"I wasn't here when you and her first started, but I was here to see that you took things much too far."

Still having no remorse, Mr. Lewis continued revealing his own brand of act-right. "So, let me get this much straight. You think not only is that ill-conceived baby of yours gonna come up in where I pay all the bills and talk to me any sort of way, but you gonna give me lip as well. Is that what you think I'm gonna stand for? After all these years, you should know me much better than that."

"Look, dear, I'm not saying that. But the family has suffered enough turmoil these past few weeks. We don't need to be divided like this." She tried reasoning with him. "I'm already upset that Tori is in the hospital bed clinging to life. I don't need any more grief added to my mind."

Mr. Lewis was not backing down. In fact, his voice not only got louder, but his contempt for Tami did as well. The more his wife tried to calm him down, the more he made sure his hysterical stepdaughter knew what he truly thought of her. "Yeah, I remember it just like it was yesterday. Here you came back from the corner store with some lie that made no sense at all."

Mrs. Lewis once again lowered her head in shame as her spiteful husband took the entire household on a trip down memory lane.

"Oh my God, help me!"

Watching his girlfriend practically fall through the front door, the young man claiming to be so deeply in love quickly leaped to his feet. "Hey, what in the hell happened to you? Why is your shirt ripped off your shoulder? Why is your lip bleeding?"

"Please help me! That man around the corner—" She openly sobbed, trying to catch her breath.

"What man? What damn man are you talking about?" He grabbed her arm, trying to get a straight answer. "Around what corner?"

"Near the store. Near the alley. He . . . He . . ."

"He what? He did this to you?" Running to get the shotgun he kept in the closet, he was hell bent on making whoever pay the price for messing with the woman he was engaged to. "I'll kill him. I swear to God I will."

After roaming the neighborhood for over three hours straight, he finally gave up and started to question his fiancée's story as being untrue. Already extremely jealous in nature, he thought that the more she told him the gory details of the attack and rape, the more she seemed to enjoy the added attention and sympathy he was giving to her. Considering the fact that she refused to go to seek medical aid, claiming she was embarrassed, the more she became a liar in his eyes.

Nine months later, she was giving birth to a bastard baby who, come to find out, belonged to a psychopath. Mr. Lewis swore he would take care of Tami and love and accept her as his own; yet less than a year later, he was treating not only the baby, but his new wife like garbage. When Mrs. Lewis became pregnant with Tori, it seemed to soften his demeanor, but not enough to soothe the ongoing verbal abuse he cast upon his stepdaughter.

If Mrs. Lewis would've have just put her foot down in the first place, maybe her oldest child would not have been up in the room now on the brink of suicide.

CHAPTER SIXTEEN

It had been a good month or so since Tami's mother discovered her passed out cold on her bedroom floor. She knew her older daughter was not built to mentally withstand the heart-wrenching blow delivered by her husband. Rightfully concerned about Tami's demeanor in the days following hearing the dreadful news, Mrs. Lewis took it upon herself to get in touch with the therapist she knew her child had been meeting with. She'd found the journals Tami had been keeping and knew her daughter had been living on the edge for some time. Understanding it was against the law to fully disclose what she and her patient had discussed, the therapist advised in no uncertain terms that Tami may need some further consulting of medical professionals and help that she wasn't able to provide at the free clinic.

Mrs. Lewis waited for the best possible time, her husband being out of town, to speak to her firstborn. Tami was totally receptive and not at all in denial about her problems. Realizing that her life was spiraling out of control and there was some sort of disconnect, she bossed up. Tami made the conscious decision to check herself into the mental hospital to get some help.

Although a part of her wanted to die most days, the other part of her welcomed the daily psychotherapy sessions at the Warrendale Health Services facility so she could fight to survive. Finding out her biological father was a sick-minded animal who not only raped her mother but had stabbed several others, including a small child with a dull screwdriver when he was high, caused Tami to grow more depressed, praying she'd never be anything like him.

"So, Tami, how are you feeling today? How did you sleep?"

"Last night was much better than the night before. I didn't have any dreams, which is good."

"And why is that so good?" The lady sat back with a pen and pad, taking notes.

"Because, like I told you before, most times I'm 'sleep I see faces."

"I know you told me that, but do the faces ever speak to you? Do you recognize these faces?"

Tami started to feel antsy even discussing the faces she'd seen whenever she got off into a deep sleep. Opting to cut the session short, Tami returned to her room to gather her thoughts. Trying her best not to obsess about Vance, she wanted to at least call him and see how he was doing. She wanted to ask her mother if she'd seen him down at the hospital visiting Tori, but she knew her mom would only lie. Tami could easily tell by the questions her mother and therapist were asking that they'd found her journals. It didn't take a rocket scientist to realize they were basing the help they believed she needed off of those sordid, drama-filled pages.

Tami was immediately placed on a special diet upon signing herself into the inpatient facility. The hope was that the on-staff nutritionist could pinpoint whether certain chemicals in the foods she was consuming were triggering bouts of severe depression or social rages. After the few weeks she was there, no traits were easily found. Even with the special diet they had Tami on, she seemed to be getting plump in the face, demanding bigger portions. By the doctor's request, several tests were performed to take blood, skin, and hair samples to send to the lab. With the aid of modern technology, hopefully the chemist and the machines they used would determine the proper medication and dosage Tami should be on to stop her rages, depressions, obsessions, and overall peculiar behavior.

"Yes, Mrs. Lewis, this is Dr. Rivers at Warrendale."

"Yes, Doctor, is everything okay with my daughter?"

"Well, Mrs. Lewis, we never like to discuss information about our patients over the phone, so I was wondering if you could stop by in the next forty-eight hours. It's not dire; we just would like you here to sit in on the next session with your daughter."

Tami's mother explained to him that she had another child, Tori, in a coma in a hospital located far on the other side of the city. She promised the doctor that as soon as she cleared her schedule where Tori was concerned, she'd make it out to Warrendale.

"How are you feeling this afternoon, Tami?" the therapist asked, wanting to start the meeting off on a good note.

"I'm doing well, but I'm kind of confused. Why is my mother here? This isn't a regularly scheduled family support group session."

"Honey, aren't you happy to see me?" Mrs. Lewis walked over to hug her daughter.

"Of course, I guess so, Mother. But once again, why is she here?" Tami directed her question to the therapist, who always looked as if she had the weight of the world on her shoulders.

Sensing Tami was not in the mood for any cat-and-mouse games, the therapist removed her eyeglasses and cut to the chase. "Well, as you both know, we've been running test after test, trying to find out if Tami is suffering from any chemical imbalances inherited, or self-made by way of food consumption."

"Okay and . . . ?" Tami was now sitting on the edge of her seat awaiting the verdict on her mental state of mind.

"Well, Tami, it seems as if we've run into somewhat of a roadblock in the way of testing."

"Which is?" Mrs. Lewis was as eager to hear the verdict and update as much as her beloved daughter.

"Okay, well, it seems as if Tami is pregnant."

"Pregnant? Tami? My Tami?" Mrs. Lewis couldn't believe what she'd just heard. Her suicidal, overweight, mentally distressed child was pregnant. "There must be some sort of a mistake. She doesn't even have a boyfriend."

"I don't know what to tell you, Mrs. Lewis. We had the test run several times because in our intake records Tami stated she wasn't pregnant."

Mrs. Lewis was shocked and leaped to her feet. "Tami, please tell this woman they must be mistaken and their tests are wrong."

Tami was dumbfounded as all eyes were focused on her. As her mouth grew dry, she got a lump in her throat. Throughout everything that had gone on in the past six weeks, she was not thinking about much of anything else. Learning who her real father was had her mind gone. Preoccupied, facing that insane, tainted-blood-line harsh fact, she'd put her obsession with Vance on temporary hold. Now, just like that, it was back.

The poorly thought-out but well-executed gameplan of getting her sister's husband to ejaculate in her the night before he left had worked. And now, getting official word from these doctors, she knew the second part of the plan obviously worked as well. She had conceived her brother-in-law's baby. With a mixture of emotions racing through her mind, Tami still sat speechless.

After being able to take no more of her mother's threats of malpractice for the doctors relaying information she knew had to be false, Tami got out of her seat. Saying no words in the way of denial or acceptance, she casually strolled out of the meeting and returned to the peaceful tranquility of her room. Tami had to get her mind right and process what the therapist had said moments prior. If she didn't have enough things going on in her chaotic life, this would definitely top them all. Placing her hand down on her stomach, Tori's big sister smiled with complete satisfaction. She was going to have a baby—and not just any baby, but Vance's.

Her mother was gone. The therapist was off duty, and Tami was left with the truth. Living with the idea that she was going to soon be someone's everything, the expectant mother went from being sad and confused to hopeful and elated. Even though she hadn't spoken to her "baby daddy" since before he abruptly left to return home to his condo, Tami was convinced that if he knew she was carrying his seed, he'd abandon all hope of Tori getting better and run to her side.

Going to the room's closet, Tami put on the same tracksuit she wore when she originally checked herself into Warrendale. It was a little snugger now, but she pulled it off. Knowing she still hadn't dealt with the demons that'd set residency in her head, Tami ignored their chattering voices. Unlocking the nightstand drawer that held her purse, Tami smirked as she checked herself out and headed toward the parking lot.

CHAPTER SEVENTEEN

Vance was weary but not broken. Despite character flaws that everyone had, his devotion to his wife was still intact. He made it one of his top priorities to visit her as often as he could and make sure fresh flowers were forever near her bedside.

Since he had returned to his condo, Vance's health had slowly started to improve. Initially suffering from some withdrawals from the various prescriptions he was on, not to mention the pills he was unknowingly drugged with, Vance was proud of the accomplishments he'd made since the tragic morning of the accident. The doctors had cut the full-length cast down to half its original size. Now, with the aid of one crutch, he was getting around like a champ. If it hadn't been his right leg that was broken, he'd even be able to drive himself around. Luckily, his best friend and frat brother, Courtney, had his back. Whenever he needed a ride to here or there, Courtney was Johnny-on-the-spot.

***

"I'm so sorry. I don't know what else I can tell you. The machines are doing all the work for her. Now, even though we can keep them going along as you'd like, I want to make it clear that slowly, day by day, it's taking a serious toll on your wife's already damaged organs." The main doctor explained several more scenarios that could occur as a small group of students looked on. "As I told you a weeks ago, when she was first brought in through emergency, her frame was so small that it was easy for her lungs to get punctured and other vital organs to shift. Had she been a little heavier in weight, who knows what trauma force she could've withstood."

Vance's demeanor was solemn. With prayer in his heart, he kept hope alive while holding Tori's tiny hand. With the doctors telling him it might be best to make sure his beloved wife's affairs were in order, he was in complete denial and made them swear to do any- and everything possible to keep Tori among the living.

With visiting hours close to being over, Vance called Courtney, informing him he'd be ready and down near the hospital entrance whenever Courtney pulled up.

"Hey, dude, they got me pulling a hour overtime because some joker done called off sick.

And you know we can't slip on the patrol times on the highway."

"Hey, it ain't no thang. I can grab a cab," Vance announced, not wanting to be a bother to his homeboy. "Work is work. Get that money. I ain't mad at you."

Courtney advised him not to call a cab. Quick on his feet, he came up with another solution that would kill two birds with one stone; especially considering his unplanned delay.

Tami had the radio blasting. Having been laid back, chilling for over a month in the quiet surroundings of Warrendale, she welcomed the ear-piercing sounds her factory speakers were kicking out. With both hands on the steering wheel, she drove cautiously, knowing that she had an extra passenger riding with her: Vance's seed. In good spirits, Tami was hell bent on not letting any of the many voices inside her head rain on her parade. Delusional, she hoped her brother-in-law would take her in his arms and tell her he was praying for their soon-to-be bundle of joy to be a boy. Tami was on cloud nine. The expectant mother was ecstatic. She was only miles away from surprising her "baby daddy," and nothing could make her happier.

***

"Okay, Shawna, you can turn left at the next block then go like two blocks down and make a right." Vance's mind was back at the hospital and focused on what the doctor had told him about Tori. He wanted to make conversation with the nurses' aide who had driven him home, but he was not in the mood. The more idle conversation she started, the more Vance ignored her.

Shawna, not needing a brick house to fall on her head, knew his wife's ongoing health issues and decided to let him be. Even though she was off the clock, she was still dressed in her uniform. Her normal routine would be to change at the hospital and get herself together for come what may, but Vance needed her, so she happily obliged.

Following his directions. she was almost at the driveway that belonged to his condo. Turning in and parking as instructed, the curvaceous, brown-skinned beauty made mention that he lived out in the boondocks where Freddy and Jason hung out. For the first time since he'd gotten in her car, Vance smiled and even laughed a little.

Just as she turned off the engine, her cell phone rang. Stepping out of her vehicle, she pranced around to the passenger door to assist him in getting out.

"Dang, thanks, girl. I appreciate you." Vance allowed her to hold one of his crutches as he attempted to balance himself.

Holding her cell to her ear, Shawna giggled, telling Vance it was no problem and she always had his back when need be. As he hobbled, making his way to the front door of his condo, Shawna popped her trunk, getting out a small Hello Kitty overnight bag. Informing the caller she was about to go inside the condo and jump in the shower real quick, she ended the conversation. As Vance closed the door behind them, neither he nor his houseguest had any idea they were being watched and heard from the moment that they pulled up.

Oh, so baby daddy wanna play it like this, huh? Like I don't exist or my feelings don't matter?

Tami couldn't seem to make herself get out of the driver's seat and act an outright fool on the man she loved. She held on to the steering wheel as if her life and sanity depended on it.

Don't do it! Don't do it! Please don't do it!

Here he was looking all healthy and handsome, pulling up in front of the condo she held down for him when he was messed up. She was his backbone when he needed one.

Ain't this about nothing! What nerve!

And to add insult to injury, he had the nerve to be with one of them shit-starting nurses' aides from the hospital who had always been giving her the evil eye.

Not this bitch of all bitches! He moved his fake ass out our house acting like he didn't need anyone anymore, and obviously that's not the case. I swear I wanna snap! I see dudes like him can't be trusted.

Tami was infuriated. Her mouth grew dry. She had a lump in her throat. She fought to control her emotions but couldn't. How dare Vance play her like this? He must've taken her for some sort of a fool, but today he was gonna learn about the consequences of cheating on his baby momma. And as for the wannabe cute whore he had up in the condo bragging about taking a shower, she was gonna feel the fever as well.

CHAPTER EIGHTEEN

Tami's patience with Vance and his bullshit had worn thin. Her warped mind was working overtime. She tried to calm herself down but couldn't. The man she loved was on the other side of the steel beige door committing what she deemed as the ultimate sin: cheating.

As her fist balled up, her taste for vengeance heightened. Tami's knees grew weak and wobbled as she stood. Banging on the door like she was the police executing a search warrant for a serial killer, she was enraged. The force of her thunderous pounds caused the frame to shake and a few neighbors to peek out from behind their curtains. Attempting to twist and turn the doorknob, the scorned female had to even the score. Her soul wouldn't let her do otherwise. Thoughts of her man behind the locked door doing God knows what to that scandalous female she'd recognized from the hospital made her seethe with anger.

The angry vixen had blood boiling in her eyes. Revenge embedded deep in her heart was evident.

Impatiently waiting for a response, Tami tapped her foot, trying to once again to calm herself down. Using the palm of her hand, she smashed it to her forehead over and over.

God, please let this man hurry up! Please don't make me think he's in there with his hands on that tramp! Please, God, I'm begging you!

Seconds later, Vance swung open the door as if he was expecting someone else. Shocked to see Tami of all people standing evil-faced in his doorway, he was at a loss for words. He'd been told by her parents that she was supposed to be locked up in some sort of nuthouse, but here she was, live and in living color.

Looking like she was ready for war, no words were exchanged between the two as Tami raised both hands. She pushed them on his chest, shoving an already unbalanced Vance out of the way. The fact that her man fell backward off his crutches and hit the floor meant absolutely nothing to the angry female on a mission.

Not caring if he broke his neck or other leg in the fall, Tami stepped over him. She had more pressing business than making sure her baby daddy was good. Tami was in search of the forever neck-rolling, gossiping shit-wiper who was constantly eyeballing her. If she thought she could just whisk in and steal her baby daddy, she had another think coming.

Vance was dazed. He hardly had an opportunity to get back on his feet after being trampled by a rambunctious Tami. Wobbly, using the aid of one crutch, the wounded Que made it into the living room. This entire day had gone from bad to worse in a matter of mere seconds. First the team of doctors delivered the tragic news pertaining to his wife, and now this: her crazy sister had just barged in acting renegade. Vance's world felt like it was crashing in.

He couldn't believe his ears. He heard what sounded like two wild cats going at it, fighting for their lives. Following the piercing trail of screams, yells, and accusations, the crippled condo owner was soon led in the bedroom. Finding his wayward sister-in-law and Shawna boxing it out, he was speechless. Not knowing who to grab, and, in a naked Shawna's case, where to grab, Vance stood back outta harm's way.

***

Of course this tired tramp is already in the shower. She couldn't wait to get comfortable in my man's house. What damn nerve! I'ma kill her!

Tami could easily hear the water running in the bathroom. Intent on murder, she burst in. Met with a thick, misty steam and a sweet-smelling fragrance of body wash, she fumed. Immediately spotting the girl's overnight bag wide open and a few of her personal items on the sink made Tami even madder.

Oh, this skank think she getting her ratchet ass together to sleep with my baby daddy? Oh, hell naw! I'll cut the bitch first!

Without further hesitation or remorse, Tami yanked the curtain to the side, allowing more steam to fill the tiny room. Tearing half of the decorative plastic off the flimsy rod, the deranged pregnant female went directly in for the kill. She'd caught her victim at a disadvantage, naked and soaking wet. Shawna had soap lathered up on her near-perfect body, but to Tami, it didn't matter. There was hell to pay, and Shawna's bill was due in full.

The big-boned menace then made her presence known. No words were passed as the two locked eyes. There were none needed. It was apparent what was going to take place.

You dirty piece of gutter trash. You got me all the way messed up! You not just gonna bounce all up in here like it's all good!

Not caring if the sleeves of her tracksuit got drenched, Tami felt her rage intensify. Snatching the stunned young woman by her long weave, she wrapped her fingers around every strand to ensure a better grip. Ready for an all-out street brawl, she roughly skull-dragged Shawna out of the hot shower, kicking and screaming.

"You little bitty whore, you got me messed up," she shouted loud enough to wake the dead. "You didn't get the memo? Vance belongs to me! He's my man. Not yours and not my sister's, but mine!"

Shawna's skin was glistening with beads of water and traces of soap as she hit the hard marble bathroom floor. Although she had no idea what the true situation was between Vance and his sister-in-law, at this point it didn't matter. Shawna was hood to her heart, and the fight was on as she quickly realized that if she didn't get over the embarrassing fact that she was nude, Tami would most certainly mop the ground with her face.

Now standing toe to toe, they boxed their way out of the wet floor area and into the bedroom. Shawna, exposed for the world to see—or at least

Vance, who'd just come in the room—started bucking as if her life depended on it. As the two feisty women went back and forth throwing haymakers that could probably knock the average man out cold, Vance didn't know what to do. Each female seemed to be having a turn at being the aggressor and getting down on the other.

Vance believed he should intervene and break it up; however, he didn't have the strength to physically do so. As he stood over to the side yelling at them to stop, he was trying to understand why Tami was even at his condo in the first place.

"I know you ain't over here trying to be with Vance. I can't believe this madness. Bitch, I'll kill you up in this damn condo! You gonna learn today!" Tami's face was full of anger. Over the top, she wildly swung her balled-up fist, connecting with Shawna's jaw.

"Who in the hell you calling out their name?" Shawna blurted out while still exchanging blows. "You must be crazy or something. Don't nobody want your damn sister's husband!"

"Guess what? Fuck my little sister and fuck you too." Tami was running out of steam, and Shawna could easily tell. Taking advantage of her overweight attacker's shortage of breath, the innocent nurses' aide went in for the kill.

Raising her bare foot, she tried kicking Tami in the stomach but missed her mark.

Tami was outdone. She took it upon herself to take two steps back from the impromptu battle royal she'd started. "Oh my God, you tramp. You trying to kill our baby?" she screamed out as both a statement and question. Going into what she thought was self-preservation mode, one of the many voices in her head stepped up, taking control. As her mind had several internal fights taking place, she saw herself losing even more of a grip on reality.

On the verge of blacking out, she felt like Shawna was trying to snatch everything she'd worked for out of her hands. Tami couldn't let that happen. Vance was hers, and no one would come between them. Tami had to end any thoughts or designs Shawna had on her man. Evilly, she reached for one of Vance's many fraternity paddles that proudly hung on the wall. Ripping the leather strap off the nail, Tami raised the purple-and-gold painted wood over her head. With all her might, the delusional female brought it crashing down across Shawna's temple and jawline.

Hearing the cracking sound of a bone or two breaking, Tami felt satisfaction watching

Shawna fall to the floor. Her now unconscious victim lay naked, still semi-wet, and bleeding from the mouth. Tami's bizarre accusations continued as she focused her sights on Vance.

"Why would you have her here in the first place? I don't understand why. The last few months don't seem like they even mattered."

"Yo, hold up, Tami. What the fuck is wrong with you? Why would you hit that girl with that bullshit? I know they said your ass done gone crazy, but damn! What in the hell?" Vance grabbed the one crutch he was using and started hobbling. He tried walking over toward Shawna to see if he could help her in any way before he called for an ambulance.

"Oh, so you just gonna run over to her like she so important? You just gonna act like she more important than me? I guess it's like forget about me and our baby." She roughly yanked at his arm, causing him to fall to the floor once more. She was obviously zoned out on some sort of power trip as she stood over her baby daddy. Instead of nurturing the seed growing inside of her, Tami socked herself in the stomach in defiance.

"Baby." Vance had heard her say the word "baby" a few seconds ago during the fight, but it'd gone over his head until now. "Yo, Tami, what the hell you mean, baby—let alone *our* damn baby?

"Wow, I never seen it until just now. I guess your sister was right when she said you was never wrapped too tight. I guess you just been playing at being normal. You a straight loon!"

Tami's hair was all over her head. Shawna had scratched her face in several places and swollen one of her eyes damn near shut; yet Tami felt she was a goddess in Vance's sight no matter what he was saying.

"Vance, sweetheart, I love you and our baby, so stop saying those things. We were meant to be together, a real family. Me, you, and the baby! It's our destiny."

"All right, listen up, you crazy bitch. On everything I love, you need to go back to that place and get your mind back straight, because you over here bugging! You done jumped on an innocent female and knocked her out cold with a damn paddle. And for what?"

Tami didn't want to hear the cruel words that were coming out of her beloved Vance's mouth. She wanted to block them out, but she couldn't. She wanted to hear some fairy tale response from him, having just revealed he was gonna be a daddy. The room began to spin quickly as she realized her fantasy was not Vance's reality. His words and insults cut like a knife. Tami felt them penetrating her inner soul as she sobbed.

"How can you say all those things to me? How? I don't understand. I thought you would be happy for me, for us. I thought you would be happy we could be a real family now: me, you, and our baby—our love child."

"A family, our baby . . . Girl, you need to be on some serious strong medication. They need to lock you up somewhere and throw away the key until they find a cure for your type of crazy." Vance was thrown off as he struggled to lift himself from the floor. His one leg was weak and the other with the cast throbbed. "Listen, Tami, I already have a family: your sister Tori. Remember her? I know you ain't that far gone in your mind. And please, damn, stop saying 'our baby' like I got something to do with whatever else madness you talking about or got floating in that twisted mind of yours."

Tami had about enough. She was sick and tired of him constantly taking up for her younger sibling like everyone else did throughout the years. As she stood tall with the paddle still clutched in her hand, she grew increasingly dizzy. She was still trying to catch her breath from the fight, and now his verbal attack. Trembling, she spoke.

"Vance, why are you trying to deny our child like this? I didn't do this by myself. You wanted this too."

"Tami, you are nuts." His reply was swift.

"Naw, I'm not. Vance, we made this miracle together in the den, you and me. Almost every night I tried to get it right when we were doing what we'd do. Well, now it's right. You gonna be a daddy."

"The den? Me a daddy? What in the entire hell is wrong with you? You sick in the head!" His voice angrily bounced off every wall as he held his aching knee.

"Yes, baby, we gonna be bonded together forever and ever. See, now you don't need that skinny-ass Tori anymore. You can just let that tramp die so we can get married like it was supposed to be in the first place—me and you!" Tami was proud, sticking out her chest as she explained their impending near future. "And of course your son, Vance Jr."

"Vance Jr.? Me and you married? Get the fuck outta here with all that madness. I'm about to call the ambulance for her and the nuthouse for you. And as for the den, bitch, you bugging."

"Look, sweetheart, I don't care if you've been over here cheating with this raggedy home

wrecker." She pointed to Shawna's still motionless body. "I can get over her. I know you a man
and needed some type of pussy since you left our
little makeshift love nest in the den. I get that
much, but I'm pregnant now, and I come first
in your life. So, like I said, fuck that thang lying
over there. And as for my sister, let them pull the
plug!"

Now back on his feet, Vance tried process-
ing all the allegations, assumptions, lies, and
possible truths a crazed Tami was spewing. He
couldn't believe the seemingly innocent-minded
Tami, who'd taken care of his every need while
convalescing, had turned out to be such a monster.

Vance wanted to snatch the paddle out of her
hands or another one off the wall and give
her the same treatment she'd given Shawna.
He was infuriated by most of the things she
was saying, especially suggesting he should
allow his wife Tori to just die. Confused and
infuriated, he thought back on the time spent
at his in-laws' house initially recuperating from
the car accident. He thought about all the pain
medication he was on and how messed up it had
him in the brain. Racking his memory, Vance
relived the countless nights he had what he'd
believed to be hallucinations about having sex

with Tami. He was stunned by what she was
claiming to be true. Here she was confessing the
many times he thought he was dreaming his sister-in-law was really giving him the best head
he'd ever felt. She was really riding his manhood
raw, and worst of all, he really could've impreg-
nated her.

"Tami, just what in the hell is wrong with
you? Why would you even try to take advantage
of a nigga and do some old slime-ball bullshit
like that in the first place? Why would you want
someone who you know don't want your lunatic
ass? You sick for real. After the police deal with
your dumb self for attacking this girl, I hope they
put you in a straitjacket for a year or two."

Tami was feeling herself. She was proud and
content with her actions. Shawna done learned
her lesson. She would know better than to come
around Vance anymore, and if she could convince her baby-daddy-to-be to give up on Tori,
the world would be perfect. Tami knew that she
was the goose that was about to lay the golden
egg. Vance might've been acting like he was
pissed now, but in time he'd get over it and come
to embrace her and their child. "Listen, sweetie,
it's all good like I keep telling you. We're going
to be a family. And to make things simpler, you
can just divorce my sister if you don't wanna pull

the plug, and we can still give our baby a proper home."

Vance had spoken his peace, but she seemed not to be getting the point. He knew there might have been a small bit of truth to what she was saying as far as them having sex in the den, but so what? He didn't owe her anything and had to make that part perfectly clear before things got further out of control. She'd already jumped on an innocent Shawna, so Vance knew she was capable of anything. "Look, Tami, what the fuck you mean proper home? I'ma keep things real with you. See, you got me all the way messed up. I don't give two red hot shits about you or no damn baby your sick-in-the-head ass claim to be mine. You can kick rocks with all that. If you truly are knocked up, then you best either go find your real baby daddy and let him know, or take a quick trip to the slaughterhouse. Either way it makes me no damn difference. That's on your silly ass. And as far as Tori is concerned, you need to keep my wife's name out your mouth before I shut that motherfucker up permanently! Female or not, I'll beat your ass to sleep!"

"Oh yeah, Vance? It's like that between me and you?"

"Yeah, it's just like that. And I keep telling you it ain't no me and you!"

"Sweetheart, it's always gonna be a me and you. Vance Jr. gonna always need his daddy. So like I said, fuck Tori! I wish she was dead. For real for real, she can die in her sleep tonight for all I care." Tami stood her ground while rubbing her belly. "Me and your son are your world now! We need you more than some nurses' aide hussy you been fucking, or that two-faced, fake-ass Tori."

Interrupting his rebuttal to his demented sister-in-law, Vance's cell phone began to ring. Leaning against the doorframe, he reached into his pocket. "Yup, hold tight, you deranged ho. We ain't done yet! I warned you about speaking my wife's name!" Realizing it was the hospital on the other end, the always concerned husband immediately took the call.

After a few brief seconds of him being silent, Vance's hands grew numb. His hands shook as he dropped his cell to the floor. Normally a medium brown complexion, Vance turned white as a ghost. His legs started to wobble and his knees grew increasingly weak.

"Oh my God. I can't believe this. She's gone. My baby is gone." The words fought to escape his dry mouth. "I just saw her. It can't be. Oh my God!"

"Who's gone, Vance? Your baby ain't gone. He's right here in my stomach, growing bigger and stronger every day."

Vance was in the zone. The room started to spin. His life seemed to flash before his eyes. He suddenly blacked out. Forgetting his leg was in a cast, the injured, emotionally spent man found the inner strength to run across the room. Without any reservations, he bum-rushed Tami. Grabbing her up by the throat, Vance lost all control. He lifted her up then preceded to body slam the shocked female to the ground, landing her overweight body next to Shawna's.

As his sister-in-law claiming to be pregnant struggled to fight him off, she quickly lost the battle. Vance had a distant, cold gaze in his eyes. Multitudes of tears streamed down his distraught face.

"Oh my God! What the fuck! You did this, Tami! You asked for that bullshit to happen and it did. It's all your fault, you crazy bitch! You killed my wife. She's gone! Tori's gone and you did it! It's all your fault."

Tami reached up, trying to pry Vance's hands off her throat. He was strong as an ox, and with every word he spoke, his grip began to tighten.

His intensity in bringing harm to her was only met by his apparent grief.

"Vance, you're hurting me. Let me go," she pleaded the best she possibly could, considering. "I can't breathe. I can't breathe, I'm telling you."

"Shut your fucking mouth, Tami! Just shut your mouth. You done said and did enough. You just said you wished my baby was dead, and now she is! She's gone! Tori is gone! "

Tami's eyes grew twice their normal size. She could hardly believe what he'd just said. Her little sister was no more. The one person who she'd constantly hated more than her stepfather was no longer alive. There would be no more teasing or judgments from her. No more making her feel like a second-class citizen in her own home. There would be no more daddy's-girl special treatment in their household. That era was now over.

"Tori is really dead? Is that what you saying?" Tami finally caught her breath to say.

"Yesssssss," Vance blurted out before breaking all the way down. Slightly loosening his hold on Tami's neck, he allowed his tears to drip down on her face. His world had just collapsed.

"Are you sure? My sister is dead?"

"Yes, I'm sure. That was one of the doctors telling me to come down there. I could tell in his voice that she's gone. It's over." His tragic sobs continued. "Why did you have to wish her dead, you no good tramp? Why? Why in the hell would you wish that on your own flesh and blood?"

"Because I hated that rotten, backstabbing trick from the beginning, that's why. Ever since my mother and stepfather brought her home from the hospital I hated her. I'm glad she's gone, probably straight to hell!" Tami taunted Vance, showing no remorse whatsoever that her little sister was dead, or no sympathy for his apparent grief. "She's the reason me and you not married now! Can't you see that? She was blocking our happiness, but now the bony troublemaker is out the way. We can finally be together—you, me, and our baby."

Vance tried to contain himself, but he couldn't. His face was totally filled with tears. His T-shirt was beginning to get drenched along the top. He couldn't see straight or think straight. The love of his life was gone, and he couldn't do anything to bring her back.

His entire body started to tremble as he listened to the uncalled-for statements Tami was making about his now deceased wife. He wanted her to stop talking, but she wouldn't. There would never be a damn her and a him, let alone no baby for them to share in raising as a family, so she needed to shut up. If she couldn't do it on her own, he'd gladly help her. Vance wanted revenge on life for dealing him such a messed-up hand.

After a few seconds more of her words of hate, Tami's lips continued to move, but he heard no sound. Wanting nothing more than to make her pay the ultimate price for the nasty things she was saying about Tori, Vance tightened his grip again. The more pressure he applied, the more temporary satisfaction he gained from watching Tami squirm to breathe. Her moving lips had now turned a dark shade of purple. Seeing nothing but the devil dancing in her eyes, Vance grew angrier. Before the usually law-abiding citizen realized what he'd done, it was over. His troubles with Tami were done. Releasing all her built-up bodily fluids, her time spent on the earth being mentally tormented by her inner demons was over. Tami, like her little sister Tori, was gone to meet her Maker. Just like that, Vance had taken a life.

"Hey, what in the hell is going on in here?" Courtney, dressed in his police uniform, came bolting through the still open front door.

Wasting no time, he rushed over to Shawna, who was nude on the floor. Lifting her head, he immediately noticed blood leaking out the side of her face. Confused as to why the female he'd been dating for the past few weeks was like this, he shook his head. This didn't make any sense. He asked her to simply give his homeboy a ride since he was running late; now here she lay in this condition.

Raising Shawna's now semiconscious body in his arms, he then noticed his best friend weeping and Tami mysteriously sprawled out next to him. "And, dawg, what in the hell happened to her? What's going on in here, dude? Tell me something! Shit!"

"Bro, I can't believe she's gone, man," Vance cried out, dropping his head. "My girl is gone and ain't coming back. She's gone. She left me."

Courtney, assuming he meant his sister-in-law Tami, laid Shawna back down. Being an officer of the law, Courtney was trained to deal with emotions of all sorts and take command of explosive situations when need be. Praying silently, he crawled over to check on Tami, hoping that what his best friend said wasn't true. Smelling the urine that formed a small puddle where she lay, Courtney knew things weren't looking good. Checking for any signs of a pulse on her wrist as well as her bruised neck, the trained cop quickly realized Vance was correct. Tami was indeed dead.

"Dude, what in the hell happened in here? Who did this to Tami and attacked Shawna? Are you hurt? Was y'all robbed? A home invasion? What happened?" Courtney defensively jumped to his feet as he bombarded a blank-faced Vance with questions.

"Man, Tori is gone. My life is over. My baby is gone."

"Tori? Dude, you confused. I'm talking about Tami and Shawna and what jumped off here. Snap out of it, dawg. Now, what happened to Tami?"

"I killed that bitch, that's what happened!"

"You killed her? Come on, man. Now is not the time for any bullshit games. Tami is dead and Shawna is over there fucked up. Now, what in the hell you talking about you killed your sister-in-law? Tell me the truth!" Courtney paced the floor, waiting for some sort of clarity about what had gone down.

"Man, she wished my Tori was dead and now she is. That dirty tramp was some sort of a witch; like she knows black magic or something. That snake killed my wife, so I killed her," Vance babbled, trying to explain his reasoning for becoming a cold-blooded murderer.

"Hold up, Vance. Wait a minute. What you saying? Tori is dead too? Is that what you're telling me?" Courtney was just as confused as the moment he'd initially walked through the front door.

"Yeah, dude, the hospital just called." Vance found it extremely hard to swallow as he struggled to speak. "They said my baby is dead. She's gone. I gotta get to her. She needs me."

Courtney had a legal as well as moral responsibility to fulfill. He was sworn to uphold the law. Not only had a murder taken place, but some sort of an attack on Shawna for which he still hadn't found out the reason or the actual perpetrator. Vance was not only his frat brother, but his best friend. He didn't want to turn him in for the crime he'd confessed to, but he knew not placing the call could possibly cost him his own job.

"Look, dude, I really don't know what went on here, but you know I gotta call this bullshit in. I mean, Tami's lying dead right in the middle of your living room floor. I just can't ignore that fact. Look, guy, just remember for your own sake, don't say anything else until you get a good lawyer. I'm serious; nothing else."

Vance's mindset was that of utter despair. He was talking out the side of his neck, claiming Tami was a reincarnation of the devil himself. Courtney didn't know what to make of his boy's gibberish, other than that he'd totally lost his mind. Vance was far from being a coward, and in any other circumstances, he'd face the consequences of whatever came his way, but this was different. This was much different. Tori, the true love of his life, wouldn't be able to stand by his side. She wouldn't be there to hold his hand or pat him on the back. His constant rock when need be was no more.

Engulfed in regret and denial, Vance buried his face in his hands, not wanting to face the truth. Seeing no other way if he wanted to see his beloved wife again, he stood to his feet. Taking a deep breath, he wiped the tears off his face. As his best friend was preoccupied placing a call to 911 as well as his shift supervisor, he snatched Courtney's gun out of his holster.

"Hey, man, what are you doing? What's wrong with you? Have you lost your mind or something for real?" Courtney knew at this point that Vance wasn't playing with a full deck. As he held the phone in his hand, he heard the 911 operator asking for the location and problem.

"I can't do this. I just can't! It's so messed up. Tori is gone, and I just wanna be with her." With no fear of dying, Vance placed the barrel snuggly beneath his chin. Despite his best friend begging him not to do it, Vance's hand trembled. Suddenly he cried out that he'd rather die than live life without Tori by his side. Just like that, he pulled the trigger. The splatter of bloodstains covered the wall. With a gaping hole in his head, Vance's near-lifeless body fell to the floor. As fate would have it, he landed near his alleged baby mother. Taking his last breath, Vance slumped over on top of an already deceased Tami. Ironically, it would be the last time the two prescription pill–popping lovers and their ill-conceived bastard baby would be together.